# ON CHRISTMAS AVENUE

A feel-good small-town romance

*NEW YORK TIMES* BESTSELLING AUTHOR
# GINNY BAIRD

*On Christmas Avenue*
Copyright © 2022 Ginny Baird

ISBN: 978-1-952210-73-0

www.hallmarkpublishing.com

*For John*

# *Chapter One*

 ARY WARD STARED AT HER boss and blinked.
    "Where did you say I'm going again?"
    Judy cocked her chin and her asymmetrical bob swung sideways. She had a slender section of her black hair pinned back on top, offsetting her dark brown eyes. "To Clark Creek," she repeated matter-of-factly, like she'd just said Atlanta or some other highly recognizable place. In addition to being Mary's boss, Judy Ramos was also her bestie, and had been for a decade—ever since they'd been roommates in college.
    They stood in Judy's tenth-story office in a corporate building on the outskirts of Richmond, Virginia. Snow fell beyond the floor-to-ceiling windows, coating the pines abutting the parking area. Davenport Development Associates specialized in fundraising initiatives for nonprofit entities, but generally not towns, so this wasn't a typical assignment.
    "Well, I've never heard of it."
    "Neither had I," Judy said, "before I got their mayor's cry for help." She stepped toward Mary, extending her cell phone, and Mary had to crouch down to see. She towered over her shorter and more athletically built friend.

1

Judy pulled up a map of Virginia and tapped at a spot in the state's western portion.

Mary's brown curls spilled forward and she held them back with one hand, attempting to get a better view of the screen. Nothing obvious jumped out at her, besides mounds of mountainous terrain. "I'm not sure I—"

"Hang on." Judy enlarged the map on her navigational app and a tiny dot appeared. The name *Clark Creek* sat adjacent to a curvy blue line, indicating a narrow body of water connected to a larger tributary.

"That looks like it's in the middle of nowhere."

"Not completely nowhere," July replied. "The Blue Ridge Parkway's nearby."

Judy was big into hiking, kayaking, and skiing…all sorts of things that meant spending time outdoors. She'd been president of the sporty Outdoors Club at their university. Conversely, fair-skinned, easily-sunburned Mary was more of an *indoor* yoga person. The only club she'd belonged to in college was the Christmas Club she'd started.

While other charities donated seasonal gifts and meals to those less fortunate, few delivered uplifting decorations, like live Christmas trees and festive garlands, to folks who wouldn't otherwise have them. Mary had been pleased to learn her club had continued operating even after she'd graduated from college.

For her part, she'd never really gotten out of the habit of buying Christmas decorations whenever she found them on sale. She loved saving them up to drop off at nursing homes or other places where they were appreciated. Her apartment closets were so jam-packed they couldn't absorb any more holiday cheer, and the cargo area of her SUV was loaded.

Judy motioned for Mary to have a seat in the chair facing her desk, and Judy sat behind it. A small plastic

Christmas tree stood on its corner wrapped in colorful lights, and the wreath above Judy's bookshelf behind her showcased a red-and-green-checkered holiday bow.

"What's going on in Clark Creek?" Mary asked her.

"Not nearly enough." Judy sighed. "The email from the mayor was honestly a little sad, and a lot frantic. Clark Creek barely has enough reserves to fund its daily operations."

"Oh no. You're talking local government?"

"I'm talking all of it. Government operations, the sheriff's office…and the shops and restaurants are hurting, too. The town council learned about our company's reputation for raising capital quickly and reached out to us for help. If they don't get relief soon, the whole town will go under."

"Bankrupt?"

Judy nodded. "Everything will take a hit in that case, including funding for parks and schools."

That sounded perfectly awful for the poor people of Clark Creek.

Mary shifted in her chair, growing uncomfortable. She normally helped smaller organizations like charities run their fundraisers, functioning as part of a team. Lately, she'd been spearheading those teams. But none of them had tackled anything this big.

"How many of us will be on this?"

"I tried to suggest sending you, Natalie, and Paul—at a minimum." Judy grimaced. "But the mayor said they can only afford one consultant."

"One?" Mary swallowed hard. "I don't know, Judy. This sounds like a challenge."

Judy scanned something on the laptop in front of her, then shut it. "Since when have you backed down from a challenge?"

Mary chuckled, feeling called out. "Never."

"See? You're perfect for the job. Smart. Determined. Innovative! Plus, you can think on your feet."

"Let's hope I land on them, too."

"You will." Judy took on a serious tone. "I'm not supposed to tell you this," she said in a whisper. "But if you pull this off in Clark Creek?"

"Yeah?"

"It could mean Seattle."

Mary's heart thumped. "What?"

"Headquarters," Judy confirmed. "And a promotion to program manager, like me. You won't even have to apply. Upper management already has their eye on you. All you need is this major victory to seal the deal, and my recommendation, of course. Which you know you have."

Anticipation coursed through Mary. This was just what she wanted—what she *had* wanted for the past year, ever since Judy had been promoted ahead of her. They'd started at the firm at roughly the same time as implementation specialists, after both having earned their MBAs and working for different universities' development offices.

Mary had been glad to move to Virginia, and extra happy about working with Judy, who'd already accepted a position at Davenport. Things became privately awkward for Mary when Judy got named her boss. Even though Judy was always kind and fair about it, being her subordinate felt weird after being equals and friends.

Then again, Judy was more assertive than Mary, and not afraid to advocate for herself. Like she had when she'd applied for the supervisory position she currently held.

Mary frowned. "But that would mean leaving Virginia. And you."

"Don't be silly, Mary! We'll keep up like we did before. Besides…" Judy playfully rolled her eyes. "You've got to know, if the shoe was on the other foot—"

"You'd jump at the chance in a heartbeat."

"Yeah."

Mary knew this was an opportunity she couldn't refuse. She really did love rising to a challenge, and moving to the West Coast sounded exciting. Virginia was great, but she'd already lived here for nearly two years, and grass was growing under her feet. While Mary wasn't stellar at maintaining long-distance connections, she'd always managed to stay friends with Judy—in part, due to Judy's bullheaded persistence. Mary loved her to death for her loyalty. Judy was the closest thing to a sister she had.

"So all I've got to do," she said, "is present this little town with some new strategies?"

"For fiscal viability, yes. That's what they're counting on. An economic reboot."

Mary inhaled deeply, thinking things through. She could do this; of course she could. Given enough time to strategize. "Okay. Why don't you send me the particulars: demographics, chamber of commerce information, that kind of thing. Oh! And forward that email from the mayor. I'll do some research on Clark Creek and come up with a proposal to run by you before presenting it to the mayor and the town council."

"Super. As soon as it gets their approval, you can go on site to implement your plan."

"How long have I got?"

"They're wanting results by Christmas."

"Christmas?" Mary's stomach clenched. That sounded impossible, even to her. She was accomplished at her job, but she wasn't a miracle worker. "That's only two weeks away."

Judy shot her an encouraging grin. "Sounds like you'd better get busy."

Evan Clark's mom greeted him as he approached the courthouse. Snow drifted through the air. A fine white powder dusted the town square with its stylish gazebo and seasonal outdoor skating rink. The impressive façade of the library stood across the way, marked by its tall ivory columns and ornate windows. Beyond the smattering of town buildings behind the library, clouds cloaked a snowy mountain ridge.

"Oh, Evan! I was looking for you earlier. Itzel said you'd stepped out," his mom said, mentioning his administrative assistant. Connie Clark wore her winter coat and held up a small umbrella while grasping a paper cup of coffee in a gloved hand. Her dark blond hair skimmed the edges of her fake fur coat collar and her blue eyes sparkled when she smiled. Despite the crows' feet at their corners, she looked a lot younger than her age. She'd been mayor in Clark Creek these past ten years.

"Yeah, I had to stop by the bank." As Evan walked with his mom up the courthouse steps, he angled his sheriff's hat forward to keep the snow from hitting his face. It was driving down harder now and growing icy, which would mean slick streets. Folks would need to take care. "What's up?"

"This is about, you know…" She dropped her voice a notch. "That little issue we have going on."

Evan would've hardly called Clark Creek's budget deficit "little." That was why he'd been at the bank, examining different scenarios for bailing out the town. Unfortunately, none looked promising, since loans required repayment—with interest, and the bank had already overextended its credit to several struggling businesses in town. They couldn't afford to help float county operations besides…not without eventually going under themselves.

As the Clark County sheriff, Evan was an elected state official, and therefore not directly involved in local government finances. Clark Creek's budgetary concerns affected the citizenry he'd been sworn to protect, though. They also had a very real impact on his office, since supplemental funding from the town council helped run it. This was the first year since he'd been sheriff that the town council had not been able to approve any additional funding. So those who worked with Evan were in financial jeopardy too.

He held open the door for his mom, then shook the moisture off his hat before placing it back on his head and stepping inside.

"I know things look bad," he told her. "But we'll find a way."

"Yes. About that!" His mom closed her umbrella. "I believe that we have."

"We who?"

"Why, me and the town council."

"Okay," he said, wondering what she was up to now. His mom was always coming up with innovative ideas, some of them less practical than others. Like the time she decided to emulate Pamplona, Spain's "Running of the Bulls" with a "Whole Hog Race" on the Fourth of July. Pigs running amok down Main Street was not Evan's idea of a good time, even if they were wearing patriotic red, white, and blue ribbons.

They'd broken loose from the barriers at the county fairground at the edge of town and stampeded straight for the courthouse. The entire event had been two things Evan couldn't stand: unpredictable and chaotic. Though it had been predictably chaotic, when he thought about it.

"This is big," his mom said. "Very big. We've hired an expert from Richmond."

"Hang on." Evan held up his hand. "Hired?"

"A consultant, yes." She nodded eagerly. "A *Christmas Consultant*. Doesn't that sound fab?"

"Uh. No." Clark Creek couldn't afford that kind of extravagance. He couldn't even pay his staff.

His mom got that knowledgeable look in her eye. "She's very skilled at fundraising."

"Funds we can use. But we can't afford to spend them."

"It takes money to make money. That's what your Grandpa Clark always said."

"That assumes you've got the cash to begin with."

"Now, don't be such a spoilsport. I'm offering you good news and all you can do is rain on my parade."

"I just want what's best for—"

"So do I and the rest of the town council members. Mary Ward comes very highly recommended. She's going to turn Clark Creek around!"

"Oh yeah? How?"

His mom patted his cheek. "I suppose we'll leave that to her."

*Christmas Consultant. What kind of hooey is that?* The last thing Clark Creek needed was some big-city woman coming in to offer her opinion, at a presumably high price tag. He'd seen her type before. She'd arrive with impressive spreadsheets and a plan that looked good on paper, but which was near-impossible to enact. Then, when all was said and done, Clark Creek would be no better off than before. In fact, it would be deeper in debt.

"And anyway," he asked, after puzzling this through. "Why does she bill herself as a 'Christmas Consultant'?"

"She didn't call herself that. I did, because she's delivering the best gift of all." His mom held a gleam in her eye. "New hope for Clark Creek by December twenty-fifth."

Now he'd heard everything. No expert was that good, no matter what her credentials. "*This* Christmas?"

"It's my favorite time of year," his mom said, undaunted by his skepticism. "So a very reasonable deadline. The rest of the town council agreed. We can't afford to wait."

"We can't afford to *pay her*, Mom."

"Now, don't you bah-humbug me, Evan. I need you on my side—and Mary's."

He forced a tight grin, knowing things had already been decided. His office had no influence over what the town council did. Not in matters like this. All he could do was complain by voicing his opinion. "How much is this costing Clark Creek?"

"The specific number is confidential." It wasn't. County spending was public record, so he could always look it up. The fact that his mom wasn't being forthcoming about Mary's fee had to mean she was commanding a hefty sum. The town was already hurting. After paying her, they'd be bankrupt. Which was just what they were trying to avoid.

Evan sighed. One of his mom's best features was her optimism. In cases like this, it was also her downfall. "When does she get here?"

"After lunch on Monday. She's staying at Marshall's place," she said, referring to Evan's brother's inn: the Clark Creek B&B.

"At least she'll be comfortable for her short stay," he said, turning to go.

His mom caught him by the coat sleeve. "Mary may need your help."

"My schedule's really full."

"Evan. Son." She pleaded with her eyes. "Please

cooperate. She could be our last hope!"

*Sure, or the final nail in our coffin.*

"Besides," she added pertly. "You've been appointed to work with her."

"Me?" Even thumbed his chest. "Appointed?"

"The town council's vote was unanimous. Of course, you can always refuse the position of Clark Creek Liaison, but I wouldn't recommend it. There are logistics involved, and who knows? Maybe some legalities…"

"What?"

"We'll want to ensure everything's in compliance."

What on earth was she talking about?

"So!" she concluded. "You're the natural fit."

Maybe the natural fit for getting rid of Mary quickly, since she was likely billing by the hour. He supposed he could sacrifice one afternoon to go over her proposal. Then he could thank her for her time and send her on her way, before she could cost Clark Creek any more money.

His mind seized on something his mom had said that didn't make much sense.

"Logistics? What kind of logistics? And what do you mean by legalities?"

"I'll let Mary fill you in on the details when she gets here on Monday." His mom beamed brightly. "The town council's all for her wonderful plan! Once you hear about it, you will be too."

*Chapter Two*

$M$ ARY DROVE INTO CLARK CREEK as snow fell gently from the sky, sifting through the trees lining Main Street. Quaint shops with awnings wore their holiday best. Garlands hugged door frames and colorful displays of Christmas lights shimmered through decorated windows. Yet businesses here were far from bustling. The town appeared nearly deserted. She tightened her grip on the steering wheel and her confidence soared. Clark Creek needed her talents, and she was going to deliver.

Yes, the challenge was huge, but she'd come up with an amazing idea. The mayor and the entire town council had been enthusiastic about it, too.

She was planning a parade. And not any old parade, but one that would serve as a superb fundraiser. In the last few days, she'd made tons of phone calls and sent dozens of emails, and everything was falling into place. Now, it was down to orchestration. Securing sponsors and volunteers, soliciting proposals for floats, and designing the parade route and other particulars.

With just ten days left until Christmas, she was under a bit of a time crunch, but she worked well under pressure. Though it was a holiday parade, Mary hoped that its benefits in putting Clark Creek "back on the map" would be realized all year through. Once more people recognized Clark Creek as a fun small-town destination for shopping, dining, and day trips, they'd only come back for more.

She needed boots on the ground to accomplish her goal, and she couldn't wait to get started. After her appointment with the mayor, she'd be meeting with her Clark Creek liaison. She was grateful the county sheriff had volunteered to help her by showing her around the town while offering his logistical support.

The smattering of restaurants she passed looked like the type that placed outdoor tables on the sidewalks in pleasant weather. Mary spotted a few art galleries and grinned at her discovery of a kids' museum. Fluttering red and green flags hung from lamp posts welcomed visitors to Clark Creek. The town definitely had potential. It simply needed to be discovered. Or, rediscovered, really.

It had been a regional hub back in the day when it had a working railroad station. One of the places she passed was called the Whistle Stop Café, which had been fashioned from an old train station. She'd looked it up online and had been charmed by its retro atmosphere and classic menu offerings. She hoped to drop by. Maybe she could do some of her project planning there.

She paused at a stop sign, noting she'd not seen a single stoplight in town. This was just the kind of place she'd always dreamed about living in when she was growing up. But her mom, Lila, was a big-city person.

Mary approached the town square, which was hemmed in by small businesses on both sides and presided over by two official-looking buildings. From the directions she'd been given, she knew that the imposing building was the courthouse, and the one with the columns, the library. A picturesque gazebo stood in the center of the square, and park benches bordered the outdoor skating rink nearby.

Mary sighed. She had a feeling she was going to love being in Clark Creek.

With a little luck, hundreds of others would soon be visiting, too.

Evan glanced out the window across from his desk. From where he sat, he could see the cupola of the snow-covered gazebo and a swath of the lights surrounding the skating rink. When he focused, he could also spot the first several shops lining Main Street, past the library and on the other side of the town square. The powdery white stuff continued to swirl from the sky and the sky was gloomy, matching his mood.

He couldn't help but grumble at the town council's decision to spend unnecessarily on a Christmas Consultant, who was apparently arriving today. The sooner she got here, the better, so he could put the inconvenience of meeting with her behind him.

Itzel Torres knocked at the door, which was partly ajar. "Visitors here to see you." From his assistant's deep blush, Evan could guess which "visitor" at least one of them was. Itzel had had a raging crush on Evan's doctor brother for the past two years. Basically, ever since she'd first laid eyes on him at the county fair, shortly after moving here.

Nash was as clueless as ever, scarcely noticing the kindhearted brunette. Nash hadn't dated anyone since losing his late wife, Becca, to cancer three years ago. Evan understood that had been rough, but he also wanted to see that carefree smile on Nash's face again.

Maybe someday.

Itzel stepped aside and Nash nodded politely. "Thanks, Itzel."

Evan's five-year-old niece, Chloe, tugged on her dad's hand, staring up at Itzel. "Thanks for the yummy Christmas cookies!" she said with a toothy grin. Evan chuckled to himself, knowing those cookies had been every bit as intended for Nash as they had been for his kid.

Nash rubbed the side of his neck as if remembering. "Right! They were very delicious, those *man-te-ca…*"

"*-ditos!*" Itzel inserted when he faltered on the word.

"Yeah, those." He smiled pleasantly enough, but Evan could tell it wasn't the kind of smile Itzel hoped for. "Sorry. I've never been any good at Spanish."

"My mother used to make them *all* the time," she said, attempting to engage Nash in conversation, but he didn't take the bait. He seemed preoccupied by something, and Evan wondered what it was.

"How nice. Well, thanks again." He turned toward Evan.

Before Itzel slipped from the room, she asked them, "Coffee, either of you?"

Evan shook his head and Nash said, "No, thanks."

Chloe dropped her daddy's hand and raced toward Evan.

"Uncle Evan! Can I wear your hat?" Her dark eyes twinkled. She had a little button nose, rosy cheeks, and two brown pigtails. If ever there was a picture of cuteness, Chloe Clark was it. Evan lightly tapped her nose.

"Only if you promise not to arrest me, Buttercup." He couldn't remember when he'd started calling Chloe that, but once he had, it stuck.

She giggled and rolled her eyes. "*Uncle Evan*. I wouldn't do that."

Nash set his hands on his hips. "Why not?" he asked his child.

"Yeah?" Evan queried, attempting to remain stern-faced. "Why not?"

"Cause you're not one of the bad guys." Chloe stated this as if it was obvious, and Evan and Nash laughed. Evan removed his hat, placing it on Chloe's small head. It swallowed up most of her forehead and covered her ears.

Evan gave the brim of the hat a tug. "I think you'll have to grow into it."

She grinned from ear to ear. "When I grow up, I want to be a sheriff just like you."

That novel bit of information touched his soul, but it worried him, too. If his niece was going to go "sheriffing," he hoped she'd pick a place as nice and quiet as Clark Creek to look after.

"A sheriff?" Nash complained, but it was all in fun. "Not a doctor?"

Chloe stuck out her bottom lip, thinking. Next she proclaimed, "Maybe I'll be both!"

"That would be a great mix," Evan conceded.

Nash affectionately eyed his daughter. "You'd keep your town healthy *and* safe."

Evan motioned for Nash and Chloe to have a seat in the two chairs facing his desk. "Did you want to see me about something?" he asked his brother. "Or is this purely a social call?"

"Yeah." Nash cast a sidelong glance at Chloe, who seemed awfully happy about something. "The parade."

This caught him off guard. "What parade?"

Chloe bounced in her seat. "The one we're having here!"

Evan pushed back in his chair and stared at Nash. "I haven't heard anything about it. How big? When and where?"

"Pretty huge, from what I gather, and it's happening on Christmas Eve. It's the *where* part I wanted to talk to you about." Chloe grinned at him and Nash clammed up. The kid was obviously excited about the notion of a parade, and Nash didn't seem to want to dampen her spirits. At the same time, he appeared concerned about something.

Evan's gut churned over the potential complications a big parade could entail. The venture sounded complicated and costly, at a time when the town was already strapped.

"Sweetie," Nash said to his daughter. "Would you mind running out there to tell Itzel I've changed my mind about the coffee? I really would love some, if it's not too much trouble."

Evan raised two fingers. "Make that two."

Chloe hopped out of her seat. "All right." She peered up at Evan, having to tilt her head way back in order to see him. "Can I still wear the hat?"

Evan smiled at her sweetness. "Of course."

Once Chloe had left the room, Nash leaned toward Evan and whispered. "It's not the parade I'm against—entirely. I'm just not sure I can stomach the thought of porta potties popping up in my pasture."

Evan felt like he'd been tossed another curve ball. "Can't say I blame you. Who says that's going to happen?"

"I heard Austin grousing to Leroy about it," Nash said, referring to two of his farmhands.

Evan set his elbows on his desk. "Who told them?"

"Marshall."

"Marshall?"

"Yeah," Nash said. "Evidently, this Christmas Consultant

lady is staying at his inn, and when she phoned to make her reservation, she requested a map of the town, along with other touristy information. He asked her what she was planning, and she was very happy to tell him. When Austin ran into Marshall at the feed and seed on Saturday, Marshall shared the news. Then, Austin told Leroy, who was not thrilled by any of it." Nash sighed. "None of us are. About the porta johns, I mean. The idea of a parade is kind of cool. We've never had one in Clark Creek."

"And one's not happening now, as far as I'm concerned. Nobody's asked me about it, and this definitely isn't the year for overextending ourselves. The town's hurting, Nash. Private businesses are hurting. We're *all* hurting, and my office…" He swallowed past the tender knot in his throat. "Is barely hanging on."

Nash's face fell. "Aw, man. I'm sorry."

Evan flattened his palms on his desk, staring down at his closed ledger. He'd just been reviewing his office's finances *again*, and they were definitely in the red. "With my tiny staff, I've got nowhere to make cuts," he said, looking up. "Itzel's still paying off student loans, and Dennis and Linda are expecting a baby." It would be the third child for Evan's deputy and his wife.

"I know Helen already mostly works from home," Nash said. Helen was Evan's dispatcher.

"Yeah, and she's got Bernie, who's on disability."

Nash's shoulders drooped, and then his dark eyes brightened. "What if this parade actually helps? I heard that it's a fundraiser."

Evan heaved a sigh. "We don't have the funds to run it, Nash. Clark Creek can't justify spending money on something so frivolous." He massaged his tight forehead with his fingers. "Policing a parade takes money. You need staffing for crowd control and traffic management.

17

Resolving parking issues." His mind snagged on the memory of what his mom had said about logistics and legalities. "Oh, ho. So that's what Mom was driving at. She must have known about this parade last week."

"But she didn't tell you?"

"The mayor? Nope." Evan set his chin. "She left that minor detail out."

"I wonder why."

"I'm guessing because she knew I'd be opposed."

Chloe pushed back the door for Itzel and the woman entered, carrying two paper cups. "Two black coffees, coming up!" She set one on Evan's desk and handed the other to Nash, her cheeks dusty rose.

"Thank you," Evan said.

Nash sipped from his cup and smiled at Itzel. "Yeah, thanks, Itzel."

Chloe scooted back into her chair, repositioning her hat. "Are you coming to the parade, Uncle Evan?"

He pursed his lips, then said kindly. "Not sure, Buttercup."

She frowned and Nash patted the top of her hat. He sent Evan a questioning glance as Itzel left the room.

"Let me look into it," Evan said, intending to do just that.

# Chapter Three

*E*VAN PICKED UP HIS CELL phone from where it sat on his desk and called the mayor, but the call went straight through to voicemail. Just like it had done the past several times he'd called. And she'd totally ignored his one-word text:

*Parade???*

Seriously. What were his mom and the town council thinking? Now wasn't the time for party-like celebrations. Clark Creek was in dire straits. Hiring a Christmas Consultant to come up with suggestions was one thing. Paying her to stay on until Christmas Eve was something else.

He thumped his pencil against his ledger, his tension mounting. Things were so bad this year, he'd had to scrap his office's annual Christmas luncheon, and institute a potluck instead. If finances didn't improve soon, he'd need to do even more belt-tightening. He just didn't know how or where. His pencil slipped from his grip and rolled off his desk and onto the floor, landing beside his right foot. He reached for it and his door swung open.

Itzel's chatter spilled into the room. "Wait! You can't go in th—"

"I'll just be a minute," a lilting voice said.

Evan spied a pair of black spiky-heeled boots approaching his desk at a fast clip.

He raised his head so quickly, he bumped it on the underside of his desk.

"*Ow.*"

"Oh! Oops!" Evan looked up and a woman's face came into view. He knew every face in Clark Creek, and this was definitely a new one. She had long, curly brown hair, creamy white skin and big brown eyes. Without preamble, she set some sort of wooden reindeer decoration on his desk. Right on top of his ledger.

*Wait a minute.*

"Sorry," she said. "I didn't know you were down there."

"No, I guess not," he said, dazed.

"Hang on one sec." She surveyed the area, her gaze landing on his coat rack in the corner. "This will go much better…here." Amazingly, she picked up the coat rack and carted it in front of the window, totally blocking his view. She removed the silly-looking plastic Christmas garland from around her neck and wound it around the coat rack. The greenery was threaded with tinsel that actually *sparkled*.

She produced a strand of miniature lights from her suit jacket pocket next and got to work twining them around the greenery before switching them on from a small attached battery pack. "There!" She grinned as their glow filled the room. "That's better."

He dropped his pencil onto his desk, stunned by her whirlwind display.

"Sorry about that," she said. "I had an inspiration." She gave him a friendly wave. "Hi there, I'm Mary Ward. Clark Creek's new Christmas Consultant."

"Mary." Evan rubbed the back of his head, which was throbbing. He must've knocked it harder than he'd thought.

"Sorry, boss," Itzel said from the doorway, not sounding sorry in the least. Actually, he suspected she was kind of enjoying the show. "I tried to stop her." Itzel was a die-hard romantic and forever chastising thirty-four-year-old Evan for not having enough romance in his life. She probably figured the tall slim brunette was about his age, maybe a few years younger. Possibly even single. Not that those things mattered to him—one iota.

His main concern with Mary was getting her out of town quickly.

"What's going on?" Dennis asked, appearing behind Itzel in the hallway. Dennis, a man in his forties with a dark brown complexion and deep-set eyes, had been made deputy before Evan had been elected sheriff. Evan could have appointed someone else in his place, but he valued Dennis's experience and the fact that Dennis was a former Army man like he was.

Dennis eyed the Christmas decorations with a grin. "Hello. You must be—"

"Mary Ward." She smiled. "Nice to meet you."

"Dennis Armstrong," the deputy said. "And this is—"

"Itzel Torres," Evan's assistant said.

Mary frowned. "Sorry about bursting in here. The reindeer were getting heavy." She whispered like this was news, "*The base is solid brass.*" She gave Evan an apologetic look. "I'm sorry I surprised you, too. I didn't know this office was occupied. I was just trying to finish up decorating the courthouse before my three o'clock meeting with the sheriff."

"Sheriff Clark?" Dennis asked. His brow crinkled and Itzel giggled.

Evan thumbed over his shoulder.

Mary's face paled when she read his name and title on

the open door. Even when viewing it from the opposite side, it was easy to make out what it said.

"*You're* the sheriff?" She bit her bottom lip, scanning his shiny gold star and the name tag attached to his uniform. "I thought your office was downstairs. On the first floor?"

"Nope. Second."

Her cheeks colored. "I see."

Itzel and Dennis swung their gazes back and forth between Evan and Mary like they were watching a ping-pong match. Evan shooed them away before they could break out the popcorn. "Do you mind?"

Itzel smoothed back her short choppy hair. "Oh, right."

Dennis took the deputy's hat he held in his hand and placed it in on his head. "I was just leaving."

"*Sure you were,*" Evan heard Itzel whisper to Dennis before she shut the door, but not all the way. She left it open a crack and then walked away *very slowly.*

Dennis seemed to be taking his time, too. He shoved his hands in his uniform pants pockets and pretended to admire the artwork that had hung on the corridor walls for as long as Evan remembered, while whistling "Jingle Bells."

Evan raked a hand through his hair, then winced when he hit the tender spot on his head. "Who told you to decorate the courthouse building?" he asked Mary, trying not to let his discomfort show.

She met his gaze and grinned. "Nobody told me to. I offered. The mayor was all for it."

Naturally, she was. Add one more thing to the check-out list. *Ca-ching. Ca-ching.*

"Um-hmm," he mumbled. "The mayor."

He slid open his top desk drawer, hunting for the roll of antacid tablets he kept on hand. He located the package and popped one in his mouth before thinking of Mary.

He extended the package in her direction.

Her eyebrows arched. "Er...no thanks."

Evan chewed on the peppermint-flavored antacid, pondering the price tag for so much fancy decorating. It had to be steep if she was covering this three-story building. Plus, it had a basement. And a large entryway with a staircase.

"The courthouse decorations didn't cost Clark Creek anything, if that's what you're worried about," she said, and motioned around the room. "This extra bit of Christmas cheer is *lagniappe*."

Evan shut his desk drawer. "Lan-yap?"

"It's what they call a business bonus in New Orleans."

"So, you're originally from New Orleans, then?"

"No. But I lived there. Lots of other places, too." She shrugged. "When I was growing up, my mom and I moved around a lot."

He considered her a moment, noticing she was nicely dressed in tailored black slacks and a red turtleneck beneath her business jacket. She had a well-put-together look that was casual yet professional. "Why the bonus?"

"Because I appreciate your business. I mean, *we* at Davenport Development Associates do." Her dark eyes shone brightly. "Besides that," she continued, "it appears that nearly every other part of this town but here is decorated to the hilt. And, oh..." She peered out his window. "The gazebo. We'll need to work on that."

"We rarely decorate at the courthouse," he informed her.

"The mayor's office looks festive."

Of course it did. It was inhabited by his mom. He moved the reindeer sculpture aside and its weight ripped his ledger. She winced.

"Look, Ms. Ward."

"Please, call me Mary."

He nodded. "Mary."

"May I call you Evan?"

"Uh. Sure," he said, grappling with his thoughts. He stared down at the reindeer on his desk and then up at her. "Look, Mary," he started anew. "I appreciate the gesture and all. I'm just not one for a lot of Christmas clutter."

"Clutter?" she asked, aghast.

"Extra fuss and glitter." He gestured to the coat rack she'd placed in front of the window. "Twinkling lights and tinsel aren't really my style." While he enjoyed the holidays as much as the next guy, he wasn't a huge fan of going overboard.

"No? Oh. Well. That's a shame." She frowned. "I guess I won't bring the rest of the stuff in, in that case."

*There's more?* "Thanks for the thought, though."

She glanced back at the coat rack and then at his desk, wearing a downcast expression, and Evan worried that he'd hurt her feelings. "Want me to—?"

"No, no. Leave it. Everything's fine." He raised both hands. "Just enough!" He paused to study her. "How did you know the courthouse wasn't decorated, anyhow? Did the mayor mention it?"

"No, I saw that with my own eyes when I got here, and I happened to have a few spare decorations in my SUV."

"Ah." What sort of person kept surplus holiday decorations in their vehicle, on the off chance they were needed? A Christmas Consultant, apparently.

"Why don't you have a seat?" He gestured toward a chair, mentally preparing his delivery. While he didn't want Mary sticking around, he aimed to be gentle in urging her departure. The sooner she left, the better off Clark Creek would be financially, and there were a lot of people Evan cared about in this town.

When she was situated, he said, "It was good of you to come here and I appreciate your efforts, sincerely I do. All of us in Clark Creek do. But I'm afraid we'll need to make this a short stay."

She seemed nonplussed by his comment. "I don't know what you consider 'short,' but if it's about ten days, then I guess we're in business."

Before he'd been apprised of her plan by Nash, he'd been thinking two days—at the outside. And even that seemed excessive, given that she'd already spent time in Richmond preparing her proposal.

Evan pushed back in his chair. "What I'm trying to say is that ten days is too long. Way too long for Clark Creek to pay a consultant, given our current circumstances." He spread his hands out on his desk, striving to sound firm but fair. "I'm sure you understand our budgetary constraints."

"I do."

"Which is why...your staying through Christmas Eve won't be necessary."

She sat up straighter in her chair. "I beg your pardon, but I believe that it *will* be necessary. So do the mayor and the town council."

He was a little thrown by her bullheadedness, but decided to carry on. "The mayor says you have a proposal?" She'd gone to the trouble to prepare one, so he might as well listen to her presentation, before saddling her with more disappointment.

"Yes." She reached into the satchel she'd set on the floor and withdrew some papers, handing him a business folder. "Here you are." She tugged at her jacket lapel, looking pleased with herself, and not the least bit intimidated by his lack of enthusiasm. She probably thought she could win him over with her glossy proposal...and that smile, like sunshine on a springtime day.

Evan averted his gaze from her mouth and opened the folder she'd handed him. As he'd anticipated, stellar financial projections filled the first few pages. Colorful bar charts showed revenues skyrocketing on Christmas Eve—not only for the local government, but also for every business in town. Yet there was no immediate indication of where that huge infusion of cash was coming from. He suspected she was paving the way for her huge reveal by starting with the promise of big money as an end result. If he hadn't been tipped off about the parade by Nash, he might have started worrying about those "legalities" his mom had alluded to.

"What are you recommending?" he asked her, deadpan. "That the council go out and rob a bank? Because if you are, I'd better warn you, the Clark Creek Savings & Loan isn't in any better shape than the rest of us are."

"Ha! You're funny." She twisted up her lips and his heart thumped. It was an unexpected thump, pounding hard against his ribcage in a manner that was oddly distant, but vaguely familiar. He really didn't like it. He found the disruption inconvenient.

She retrieved her folder, flipping to another page. "No, Evan," she said. "I'm proposing a *parade*."

The sass in her tone made his neck warm. Yet another inconvenience. He tugged at his uniform's necktie as Mary continued.

"The town council and the mayor loved the idea," she said. "We're going to recruit sponsors from the neighboring town with the ski resort."

Evan cleared his throat which felt scratchy and dry. "Hopedale?"

"Yes. They're doing very well as a tourist destination. I talked to the director of their Chamber of Commerce and she was totally supportive."

She handed her folder back to him and he set it on his desk beside that unwieldly reindeer sculpture. "I'm afraid you don't understand," he said, focusing on the facts. Much better to do that than contemplate the shimmer in her warm brown eyes. "I don't have the resources to patrol something like that. My office is very short-staffed as it is."

"Then, we'll recruit volunteers to help out. And the payoff will be *so,* so worth it." She angled toward him, becoming more animated as she cranked up her spiel. "We're planning three sponsorship levels: Reindeer Team, Elf League, and Santa's Circle. We'll sell tickets to raise money, and—"

"Mary, wait." He hated being the bearer of bad news, but he also didn't want to waste more of her time. There was no earthly way she was going to convince him to endorse her parade plan. Even if she was a very convincing individual, certain things mattered to him more...like the future of his town. He was not going to sacrifice that.

"I'm really sorry to have to tell you this," he said, "but there's not going to be any Christmas parade. Not this year. Not in Clark Creek, anyway."

She stared at him blankly, like she was a kid and he'd just told her there's no Santa Claus. "What? Why not? This parade could save Clark Creek."

His stomach roiled. "What if it sinks it?"

She blinked. "I don't know what you mean."

"You're talking complicated logistics. Traffic, parking, crowds that need regulating...an entire influx of visitors into Clark Creek—"

"Yeah, that." She leaned toward him, pointing to her proposal folder. "Holiday tourists happy to spend money. People who will boost the local economy at a crucial time of year."

She locked on his gaze and a for a moment he lost his bearings. He drew in a breath, willing himself back on track. "*And* they'll overwhelm our roadways. And our scarce resources, while making a major headache for my already stressed office."

Mary gasped. "I thought you were supposed to help me."

"I am helping," he said. "By helping you understand our limitations."

"You'll have fewer of those once the parade is successful."

"I'm afraid I'll need to talk to the mayor and the town council. Express my concerns."

"No problem." She tucked her satchel under one arm and stood, smiling cordially. "Express away!"

"You do see where I'm coming from?" he asked, as she prepared to go.

"Uh-huh, I think I do."

"Good. That's good." Evan shot her a parting wave, glad that she was going. He didn't enjoy butting heads with anybody, especially when they persistently believed themselves to be right. At least he'd gotten his message across. "I appreciate your understanding."

"My pleasure. Yours too."

Wait. A warning flag skittered up the pole and Evan wondered what she meant by that. Next, he told himself to relax. This was finally over. All he had to do now was talk to his mom and the town council about planning their next move. One that would involve bringing money into Clark Creek, rather than further draining its coffers.

"Safe travels back to Richmond," he added, as she traipsed toward the door. "And thanks for the lan-yap!"

She reached the threshold and peered over her shoulder.

Her chestnut-colored eyes held a determined gleam, and his pulse raced. "Oh, I'm not going anywhere," she said. "At least, not yet. I've been hired to do a job and I'm going to do it well."

Evan swallowed hard. It was like she hadn't heard a word he'd said. Had she been oblivious to their whole conversation? She couldn't just bulldoze her way into his town and walk all over it in those high-heeled boots of hers. Despite what his mom and the town council thought. He should have some say in this too.

"Mary," he said, pleading. "You need to consider what you're asking of Clark Creek. Your parade will stretch its resources too thin, and—just like an overstretched rubber band—it could completely *snap*."

She turned to face him fully. "Or bounce back."

*Chapter Four*

MARY HURRIED AWAY FROM EVAN'S office, clutching her satchel under one arm. She couldn't believe she'd had the nerve to stand up for herself. Not just for herself: for the parade. *Yay!* It was so unlike her to be confrontational, but she hadn't been, really. She'd been more like…professionally assertive. Maybe Judy's self-assurance was finally rubbing off on her. Or, possibly, the contrary sheriff brought out this more dynamic side in her.

She'd never met anyone so intentionally irritating in her life. Suggesting that she make this a "short stay." Uh-huh, she knew what that was about. He thought Clark Creek was wasting its money on her services, but this project had nothing to do with her consulting fee. It was all about saving Clark Creek. Okay, it was true that she would benefit too, if things went well. But now that she was here and had seen the town, she felt a personal obligation to its people.

You'd think the sheriff would share that sense of obligation and open his mind to new possibilities. Possibilities that could help Clark Creek get back on its feet again. Instead, he'd stubbornly refused to even consider her proposal. It was like the man had set up a roadblock in his brain before their meeting had even gotten started.

It was a shame he was so impossible, too. In another universe, she would've considered him good-looking, with his sandy brown hair, ruddy complexion, and those deep blue eyes. But nuh-uh, she wouldn't go there. She refused to have any even *modestly appreciative* thoughts about the sheriff. He'd certainly not thought one positive thing about her, or her proposal, which she was on fire to defend.

She rounded the corner and found Itzel at her desk in the reception area. Mary now saw that this suite housed offices for both the sheriff and his deputy. Her arms had been so loaded down with Christmas decorations coming in here, she hadn't been able to see above the tops of those reindeer antlers. She peeked into Dennis's open doorway, but the outgoing deputy was nowhere in sight. Itzel's expression was just as friendly as Dennis's had been. In fact, everyone around here appeared welcoming except for Evan, who was acutely eager for her to *go*.

"For the record," Itzel said, whispering behind the back of her hand. "I think your parade's a great idea."

Mary wondered how she'd heard about it. "Thank you."

"My mom's on the town council," Itzel explained. "Vivi Torres."

"Oh, right." Mary hadn't met Vivi in person, but she'd delivered a virtual presentation to the pleasant woman and the other town council members at the end of last week.

"I wouldn't worry about Evan. He'll come around."

"Hope so," Mary said, bristling at the thought of his dismissal. "In the meantime, I'm going to speak with the mayor."

"Good idea." Itzel's eyebrows rose. "But you'd better hurry so you get there before he does."

From the corner of her eye, Mary saw Evan approaching at a brisk pace, but he didn't see her. His gaze was on her presentation folder, which he held in his hands, as he hustled along.

"Oh, no."

"Elevator," Itzel said quietly. She pointed down the hall. "That way."

Mary nodded her thanks and hurried out of the office suite, hearing Evan speak to Itzel as she did.

"Just popping upstairs to see the mayor," he told his assistant. "Be back shortly."

Mary scooted down the hall and punched the elevator button. Luckily, it opened right away, and she pressed the button for the third floor. She needed to speak with Connie before Evan could get there and undo all her hard work.

What was it with the guy? And why couldn't he see reason? He'd scarcely looked over her proposal before deciding it wouldn't work. She was going to show him. Her parade wasn't just going to "work," it was going to succeed exponentially. Then Sheriff Evan Clark could take back all his doubting words.

She peered through the closing elevator doors as Evan beelined in her direction. He stopped short, his gaze flitting to the lights above the elevator and the illuminated arrow, which Mary knew was pointing up. "Wait! Hold that—"

Panic seized her and she couldn't move. Her hand froze in place as it hovered above the button that would open the door. If she held the elevator and let him in, she'd never reach the mayor first. She met his eyes with feigned apology, and he set his jaw as the elevator doors clamped shut.

Mary's heart pounded when it occurred to her he might take the stairs, and when the elevator doors opened, she saw that he had. Evan leapt up the top step just as she exited the elevator and hustled down the hall. Mary scurried faster to keep up with him. And then, thanks to Dennis, who accidentally got in Evan's way, Mary passed him.

"Sorry, Sheriff," Dennis said, surveying Evan's furrowed brow. "Everything okay?"

Evan huffed as Mary rapped at Connie's door. "Yes. Fine."

"Come in!" Connie called. She smiled at Mary, then saw Evan standing beside her.

Connie's office was the only one in the entire building that hadn't needed Mary's decorating touch. It was adorned from floor to ceiling in Christmas pageantry. The mayor even had two fake Christmas trees, one on either side of her desk. "Did you both want to see me?"

"Yes," Mary said at the same time that Evan said, "No."

Connie looked from one of them to the other. "Well, which is it?"

"It seems there's been some miscommunication," Mary said, keenly aware of Evan's proximity. He stood so close they nearly touched elbows, and he radiated some sort of current in her direction. Antagonism, probably.

"A very big mix-up, yes," Evan agreed. "I'm afraid there's no way——"

"The sheriff here is not very enthusiastic about——"

"The parade?" Connie cocked her head to one side and studied her son. "Why not?"

"I've got a half a dozen reasons and more, starting with money," Evan said. "There are parking issues besides, and traffic concerns. Crowd control and congestion, not to mention no place for all those folks to stay."

"And I've got just one!" Mary smiled deferentially at Evan, who gave her a suspicious side-eye. "Mind if I borrow this?"

He handed her the folder and Mary strode right up to Connie's desk, feeling her courage surge. Evan wasn't her adversary, she told herself. He was merely a part of this larger challenge. Once she adjusted her thinking, she'd find a way to handle him, too.

She laid the folder down on Connie's desk, open to her financial projections. She tapped the large dollar figure with her pointer finger. "It's right…here," she said smoothly. "Our bottom line. This is what we can achieve for Clark Creek by Christmas. And it's just what this town needs: a huge financial boost from the parade, which actually…is going to be a whole lot of fun." She added that last part for Evan's benefit, heavily suspecting that his definition of fun was only something he'd read about in a dictionary. If the sheriff knew how to enjoy himself, he did a good job hiding it. Mary looked up to find Connie grinning.

"I like your can-do attitude, Mary. You make a very fine Christmas Consultant."

Evan looked like he wanted to groan. "Mom—"

"It's all right, Evan," she said. "The council and I are well aware of the financial risks." She leveled her gaze on his. "But more importantly, we're aware of the potential benefits. So there *will be* a parade and Mary's going to run it. I'd like for you to help her, but if you won't, maybe Dennis will."

"Dennis has a lot on his plate," Evan said. "And a baby due in late December."

Connie threw open her hands. "Well then, it's all down to you."

Evan squared his broad shoulders. "I want you both to remember that I was against this."

"Oh, I don't think we'll forget it," Connie said. She handed Mary's proposal folder to Evan. "You might want to keep this."

He grumbled. "Thanks."

"Mary," she said, "don't be daunted by my son. He only cares for Clark Creek and its people."

Mary's heart hammered, her determination to prove Evan wrong growing by leaps and bounds. She understood that he had his objections, but she was on task and didn't intend to let anyone down. "It's Clark Creek's people I'm trying to help."

Evan thumped her folder in his hands. "I guess we'll see about that."

Mary held his gaze, and electricity crackled between them. For an instant, she couldn't think or breathe. "I guess we will."

"Evan!" Connie said. She gave an exasperated frown. "Really."

"Sorry," he said, like a scolded kid.

Mary smoothed back her hair, wondering what had just happened. The way Evan had looked at her had been so intense. So heavy, but it had made her feel so light. Uh-oh. *Oh no*.

"I expect the two of you to work this out," Connie told them. "And Evan, I'm leaving it to you to make Mary to feel welcome and for things to run smoothly."

"No problem," he said, casting a sidelong glance at Mary. "Of course."

Mary nodded. She'd expected a certain degree of complication with this endeavor, because those always arose with any undertaking. She just hadn't expected one of those complications to be the sheriff. The ultra-difficult but still somehow mysteriously appealing sheriff. She'd have to watch her step around him.

Now that the mayor had set him straight, things would settle down and they could get to work. Mary clutched her satchel strap harder. In a businesslike fashion.

"So," she said, as they strolled away from Connie's office. "What are you doing in the morning?"

"I have my regular patrols to do and some paperwork."

"And after?"

He stopped walking and crossed his arms in front of him. "I suppose I'm meeting with you?" he said mildly, like he hadn't experienced that lightning-bolt connection between them. *Whew.* Well, maybe he hadn't. Which was all to the good. She was here for her job, after all, and already had enough to do, without worrying about romantic involvements.

"That would be fantastic." It was a small start, but a beginning. "I want to tell you about our sponsors and discuss the parade route. Oh! And I have some great ideas for the floats."

"Anything you wish," he said like he didn't mean it, and Mary's energy flagged. The next instant she rallied.

"I saw a cute coffee shop in town."

"The Whistle Stop?"

"Yeah, that's the one. It's near at the end of Main Street and I thought the parade might start there."

"Why not at the town square?"

"Well. I suppose that could work too." She liked that he was getting into this, becoming invested.

"We could *start it* and *end it* at the same place," he said, "sort of like one-stop shopping."

Or not. "That's hardly a parade, Evan."

He sighed. "Fine. The Whistle Stop it is. Want to say ten?" He checked his watch. "I can give you half an hour."

*How very generous of you.* She pursed her lips, concealing her agitation. "Thirty minutes sounds fine. Don't be late."

He motioned grandly toward the elevator, then headed for the stairs. "I never am."

Evan sighed when he returned to the second floor. He'd told his mom he'd agree to help with Mary. That didn't mean he couldn't continue working on her about scaling back her parade. Maybe if she kept it to a reasonable size and a short timeframe of, say, under an hour, it wouldn't take such a huge toll on Clark Creek. Mary could still deliver her dose of holiday cheer and optimally make the town a little money in the process.

He rubbed the back of his neck, feeling oddly discomfited by that prolonged stare-down he'd had with her. That had proved fairly inconvenient, too. He couldn't let her get under his skin. Professionally, or personally. And he wouldn't.

"Hi, boss." Itzel wore a cheery grin. "How'd everything go?"

"Exactly as I thought it would. The mayor is totally sold on Mary's idea."

"I'll do what I can to help."

"Thanks, Itzel. I might need to take you up on that."

He passed down the narrow hallway and entered his office, where an unnerving sight greeted him. His Christmas light-wrapped coat rack completely blocked the window and an ungainly stand of reindeer occupied most of his desk. Mary Ward might be exerting her influence over the mayor and town council, but she was not exercising her Christmas Consultant "magic" here.

Evan strode to the coat rack and flipped off the lights, before carting the coat rack back to its assigned space in the corner. Next, he glanced around the room for someplace else to put the reindeer, but his bookshelves were occupied by procedural manuals, and the coffee table by the small sofa on the opposite wall was where he sometimes liked to rest his feet.

Evan hoisted the heavy reindeer decoration and carried it to Itzel's desk. "Here you are," he said, setting it down in front of her. "Merry Christmas."

She stared up at him in surprise. "What's this?"

"A little *lan-yap*."

# Chapter Five

MARY LEFT THE COURTHOUSE BUILDING, feeling drained. She needed to check in at her B&B and grab some downtime to prepare for her day tomorrow. Connie had told her about a place that offered delivery pizza nearby. Staying in and eating cozy in her PJs sounded great. Now that the drama of meeting with Evan had passed, Mary realized she was really hungry.

It was still snowing heavily when she made it down the courthouse steps to where she'd parked her SUV. Fortunately, it was an easy drive to Maple Street, which was just off Main. She found her destination three houses down from the corner, and on the righthand side. A wooden sign, supported by two hefty posts, stood in the snowy front yard, proudly displaying its name: *The Clark Creek B&B.*

The lovely Victorian, with its fresh yellow paint job and glossy black shutters, stood out against the wintry backdrop of the day like a bright ray of sunshine. The inn was every bit as pretty as its pictures, with a covered front porch and a freshly shoveled walkway. Darling Christmas wreaths hung in every window and an even larger one adorned the cranberry-colored front door, which was flanked by stained glass sidelights. There was even a turret on one side, and cheery light beamed through its elongated windows. Mary sighed. The inn was storybook perfect. She couldn't wait to see the inside.

Mary entered the Clark Creek B&B and its front door chime sounded. An attractive dark-haired guy with a beard and a mustache looked up from the reception desk. He wore a red flannel shirt and appeared to be in his thirties.

"Welcome! You must be Mary."

"I am." She grinned at his warm greeting. "Are you Marshall?"

"Guilty as charged." He strode around the desk to help her with her bags, since she'd already checked in online. She only had two: a small suitcase and her satchel, which contained her laptop and work papers. "This all you got, or do you have more in the car?"

"This is it for me."

He picked up her suitcase and she thanked him. "I'll show you to your room. Did you park on the street?" When she nodded, he said, "We've got parking around back. The sign's a little hard to see when it gets covered with snow."

Mary smiled, taking in the cheery decor. The inn was all done up for the holidays and looked amazingly homey, despite its grandeur. "This place is fantastic."

"Thanks. I call it home."

"How long have you been in business?"

"Just over three years."

She spotted three framed awards on the wall behind the reception desk, each with a seal and a shiny blue ribbon. All read *Most Romantic Getaway* in swirly gold letters.

"Yep," he said proudly, seeing her gaze on the awards. "We've won each year we've entered." He added jovially,

"Although we treat our single guests very well, too."

She laughed. "I'm sure you do." Mary noticed that he'd said *we*. "Who else helps you run it?"

"Andrea is our cook and Jeremy helps with the cleaning. I fill in for them on their days off, and otherwise handle guest relations and routine upkeep and repairs."

"A regular Jack of all trades!"

"That's me. Jack. Only you can call me Marshall," he said, teasing, and Mary laughed again. Marshall was very good at putting people at ease. From the looks of the place, he was great at keeping the inn up, too.

"Did you do all the renovations yourself?"

"I did. When I bought this place, it was fairly run down, but I knew it had potential."

"Well, you've done a great job."

He led her up a carpeted stairway with an exquisitely carved wooden banister, then down a long hall dripping with chandeliers. "You're in Room 7. I hope you'll like it. It's one of our best and has its own bath."

"Sounds great. I'm sure I will."

Marshall pushed opened the door to her room and turned on a few lights. She was charmed by the quaint four-poster bed with a fluffy comforter and big pile of comfy pillows. The small table beside it held an antique-looking lamp, and a settee by the window afforded a view of the peaceful street. There was even a small refrigerator. And—perfect—a secretary-style writing desk with a sturdy chair in one corner.

"All right?" Marshall asked her.

"It's awesome."

He placed her suitcase on a stand by the window. "If you need anything, just let me know."

"Full up this week?"

"It's Monday, so it's slow. Things will get busier later

in the week. I hope."

Mary frowned at his downcast expression. "Times a little tough, huh?"

Marshall shoved his hands into his jeans pockets. "We've had better seasons, to tell you the truth. Much better seasons than this."

"I'm sorry about that. That's why I'm here to help."

"That's what my mom tells me."

Mary knew from her conversations with Connie that Marshall was her son, like Evan, the sheriff. She'd bragged about a third son, too. Nash, whom she'd called a country doctor.

"Your mom's very proud of all you boys."

"How about you? Brothers and sisters?"

"Not a one."

"Maybe it's safer that way." He shot her a teasing grin. "Siblings can be meddlesome."

Mary chuckled. "I've heard that before." She added sincerely, "But it's nice to have people who care about you."

"Yeah." Marshall hesitated, as if deciding whether to say something further. Finally, he did. "I heard you met up with Evan."

"This afternoon. That's right."

"Hope you didn't take anything he said too personally."

"Personally? What do you mean?"

"My brother, ah…" He stalled, shifting on his feet. "Can be a little hard-edged sometimes. Tough, but not in a bad way. Mostly because he loves this town."

"Yeah," Mary said. "I got that."

"Not that Evan's a bad guy, mind you," Marshall said. "He simply likes staying organized. Sticking to the letter of the law."

"That's super. So do I," she said, meaning to put a positive spin on things. Who knew how much of this would get back to Connie—or Evan? "That's why I'm sure that he and I will get along great working together."

"How did he take it about the parade?"

Mary frowned. "Not as well as I expected."

"I'm sorry that Mom left that to you and didn't tell Evan about the parade herself."

"What? She didn't? But why?"

Marshall chuckled. "Our good mayor sometimes has a hard time convincing the sheriff of things. She probably thought you'd do a better job with your professional presentation."

Mary hadn't realized she'd ambushed Evan with her proposal. "Evan didn't seem completely surprised about the parade," she said to Marshall. "It was more like he'd heard about it, and had time to think up his objections."

"Could be. Small town." Marshall rubbed his chin, then spoke confidentially. "You know, Evan's a really great sheriff, but he's good with the status quo." His forehead rose. "Not big on changes."

"You mean, he's risk-averse?"

Marshall smiled softly. "That's one way to put it."

"Hmm," Mary muttered, unsure of what else to say. She hoped that Evan would at least bend a little. Otherwise, this was going to be a very long ten days, with her working hard on the parade, and him working twice as hard to oppose her.

Marshall seemed to intuit her distress. "Don't worry," he said kindly. He thumped the doorframe, preparing to make his exit. "Once Evan understands that this parade's going to work out to Clark Creek's benefit, he'll climb on board. You just need to help him see the upside."

"The upside." She set her chin. "Right. Thanks, Marshall."

After her eventful day, Mary was excited to catch up with Judy. She answered the call on the first ring. "Judy! Hey."

"Hey you. How was your drive?"

"Pretty good. It snowed a lot on the way here."

"I'm glad you got there okay."

"Yeah."

Mary sat back against the pillows on her bed and pressed her cell phone to her ear. She held a slice of pizza in her right hand and it smelled delicious. She bit off a huge piece, diving into its cheesy goodness. Oh wow, this was just what she needed. Carbs.

"*So*," Judy asked directly. "How was your meeting with the sheriff?"

"Extremely annoying, but I'm dealing with it."

"Wait a minute. Are you eating something?"

"Yeah, sorry. Pizza."

"Well, save a slice for me!" Judy laughed. "What kind?"

"Pepperoni and mushroom," Mary said, taking another bite and trying very hard not to talk with her mouth full. But seriously. She was starving, even hungrier than she knew.

The mound of clothing she'd unloaded from her suitcase sat beside her on the bed. She'd already cluttered up the desk with her portable printer and legal pads, her hairbrush, and the flashlight she took with her each time she traveled for late-night emergencies. Not that she'd ever had any, but it paid to be prepared.

Her yoga pants and stretch top draped over the settee, ready for her pre-breakfast morning session, and her boots and various pairs of shoes were strewn across the floor. She'd tidy up eventually—or not. The important thing was, she was staking her claim here, settling in.

"Annoying? I don't get it," Judy said. "I thought the guy was supposed to be your liaison, the person selected to work with you?"

"I don't think he got any say in that selection. Judging by his reception."

"I'm sorry," Judy said. "But you'll work it out. You've dealt with difficult personalities before." Mary had, that was true, but none of them had gotten her blood pumping the way Evan had. He'd definitely gotten her adrenaline going while racing her upstairs to see the mayor. What an aggravating man.

Judy went on to say, "What's important is that the mayor and the town council are behind you, and they are the ones footing your bill."

"That's the part that worries Evan."

"Evan?"

"He's the sheriff," Mary said.

"An old curmudgeon, huh?"

"Acts like one, but no. He's youngish."

"Ish?" Judy prodded.

"In his thirties."

"Ooh. Single?"

"Let's hope so." Mary giggled, trying to envision Evan with someone. Anyone. But out of pity for the poor imaginary woman, she couldn't. He just seemed so buttoned up somehow. Inflexible.

Judy digested this and then asked, "Handsome?"

Mary's heart stilled when she recalled the electricity in his deep blue eyes. They'd practically peered right through her, straight into her soul. If he'd been any other guy, and she a different woman…but no. None of that was happening. It was a good thing she was the only one who'd felt it, which also meant she might have imagined the whole thing to begin with.

"He's probably nice-looking enough for somebody who *might be* interested."

"Which is not you."

"Which is definitely not me." Even if Mary was interested in seeing someone, it certainly wouldn't be Evan. He wasn't her type. She'd done "difficult" before and had come to regret it. Difficult was impossible to reform, and men like him tended to become annoyed by her positive outlook, which was just about as difficult as anyone could get. Only the most negative man could be opposed to positivity. The very idea dumbfounded her.

"Better not to mix business with pleasure," Judy said. "Especially with…" Her voice took on a sing-songy tone. "…your pending move."

Mary was jazzed about relocating to Seattle. She'd started researching it online and the city sounded amazing, with its cool art scene and awesome Pacific Northwest location. But she had Christmas in Clark Creek to contend with first.

She'd been so pumped about the parade on her way here, then Evan's contrary attitude had brought her down. She was rebounding from that, though, and eager to do a good job for the town and its people. She couldn't wait for the big day, but knew there were loads of preparations to tackle first.

"I agree," Mary said, concurring with Judy's advice not to get involved, which was sort of second nature to Mary, anyway. "Besides that 'not mixing business with pleasure' thing, my timeline here's awfully short." She bristled at the memory of Evan suggesting that it should be even shorter. Then she rolled her eyes, when she realized it scarcely mattered what he thought. Judy was right. She had the critical endorsements from the mayor and the town council.

"True," Judy answered. "But long enough for you to get the job done. I was really impressed with your proposal. The folks at headquarters were, too. They called it ambitious. Innovative. Once you pull it off, they'll be singing your praises even louder."

"As long as their tune carries me to all the way to Washington state, I'm happy."

"I'm going to miss you, girl," Judy said after a pause. "Which is why I'm going to have to come visit."

"Oh!" Mary squealed. "Please do. Just as soon as humanly possible. We can have so much fun exploring the town."

"You'll have to get there first." Judy laughed and Mary laughed along with her. "Now that you're settled in, I suppose you'll begin the implementation phase."

"Yep. Getting started tomorrow. I'm seeing Evan at 10:00 a.m."

"Maybe I should say good luck."

Mary grinned, because after she'd left the courthouse, she'd begun devising a plan.

"Thanks. But I might not need it." What she needed was a way to make Evan her ally, and not her adversary. The best way to do that was by helping him see that some of the benefits of the parade would fall on his office. Marshall was on point with that.

She'd flesh things out after she got off the phone with Judy and finished her pizza. Then make some quick notes so she could present her ideas to Evan in the morning. Surely, he'd see things her way one he'd been shown the big picture. And that picture was going to involve one totally glorious, happy-heart-making—*and* revenue-producing—Christmas parade.

# Chapter Six

*E*VAN ENTERED THE WHISTLE STOP Café and found Mary sitting at one of the tables by the front window. He spied her the moment he stepped through the door, but she was so engrossed in her work, she didn't see him. She was sketching out some kind of drawing on a legal pad, and a coffee cup sat at her elbow on top of an open town map. There was basically no place for him to sit. Not if he wanted to put his own coffee cup down somewhere.

He hoped to make this meeting as painless as possible. He'd tried talking to the town council members, and every last one of them, including the generally amenable Vivi Torres, had sent him packing. They all loved Mary's plan and admired the positive energy she brought with her. If anyone could reinvigorate the flagging financials of Clark Creek, it was Mary Ward. Their first, only—and last, if Evan had his way about it—Christmas Consultant. Since he couldn't stop the parade, he could at least try to keep it scaled down to a reasonable size. That was his mission this morning: to keep things under control.

"Morning," he said, and she looked up. He wasn't sure what sort of greeting he'd receive, based on his aversion to her ideas yesterday, but she welcomed him with a warm smile.

"Good morning!"

Good. She wasn't the sort to hold grudges. At least that was something. Given that he was being forced to work with her for nine more days.

Evan pulled out a chair and her eyebrows arched. "Don't you want coffee?"

The aroma of fresh-roasted beans travelled his way. Coffee did sound good. The Whistle Stop Café was all self-serve from the counter, and when he glanced over, he saw the line was short. "I think I will grab myself a cup."

"Don't take too long," she teased. "We've only got thirty minutes."

"Ha." He grinned, feeling the jab.

Okay, so maybe he could have given her forty-five minutes. Probably still could. Things weren't *that* busy on his docket for today. Frankly, they were a little dead. He'd completed his morning drive through town, and everything looked tranquil under a blanket of snow. That was after visiting farmer Jeb Wilson, who'd put in a panicked early-morning call to Helen about a stolen cow. Turned out old Bessie had found a hole in the fence and sauntered through it to visit with a bull in the neighboring pasture. Evan had grinned to himself when he'd discovered that, thinking that spring wasn't even in the air yet.

The only thing Evan had going on this afternoon was a presentation at his niece's elementary school for Community Helpers' Day. Marshall's pal Donny Jones would be there representing the Volunteer Fire Department, and Megan Parks, a nurse practitioner from Nash's clinic, was scheduled to attend. One of the town librarians, Shirley Watson, had promised to show, and Evan's dad, Jesse, was putting in an appearance on behalf of the Department of Public Works. Those guys were staying extra busy on account of this heavy snow.

Evan returned to the table with his coffee, seeing that Mary had folded up her map, clearing a spot for him. "I'm sorry about the mess," she said. "I tend to make myself at home. When I'm in a hotel, my stuff is everywhere."

Evan took a sip of his coffee, glad that he'd gotten it. Something told him he'd need a ton of caffeine to keep up with her. She sat there looking as bright-eyed as a frisky kitten, energy oozing out of her. Mary was clearly a morning person. "Spend a lot of time in hotels, do you?"

"Not as much as I used to. I basically grew up in them. My mom's a corporate chef, and my dad wasn't really around. So." She shrugged. "I guess that was the life I knew."

His instinct was to feel sorry for her, because to him that sounded depressing and so different from how he was raised: on a big family farm with two supportive parents and his brothers, and lots of time spent outdoors. Yet, in an interesting way, she didn't seem bothered by the memory, merely reflective about it. "That must have been different."

"It had its positive aspects, and its downsides," she said. "It wasn't easy making friends, for one thing. Not many other kids live in fancy hotels, and we never really stayed anyplace for too long."

Those all sounded like negatives to him, but he didn't say so.

"The upside was that I got to travel a lot and we lived in some cool places."

"Oh yeah? Like where?" He held up a hand. "Wait. Let me guess. New Orleans?"

"I give you an A plus for listening." Her lips pulled into

a grin and he felt that inconvenient jolt in his chest—
again. He pounded it with his fist, thinking he needed to
slow down on the coffee. He definitely wasn't attracted to
her. That would be lame. She was only here temporarily,
and he wasn't in the dating game anyway.

"Are you okay?"

"Uh-huh. Fine."

"So, anyway," she went on. "Apart from New Orleans,
there was Washington, D.C., and then Atlanta. Richmond, but only for three months."

"Three months?"

She waved his concern aside. "I eventually moved back
there on my own. Two years ago last May."

"Ever live anywhere outside the country?"

"The Caribbean, yeah. We were in Saint John for a
season." Her face took on a dreamy cast. "I was twelve
and thought we'd landed in heaven." She drank from her
cup. "Have you travelled much?"

"Just with the Army. Hot spots in the middle of deserts.
None of them were what I'd call heaven. Except for that
last post in the UAE. That assignment was cushy. No
tents. I got to stay in a very nice hotel. I'm guessing it
had a corporate chef."

"If it was a five-star establishment, it most certainly
did." She grinned and dimples settled in her cheeks.
Extremely enchanting dimples that he'd failed to notice
before. He didn't know why he'd noticed them now,
other than that they were very apparent when she smiled.

He checked his watch, seeing that fifteen minutes
had elapsed and they hadn't even started talking about
the parade. It was weird for him to lose track of time,
but he'd found himself caught up in her story about her
upbringing. Not to mention her big brown eyes.

His ears burned hot at that last thought and he cleared

his throat. She observed him in a curious manner, like she was wondering what he was thinking, and he definitely didn't want her to know. He had no business contemplating her big brown eyes. What on earth was wrong with him? "So. About your parade…"

"It's your parade too," she said, clearly wanting him to take ownership, which he was not, in any way, shape or form, going to do. "I believe, when I explain my ideas, you'll appreciate how much."

He set down his coffee cup. "I'm not sure I follow."

"I've thought of a way to raise money, not just for Clark Creek in general, but for specific parts of it, like your Sheriff's Office."

Now she had his interest. "Go on."

"Today is Community Helpers' Day at your niece's school, isn't it?"

"Yeah, but how did you know that?"

"Marshall told me this morning. He was invited to go, due to his inn's support of the soup kitchen. But because of his hours at the soup kitchen—"

"There was a conflict," Evan said. "Yes. I know."

"In any case," she continued. "The whole Community Helpers' thing sparked an inspiration when I heard about it yesterday."

"Ah. Another *inspiration*." He held her gaze and it looked like she was trying not to blush. He hadn't meant for that to sound flirty, but he worried that it had.

"Yes. Well." She licked her lips and tugged her gaze away from his, focusing on her satchel, which she lifted off the floor. She extracted a piece of paper and handed it to him. "Here." It was a printed list with organizations' names on it, like the Community Church, the Clark Creek Library, Miller's Bake Shop, the Volunteer Fire Department…and—yep, there it was, smack-dab in the middle—Clark County's Sheriff's Office, along with the names of lots of town businesses, and—hang on—even the local animal shelter.

He raised his eyes to hers. "What's all this?"

"My ideas for the different floats."

There had to be at least twenty-five names on the list, and there was a second stapled page…and a third. "Oh, no," he told her. "No, no, no, just no. I'm sorry, Mary. Clark Creek definitely can't handle a parade of this size."

"You don't understand. It's all voluntary. And all participants stand to benefit in terms of parade proceeds. Each float will receive a prorated amount from ticket sales, in addition to any direct donations as designated by sponsors. So, the more floats the better."

He wasn't so sure about that.

"Clark Creek's general operating budget will earn the lion's share from ticket sales: sixty percent. It will also secure a ten percent portion of float sponsorship earnings to help offset parade costs and further bolster town revenues."

She clearly showed acumen with the fundraising angle, but was not at all focused on the fallout. The proportions of this parade she was putting together only doubled or tripled his problems regarding logistics and crowd control. And nobody—from his mom, the mayor, down to Mary—seemed to be giving any consideration to that.

"Think about it!" she continued. "Each float could be a cool project for any organization or office. School groups can participate too, like the high school band… but they'll be marching, of course. And a float doesn't have to be a 'float' in a traditional sense. The library could use its mobile book unit and decorate it with streamers and balloons…big painted signs with messages in support of books and reading. The Feed and Seed could use one of their flatbed trucks, and—"

"That's a lot of last-minute planning. Christmas Eve is less than two weeks away. At this late date, who says that anybody would be interested?"

"They already are."

"What?"

She smiled in a self-congratulatory fashion. "I spoke to several people this morning, including the high school band director. The library and Miller's Bake Shop are also on board. The Feed and Seed, too."

"How did you accomplish all this?" Evan checked his watch again, which was a regular habit of his. He wasn't one for wasting time, so always minded it. "It's only ten-twenty."

"I started early."

Evan raked a hand through his hair and the back of his head throbbed, reminding him of the headache Mary had caused him yesterday. Something told him it wasn't half as big as the ones that were coming.

She leaned toward him, growing increasingly animated. "The people at the shelter were super nice. They asked about putting adoptable dogs and cats on their floats and I said yes! What a fantastic idea."

Evan's jaw dropped. "Live animals?"

"Most of them will probably be in carriers. They have a very well-trained half Dalmatian-half Collie," she reported. Evan found it hard to envision this. "Her name is Harriette. And a Corgi mix named Rex. Those two are to be mascots, because they're older and extremely well-behaved. The cats they're not so sure about, except for Louie."

"Louie?"

"He's their big old tabby tom who sleeps a lot. Totally chill. They thought maybe he could ride in the cab of the first truck."

"First truck?"

"They'll need at least three or four pickups to fit all the animal cages in and not crowd them. Each and every one of those little guys deserves a chance for adoption. You can't tell me that you disagree?"

This was tricky business. Now, she was making him out to be an animal hater. "No, I don't disagree. I mean, I do agree with you about adoptions. In general, and responsible pet ownership in particular. Neutering and spaying, all of that."

Her face fell in understanding. "But you hate the idea about the rescue floats."

"No, no. I think it's good. But *four trucks*?" He grimaced. "Maybe a little over the top?"

She huffed. "These are little lives we're talking about, Evan."

"Right." He frowned, understanding animal rescue was an important issue, and that he should support it. Still, this was just one more complication. "How do you propose to work that, anyway? The adoptions?"

"I was hoping we could set up an adoption booth at the end of the parade route," she said. "Maybe alongside Santa's workshop?"

*Santa's what?*

She didn't seem to notice his confusion. "I flew the idea by the town council, and they loved it. Your mom adored it, too. So many needy animals finding their forever homes by Christmas. This is so exciting! By the way." Her eyes sparkled. "You were absolutely right about the parade starting at the town square. The gazebo is the perfect place for selling tickets."

*Oh, no.* He was *not* taking credit for *any* of this.

He started to speak, but her phone buzzed and she

stared down at it. "I'm sorry." She frowned. "I'd better take this."

Things were getting out of control here, which was definitely not what Evan wanted. A potential sixty or more floats wasn't a manageable parade, it was overwhelming for a town the size of Clark Creek. And what about those *rescue floats*? What if something went wrong and they experienced an encore of animals stampeding down Main Street?

"Hi, Nash!" she crooned into the mouthpiece, and Evan was sure his eyes bugged out. What was Nash doing calling Mary? "You can?" she said, looking pleased. "Oh, absolutely! Tomorrow at noon would be perfect. Thank you…Evan? Yeah. I'm sitting right here with him." She covered her phone. "Nash says to tell you hi."

Evan rubbed his temples. Now his brother was lining up against him. Who would be next? Marshall?

"Oh yeah," she told Nash, "That's what Marshall said too. A real landmark occasion. Clark Creek's first parade ever. Aww, did little Chloe ask that, really? You can tell her that of course Santa Claus will be there." She winked at Evan. "Santa always finds a way."

Her phone buzzed again and she stared down at the display. "I'm sorry, Nash, I've got a call coming through from your mom…okay, great, thanks!" she said. "See you tomorrow."

Seconds later she was on with the mayor. "Hi, Connie…ooh, fantastic! For the gazebo? Yes. Yes. That's just what I asked for. Hang on. Right now? He's there taking measurements? Oh wow. I need to meet with him. Ask him not to leave, will you? I can be there in ten." She finished her call and shoved her things into her satchel. "I'm really sorry, Evan," she said. "Do you mind if we continue our discussion about the parade route tomorrow?"

Continue? That particular discussion hadn't even gotten started. They also hadn't gotten around to the notion of ticket sales and how Mary planned to coordinate those. He was so dazed, all he could say was, "Uh-huh." How had she done all of this so quickly? Somebody was decorating the gazebo? Who? And why was she meeting with Nash? It couldn't seriously be about those portable bathrooms?

"The Holly and the Ivy Nursery in Hopedale has done the most amazing thing," she told him, standing. "They're donating a huge fir tree for the town square and a grouping of smaller trees and greenery for the gazebo. All gratis! *Lagniappe.*"

"I thought *lagniappe* was that little extra bonus paid when you did business with someone?"

"Clark Creek *is* doing business with the Holly and the Ivy. They're one of our new sponsors for the parade. Elf League level!"

"Sponsoring one of the floats?"

"Nope. Not a float. Just serving as a general sponsor for the parade in exchange for advertising. They get their name and logo on some banners and in the parade program."

"There's going to be a program?" Evan asked weakly, and all he could picture was piles and piles of post-parade litter swirling down Main Street through the snow.

"Don't worry." She tilted her chin. "Won't cost Clark Creek a thing."

"I…see," he said, feeling like he'd walked into some sort of dreamworld orchestrated by Mary. A dreamworld that more and more people seemed to be getting sucked into. "What are you talking with Nash about?" He wasn't jealous of his brother, or anything. Even if Nash was a decent-looking guy and a well-paid doctor, who ran his own farm...

"Oh, lots of things," she said mysteriously.

Tons of women found Nash attractive, including—very plainly—Itzel. Maybe Mary would too. Which shouldn't be a big deal. Seriously. Nash hadn't looked at a woman with interest in a while. At the same time, Nash hadn't yet met Mary, with her perky grin and that endless optimism that could drive a man wild.

Evan's neck warmed and he rubbed the back of it, knowing he was blowing things out of proportion. Mary was staying at Marshall's, after all, and Marshall was a well-known eligible bachelor too. All three of the Clark brothers were, only none of them was looking.

Not seriously. Not at the moment. And Evan was looking the least hard of all.

She glanced at the exit like she was in a hurry to go, which she was. Obviously. "Same time tomorrow work for you?" she asked. "Or is the afternoon better?"

"Let's make it afternoon," Evan said, wanting more time to collect his scrambled thoughts. He also planned to talk to his dad, Jesse. Jesse was an extremely grounded man and also a manager for Public Works. Surely, he'd foresee the disaster that was coming from Mary's scheme and be on Evan's side in tamping down her exploding debacle of a parade.

"Sounds good." Mary smiled. "Four o'clock? Here?"

"Sure," Evan replied. "Why not?"

She breezed out the door and into the swirling snow, popping open her bright red umbrella. Evan stood and gathered his trash, still lost in the hazy fog caused by whirlwind Mary. It was only when he picked up his empty coffee cup that he realized that fifty minutes had gone by and that it was almost eleven o'clock.

# Chapter Seven

WHEN MARY ARRIVED AT THE gazebo, Connie was there chatting with two men. The younger guy was athletic-looking with light hair and a beard, and the older heavyset man with gray hair seemed about Connie's age. He slightly resembled Evan, and Mary wondered if he was Connie's husband and dad to their three boys.

"Mary, come on over here!" Connie waved her toward them. "I want you to meet Ken Larsen from our neighboring town, and this is my husband," she said, motioning to the man beside her, who held out his hand.

"Mary," he said. "So nice to meet you. I'm Jesse Clark."

"Mr. Clark—"

"Please," he smiled warmly, and this time he reminded her of Marshall. "Jesse is fine."

"Then Jesse it is," she said, grinning.

Ken nodded a polite hello. "Good to see you, Mary. I'm the one you spoke with on the phone at the Holly and the Ivy."

"Of course." She studied his expressive face, which was tanned like he was used to spending lots of time outdoors. "Thanks so much for your sponsorship."

"Ken was the first one to sign up as an official sponsor,"

Mary said to Connie and Jesse. "Elf League."

"It helps that I have a thing for our new Chamber of Commerce director." Ken lowered his voice in a whisper. "Apart from doing a good deed, I was hoping to impress her."

Mary giggled at his frankness. It seemed people in these small towns told each other everything, even when they weren't from the same small town. "I actually think I spoke with her, and she was so nice. Gave me contact information for several business owners, and even one local developer."

Connie addressed Ken. "She's Sara Rose's little girl, isn't she?"

"Dusty, that's right," Ken said. "All grown up now and recently moved back home."

"How nice," Jesse chimed in. "Old friends reunited."

Connie grinned in an enigmatic way. "Or maybe they'll be more than friends one day?"

Ken smiled. "You always were an old romantic, Mrs. Clark."

"Now, don't be calling me 'old'," she teased, and the rest of them laughed.

Ken rubbed his gloves together, seeming to weigh his confession. "Wouldn't mind that," he said a bit sheepishly. "Me and Dusty, the long haul…" He shrugged. "You know."

"Well, your impressive sponsorship of Clark Creek's Christmas Parade is a very good way to catch her eye," Mary told him.

"From the look on his face," Connie said slyly, "he's already got it."

Ken chuckled and nodded his head. "Yeah."

Jesse studied Ken. "Will you bring Dusty to our parade?"

"Would if I could, but we've got another date for the holidays."

"Oh yeah?" Mary asked him.

"Colorado."

Jesse whistled. "That's a long ways to go for a latte. What's there?"

"My sister and her husband, and their kids," Ken said.

"So, it's looking serious then?" Mary asked with a nudge. She'd barely met Ken, and yet, he was so accepting and warm, she already felt a familiar kinship with him. In Clark Creek it was so easy to fit in, with everyone but Evan.

"I'll be sure to let you know." He surveyed the group and gave a happy grin. "In fact, I'll probably be shouting it from the mountaintops. You might even hear the good news all the way back in Virginia. Assuming there is good news."

This brought laughter all around.

Now that he'd gotten started, Ken couldn't resist sharing more. "My friend Sam Singleton set me up with a diamond. Totally elegant and one of a kind. Sam's our jeweler in Hopedale and his shop is known for its engagement rings. If you haven't seen one of his TV spots already," he told Mary, "you probably will while you're here. They air throughout the local area."

"How exciting for you," Mary said. She held up her fingers and crossed them. "I hope all goes well."

"Thank you," he said, and Mary felt like she'd made a friend. Three friends, counting Connie and Jesse. Itzel and Dennis had been super friendly too. Then, there was welcoming Marshall. She hadn't met Nash in person, but he sounded kind and approachable on the phone. The only holdout among them was stand-offish Evan, although she had noticed a *slow thaw* happening with him this morning. He'd essentially agreed with her about the animal floats, so he seemed to be coming around. Baby steps. But still.

"Oh, Ken," Connie said, and Mary realized she'd missed some of their chatter. "It's good to see you again." She turned to Mary. "I was friends with Ken's late mom when we were growing up."

"Connie's from Hopedale, you know," Jesse explained.

"No," Mary said. "I didn't know that."

Connie grew wistful at the memory. "Lived there a *long* time ago."

"Wasn't that long, darling," Jesse said. "She was sweet sixteen when her family moved to Clark Creek and she stole my heart away."

Mary was touched by his confession, and Ken couldn't help but smile.

"The stealing was mutual, honey," Connie said.

"You haven't changed a bit." Jesse twinkled at his wife and patted his ample belly. "I, on the other hand…" He chortled good-naturedly. "Thanks to your good cooking."

Connie became reflective a moment. "Ah yes, Hopedale," she said, reciting as if from memory, "*Home of the Hopedale Honeybee.*"

"The town's motto is 'Where Love Springs Eternal' now," Ken said, and the others smiled at his correction.

"Then, it seems the town motto's on your side," Jesse quipped.

Connie sighed. "How times have changed."

"For the better in Hopedale," Ken told her and the others. "I was really sorry to learn of Clark Creek's hard times."

"We don't have your ski resort here," Connie said. "Or those mineral springs that draw tourists."

Mary glanced around at the attractive string of businesses

framing the town square, and then at the nearly empty skating rink, which she suspected might fill up later once kids were out of school. In the falling snow, the setting appeared magical. Like something you'd see on a holiday card, only it was beautifully real.

The library was at one end of the square and the courthouse at the other, facing Main Street. She stared up at a second-floor window, thinking from its location that it must be Evan's office. He hadn't turned on the Christmas lights she'd wound around his coat rack. If he had, she'd see them twinkling.

Evan seemed pretty wound tight about lots of things, especially her parade. But there'd been that moment at the café when he'd nearly let his guard down: when he'd teased her about her inspirations. Mirth had flickered in his eyes and he'd almost seemed flirtatious. Almost, but not quite. Flirting was probably as foreign to Evan as having fun.

She tried to imagine him cutting loose and having a really good belly laugh, or doing something goofy like playing in the snow. Even for her great imagination, that was a stretch. And yet, she had to believe that it was possible and that he had his fun-loving side. Mary's cheeks heated when she realized what she was wishing. She was hoping she'd see that side of Evan personally. At least one time before she left Clark Creek.

"Clark Creek has a lot to offer," Mary said, rejoining the conversation.

"Yeah," Jesse said. "I hear you've come to make the most of that."

"Her parade's going to be the bomb," Connie said.

Ken shook his head. "I'm really sorry I have to miss it."

"Maybe it will become an annual event?" Jesse suggested.

Connie's eyes shimmered with delight. "Wouldn't that be cool?"

"Yeah," Mary said with a happy heart. "It would." If a certain sheriff shared that view, her life would be perfect. But she honestly didn't need Evan's stamp of approval for her parade to be successful. If all she could get was his grudging cooperation, she'd take it, and find a way to make lemonade out of his lemons.

"You should give Sam a call," Ken said to Mary. "See if he'll help out. He and his wife Angie own their shop together, and they're really good people. They'd probably be happy to contribute to your parade. I can talk to them beforehand. Give them a little heads up."

"Really?" Mary's heart lifted even higher. "That would be amazing, Ken. Thanks. I saw Singleton's Jewelers on my list, but I haven't called them yet."

"Tell you what," Ken said. "Why don't I ask Dusty for a copy of the list she sent you. I don't mind doing a little legwork around Hopedale. Talking to folks who might not have heard about your parade."

"That's a great idea," Connie said. "Thank you, Ken."

"Yes," Jesse added. "Thank you so much—from all of us in Clark Creek."

Ken nodded like it was no problem, then asked Mary, "Do you have any flyers I can hand out? Like that sponsorship form you emailed me."

Mary grinned. "Sure do. I've got dozens more in my bag." She pulled some from her satchel and Ken tucked them away in his jacket.

"Thanks."

Then he and Mary got to work, as she told him about the type of tree she wanted for the town square and the other sorts of decorations she'd love to have for the gazebo. While they were talking, Jesse walked up to Mary before leaving with Connie.

"I say, I was wondering..." He stroked his heavy chin. "What's your thinking regarding there being a Santa Claus in this parade?"

Mary beamed at him. She had to look up, because he was over six feet tall like his boys, while she was only five-nine. Even in her high-heeled boots, Jesse still had a couple of inches on her. "My thinking is that a Santa Claus float is a must."

"For a Christmas parade," Connie said, joining her husband. "Absolutely." She considered Jesse. Then, she stared at Mary. "Jesse always plays Santa for the kids at our church during our Advent Festival. It's the first Sunday after Thanksgiving every year." She smiled like a light bulb had just gone off in her head.

"So...*ho-ho*." Jesse grinned a jolly grin, cinching the deal. "I already have the suit."

Evan caught up with his dad as he strolled out of Clark Creek Elementary holding his granddaughter's hand. Jesse was taking Chloe to her dance lesson after school, since he was semi-retired now, and Nash was working at his clinic. The little girl skipped along beside her grandpa, her dark pigtails bouncing against her puffy purple coat with every step.

"Nice job with your presentation," Evan told his dad.

"Thanks. Same with yours."

Chloe's big grin displayed a gap where her two upper front teeth had been. "I love my sticker, Uncle Evan." She patted the sticker with her mitten where she'd affixed it to her coat.

"You make a very fine sheriff, Buttercup," Evan said, and Chloe giggled.

She stared hopefully up at him and he knew what she wanted.

"Okay. Here you go." Evan chuckled and removed his hat, placing it on Chloe's head. She held it on either side by its brim, as it got buffeted by the wind.

"Thanks, Uncle Evan!" she crooned, looking up.

Evan tapped the top of the hat. "You're welcome."

Community Helpers' day had gone just fine, with hordes of kindergartners through second graders sitting at rapt attention in the auditorium. Evan had come prepared with sheriff badge stickers to hand out to the kids. Last year, he'd given out toy plastic badges, but those were now too costly per item. Evan had talked about his daily duties as sheriff, underscoring important safety rules, like not talking to strangers and looking both ways before crossing the street.

Jesse had explained to the kids about how his crews helped keep the town tidy by maintaining clean streets—and clear ones, in snowy and icy weather. He'd gifted the children forest green pencils marked with Clark Creek's golden emblem of a shady oak tree, like the landmark one that sat on the banks of Clark Creek where it joined the James River tributary. Evan knew these pencils hadn't cost his dad anything, since his mom had had them made up in abundance for all county employees two years ago, and they were still enjoying an excess.

The librarian had brought bookmarks, which she'd also had in oversupply, and Donny had delivered the cardboard fire hats he had left over from last year's county fair, where kids had been allowed to climb aboard the hose and ladder truck. The pediatric dentist handed out travel toothbrushes, while the other medical professional there, the nurse practitioner, supplied mini hand sanitizers, with reminders to the kids to always wash their hands before eating.

The adults in attendance were doing what they could to keep the children unaware of the town's financial woes, but Evan suspected that some of them picked up on the stress being experienced by their parents. Evan gave the school's teachers and staff full credit for maintaining an upbeat educational atmosphere. The parent volunteers were trying hard, too; a number of them served the homemade refreshments they'd brought in after the lower grade assembly.

But Evan knew the friendly faces of those familiar townsfolk masked their secret worries. With commerce down, and so many businesses hurting, would this really be a merry Christmas for all? Beyond fretting about the extra expense of presents, people had very real concerns about putting food on the table for their families and making ends meet.

"I met our new Christmas Consultant earlier," Jesse said, when they reached the parking lot.

Evan spoke above the wind. "Funny you should mention that, because I actually wanted to talk to you about her."

"She's doing a splendid job." Jesse grinned. "Very impressive."

"What?"

"She's going to get the town square all done up for Christmas, and at no expense to Clark Creek."

"How did she manage that?"

"By working a bit of holiday magic." Jesse opened the back door to his truck which already had a child's car seat strapped into the back seat. Chloe scrambled right into it, knocking off the sheriff's hat when it bumped against the roof.

"Sorry, Uncle Evan," she said, buckling herself in.

Evan shot her a wink and scooped his hat off the icy ground, seating it back on his head. "No worries, sweetheart." He returned his attention to his dad when his dad shut Chloe's door. "No, really," he asked again. "How did she?"

Snow drove down harder, dusting both their hats. "Mary's made some connections in Hopedale," his dad said. "Ken Larsen was here taking measurements for a town tree."

"Ken? From the nursery over there?"

His dad nodded. "That's the one."

"And all for free," Evan added skeptically.

"Not no-strings completely. There was something about his business being one of the parade sponsors, so I reckon he'll get some publicity out of this."

The premise sounded good, of course. Doable. Have those sounder businesses contribute to Mary's parade in exchange for self-promotion. It was a canny form of advertising. Only, that didn't solve the major problem of the parade size Mary had planned, and its related logistical issues.

"I know Mary means well," Evan said. "But I'm afraid some of her parade ideas are getting out of hand."

Jesse's bushy eyebrows arched.

"She's talking dozens of floats, Dad. I don't think our small street structure can handle that."

"All it will take is some advance planning," his dad said.

"Planning costs money."

"Money that Mary's going to make us back tenfold, according to your mom."

"There's no guarantee of that, and in the meantime…" Evan exhaled sharply. "Clark Creek is in a state of financial collapse."

"Precisely why we need a miracle." His dad walked around to the driver's door on his truck, as though their conversation had ended. "I want you to be nice to this woman, son. Do your best to help her, because she's working her hardest to help all of us."

Evan could see he was getting nowhere. "She's talking animal floats!" he tossed out in desperation. "More than one! Rescue cats and dogs from the shelter riding right down Main Street! Can you imagine anything so—"

"Beats those pigs your mom had running loose on the Fourth of July," Jesse said with a chuckle. He climbed into the cab.

Evan grumbled when Jesse waved goodbye, and little Chloe did the same from the back seat. It was all well and good for his dad, mom, and the entire town council to be swept away by Mary's glossy parade plans. But what if they didn't work? In spite of businesses like Ken Larsen's making generous contributions?

Even if he waived his own salary for the event, which he was willing to do, Evan would still have to pay his deputy overtime for working on Christmas Eve. Helen, too, for the predictably higher demand for dispatch. Who knew how many fender-benders might ensue on the traffic-jammed streets? He'd probably also have to recruit Itzel to help with parking, or that ticket-taking Mary mentioned, and there went another overtime salary allocation. Volunteer workers were great, but volunteers could only go so far without official supervision to ensure the event ran safely.

What about public works? Had his dad not given one thought to the condition Clark Creek's streets and sidewalks would be left in after such a sizable parade? After the crush of the crowds, and given any parade debris left behind, they certainly couldn't remain a mess for Christmas. Those street crews would have to be afforded holiday pay as well, to attend to the cleanup, including hauling away temporary trash containers.

And, if the big parade attracted gobs of tourists, like Mary promised, where would all those folks stay? Would they sleep out in their cars, pitch tents, or park campers at the county fairgrounds and on Nash's farmland, right alongside those porta potties?

Evan groaned and trudged through the snow to his sheriff's SUV. It seemed like he was the sole rational individual in town who could predict the negative impact of Mary's plan. When it all came crashing down, and the parade wound up costing Clark Creek more than it made, it would be up to Clark Creek's disappointed—and far poorer—citizens to pick up the pieces of the shattered town and try to put it back together again.

What a very sad Christmas that would make for everyone concerned. And sadness and Christmas were a bad mix. Evan knew enough about that firsthand, and he wouldn't wish that sort of holiday on his worst enemy, not to mention his fondest friends.

# Chapter Eight

*M*ARY REACHED NASH'S FARM THE next day at a little past noon. The front of his property sat at the edge of town beside the county fairgrounds, at the juncture where Main Street formed a T-intersection with Three-Notched Pass, which eventually connected to a rural highway at its northern end. Mary drove down a dirt road through an open gate. The rustic wooden sign overhead read *Meadowmont Farm*. From its rolling pastures and picturesque mountain backdrop, she could see where it got its name.

Nash had agreed to meet her during his lunch break from the clinic because she wanted to discuss her parade plan and how it might impact his property, while requesting his permission to use a small portion of it on Christmas Eve. He'd initially been hesitant about seeing her, but her cheerful optimism about the parade's outcome had eventually won him over.

She'd always found you catch more flies with honey than vinegar, so she'd heaped on the sweetener when chatting with Nash, telling him all about the sponsors who'd already pledged their help, including those big-name ones from Hopedale. When she'd mentioned the developer who'd built the ski resort, Nash had seemed impressed. By the time he'd called her back to arrange their meeting time, he'd sounded swayed to her way of thinking. Since he'd shared news about the parade with his daughter, it would be hard for him not to get behind it now.

She passed a barn and a couple of outbuildings as she approached the farmhouse: a lovely two-story structure with a covered wraparound porch. It was a historic-looking place, probably built in the early 1900s, with its original beveled windows catching the midday light. On the far side of the house, she saw a set of stables, adjoining a riding ring and a large snowy field. The snow had briefly let up, but more was predicted later.

Three men rounded the house from the backyard. One was an older, grizzled-looking guy who led a horse by its bridle. A middle-aged man in a scruffy blond beard and hat walked beside him, and the third man wore a field coat, cowboy boots and jeans. He wasn't exactly dressed like a doctor, but the attractive dark-haired man in his thirties had to be Nash.

Mary parked her SUV in a spot by the front of the house, and Nash broke away from the others, striding up to her driver's side window. "Mary," he said when she lowered it. "Welcome to Meadowmont Farm." He had very dark eyes, solid cheekbones, and a sturdy jaw. He looked just like a younger version of Jesse.

"Thanks for agreeing to see me," she said.

"Won't you come in for coffee?"

"I don't want to take up too much of your time. Besides, I'm meeting Evan for coffee later."

"Ah."

The other men approached, curiosity apparently getting the better of them. "These are two of my farmhands,"

Nash said. He indicated the older guy. "Leroy." Then nodded toward the guy in the hat. "And this is Austin."

Mary climbed out of her SUV to greet them. "Very nice to meet you."

"You as well, Miss Mary," Leroy said, stopping his horse beside him.

Austin tipped his hat. "Hello."

"Austin here looks after my fields," Nash told her. "Leroy cares for the horses."

Mary had always wanted to ride and had begged for lessons as a child. With the lifestyle she'd had growing up, that had had never been possible, though. "How many have you got?"

"Six at the moment," Nash said. "This one's Nellie."

Mary tentatively stretched her hand forward and Leroy nodded. "You can go on and pet her. She won't bite."

Mary stroked the animal's nose, which felt scratchy and a little silky all at once. Nellie raised her nose in the air and snorted, and Mary jumped back. "Oh!"

The men chuckled. "She's just saying hello," Leroy told her.

Nash turned toward her. "You wanted to talk about the parade?"

"Yes, well…" She eyed his farmhands uncertainly. They didn't seem ready to go anywhere and Nash didn't act like he was going to dismiss them. "After starting at the town square, I was thinking that the parade could wind up here."

Nash folded his arms across his chest. "Here?"

"It's a straight shot from the courthouse, so easier on the floats and such not to have to turn corners—especially the large ones. The mayor plans to open up the fairgrounds for parking, and also designate an area that's large enough for the floats to turn around when they're ready to head home."

Leroy rubbed his chin. "How many floats you planning?"

"So far, I've got sixty," she said, "but I'm hoping for more."

"There's something fun about a parade," Leroy said to the others. "My ma and pa used to take me to the one in Valley View when I was a kid."

Mary hadn't heard of that town. Then again, she'd never heard about Clark Creek until recently.

Austin nodded at Leroy. "I recall those parades. My folks took me and my sister to a couple of 'em." His shoulders sagged. "Don't think they have 'em anymore."

"Nope." Leroy shook his head. "Haven't in years."

"Shame," Austin and Leroy said almost simultaneously.

Mary latched onto their sense of nostalgia. "I know what you mean. Big parades are the *best*. So much fun, and festive. And Christmas parades are the best of all, because they involve Santa." She glanced sheepishly at Nash, then leaned toward the group. "I was thinking—*hoping*—that Santa could come here?"

"Here?" Nash cocked his head and Austin guffawed.

Leroy just said, "Santa? What?"

Mary gestured toward the road. "You've got space at the end of your pasture, right where Main Street deadends at the T-intersection with Three-Notched Pass."

"Yeah? So?" Nash asked, and Mary's pulse pounded because he seemed intrigued.

"So, I was thinking we might set up a Santa's workshop there? Someplace where kids could come and meet Santa Claus?"

"What kind of workshop you talking?" Austin asked.

"Don't think she means an actual one," Leroy told him. "More of a stage-type thing."

"Exactly." Mary nodded. "Nothing elaborate. Just a nice comfy chair for Santa to sit in under a covered space, probably made of wood. The art teacher at the high school said her kids might be able to put something together. Some of them build sets for school plays. A few of the handier parents sometimes help them. We don't have much time, but she thought it was such a worthwhile project…"

"So will Santa be here, or ride in your parade?" Nash asked.

"Both." Mary smiled. "My idea is for him to ride on a float decorated like Santa's sleigh from where the parade starts at the town square. When he gets here, he can greet any children who want to see him and hand out candy canes from his workshop."

"A Santa Claus parade, right here in Clark Creek," Austin said. He glanced at the older guy and grinned. "Say, Leroy. Maybe you can play one of his elves?"

The old man snorted. Then he reddened and peered at Mary. "Truth be told, I wouldn't be disinclined, if it would help."

Mary wanted to hug him. "That would be awesome, Leroy. Thank you!"

"Who's playing Santa?" Nash asked.

"Your dad."

Nash grinned. "Right. He already has the suit."

"That's what he said." Mary shrugged, feeling happy. This was going tons better than she'd expected. Nash was being incredibly cooperative, and even Leroy and Austin were getting into the act.

Austin adjusted his hat. "Well, if it's elf-playing ya need…" He cleared his throat. "I don't mind partici-pating."

Nash dropped his jaw.

"That would be amazing, Austin," Mary said, feeling like she'd just achieved a triple-score. "*Such* a huge help. Thank you."

"No problem, Miss Mary," he said deferentially, and Nash raised his eyebrows.

"You seem to work wonders around here," he told her.

"I'm hoping those wonders help Clark Creek out of the pinch that it's in."

"Hmm. Yeah."

Leroy's eyes twinkled. "What about the horses?"

"What about them?" Nash asked.

"Those parades I mentioned over in Valley View... they sometimes had horses done up like reindeer. You know, wearing sleigh bells and such and with fake antlers on their heads."

"I *love* that idea." Mary's blood pumped harder, because just imagining this made her feel so inspired. This was going to be such a wonderful parade. Even Evan had to agree, once he learned of the progress she'd made.

Nash chuckled. "Can't see the harm in dressing up the horses. As long as they don't get too vexed about it."

"I'll talk to them first," Leroy said.

"Leroy's something of a horse whisperer around here," Nash told Mary. "They're very good at listening to what he says."

"Well, if the horses won't mind..." She shot Leroy a happy grin. "Then I think that would be super cool. Could they be tied up near Santa's workshop?"

"Yes ma'am."

"We could even offer kiddie rides," Austin said.

Mary laughed with delight. "Are any of your horses tame enough?"

Leroy patted the horse beside him. "Nellie will do just fine."

76

Nash addressed Mary. "Nellie's my daughter Chloe's horse. Really great with kids."

"Belle's an easy rider too," Leroy added. "In case we get a big demand."

"Two horses are probably better than one," Austin agreed.

Nash thought a moment and stared toward the road. "Shouldn't be any problem having you use that bit of land. I can clear out some additional space for parking in my front pasture, by opening that big gate." He pointed in that direction. "In case there's an overflow at the fairgrounds."

"That would be so helpful, Nash. Thank you." She bit her lip because this was the hardest part to ask about. "There's just one more thing."

Leroy snickered. "Bet it's 'bout those porta-potties."

"Not so sure about those," Nash said with a grimace. "Honestly."

"People will need to have somewhere to go," Mary said. "The stores in town will probably be packed to the gills, with their restrooms overrun. The company I found is into green initiatives. Everything's handled in an eco-friendly way."

"Eco-friendly," Austin said wryly. "Sounds like that natural fertilizer we use."

Leroy elbowed him. "Mind your manners around the lady."

Nash pursed his lips. "I'll need to see the particulars."

"Of course," Mary said. "I can email you the information this afternoon. And they won't be here very long. Everything will be collected by five o'clock on Christmas Eve."

"Not making any promises." Nash repressed a grin. "But I'm not saying no, either."

Which was as good as a yes to Mary. She seemed to be batting a thousand. After all, Nash's two rough-hewn farmhands had just offered to dress up as elves, and she never could have predicted that.

"Thanks, Nash!" she said, grinning. "I'll get you that information by the end of today."

Mary pulled away from Nash's farm and turned onto Main Street. There was an empty parking spot on the side of the road beside the Kids' Museum, and she snagged it. She couldn't wait to call Judy to update on her on her progress. Things were going so much better than she'd hoped. This was going to be a wonderful parade.

"Tell me you're calling with good news," Judy said, without even saying hello.

"I'm calling with great news. Things are really falling into place."

"Fantastic. With the sheriff?"

"Um, not entirely," Mary said, feeling happy. "But that's okay. We've got all the town angels flying in."

"What do you mean by town angels?"

"People in Clark Creek. Everyone's being so helpful. Even Evan's contributing, in his own grudging way."

"I…see?"

"Jesse Clark's offered to play Santa Claus!"

"Who's that?" Judy asked.

"Evan's dad and Connie's husband."

"Sounds like he had an edge on the part."

Mary laughed. "Yeah."

"What about sponsors?"

"They're lining up! And, I keep getting emails from

folks wanting to enter floats."

"Love it."

"I know. Me too. It's really fun to see the whole town coming together. People in Hopedale—that's the next town over—are helping out in a big way too."

"I know that was part of your proposal," Judy said. "To encourage those more prosperous businesses' neighborly support."

"I just didn't realize how generous folks would be." Mary sighed happily. "It really feels good to see people chipping in."

"You're going to pull this off. I can just feel it."

"I really hope so, and not just on account of Davenport's reputation, but because of Clark Creek. It's such a sweet little town." Mary glanced out her snow-dusted windshield at the tree-lined street and the darling shops on both sides of it. The Whistle Stop Café was right across the way, and there was a sandwich shop a few doors down that looked enticing. Mary decided to have lunch there, then walk the parade route she was planning to follow later with Evan, so she could be prepared for his questions, or—more critically—his objections. "And most everyone here is so friendly."

"I notice you left the sheriff out."

Mary hesitated. "I have a feeling he's not so bad."

"Oh? Why? Did something happen?"

She thought again of the way he'd teased her about her inspirations. "Not exactly. It's just that sometimes there's more to people than meets the eye."

"Spoken like the sage you are."

"Ha ha," Mary said. "He's very unlike his brothers. Evan. Really different from the rest of his family."

"Maybe that's why he's the sheriff and they're not?"

"Hmm. Maybe."

"What are you doing about advertising?" Judy asked.

"Well. Since I already have a number of sponsors lined up and floats on the schedule, I put together a preliminary announcement for the local papers in several nearby towns this morning. There's also a regional tourism blog that lists weekly events. I've been in touch with them and am writing something up to submit about the parade. Word of mouth is spreading too. People here are getting excited and telling their friends and families."

"Nice. Sounds like you've got all your bases covered."

Mary felt a twinge of unease. "Yeah. All but one."

"What's that?"

"Lodging. Clark Creek only has one B&B, and that's where I'm staying now. It's quaint but not enormous. Only eight rooms."

"Oh, wow."

"Evan's big on complaining about parade complications, and I've thought my way around most of them, but not that. He mentioned lodging before and I'm sure he will again. The man's mind is like a steel trap when it comes to remembering all the negatives."

"Will people need to stay in Clark Creek? Couldn't folks from nearby towns make it a day trip?"

"Yeah, but it would be better if some did stay over. Better for the businesses here, I mean. My idea is for the parade to begin at nine on Christmas Eve morning. If tourists arrived a day or two before, they could last-minute Christmas shop or dine in Clark Creek, providing another boost to local businesses."

"You said Hopedale's not far away, and that ski resort. Could people stay there?"

"Sure, but then they'd eat and shop there."

"I get your point." Judy sighed. "Well, stick with it. You'll come up with something."

Mary bit her bottom lip, at a loss. Everything else was going so great except for this.

There had to be a solution somewhere. All she had to do was find it.

# Chapter Nine

*T*HIS TIME, EVAN REACHED THE Whistle Stop Café before Mary. She bustled in the door while he was standing at the counter. Her coat and hat were sprinkled with snow and tiny white flakes dotted her long brown hair.

"Great news!" she said. "We've got our first Santa's Circle level donor."

"That would be…"

"The top category of donor." Then she added in low tones, "Ten thousand dollars."

Evan nearly swallowed his tongue. That was way more than he'd expected from any single contributor. "Which business is it?"

"Not a business. A *business owner*. Very wealthy gentleman over in Hopedale. He developed the Hopedale Valley Springs Ski Resort." She grinned, displaying those hard-to-ignore dimples again, and it was easy to see how she'd secured so many donations. Mary Ward was as charming as the day was long.

Evan had heard of the benefactor: an older man, reputed to be a billionaire. "Wow. Really generous of him." Evan's order came up and the server set it on the counter. "Can I get you something?" he asked Mary, preparing to pay.

"No, thanks. I'll get it myself." She nodded at the café worker, requesting a peppermint mocha, and Evan offered to get them a table. He selected the same one near the window where they'd sat the day before.

When she joined him, she said, "The Singletons are making a generous contribution too. I saw one of Sam's commercials on the TV in the den at the inn." She heaved a sigh. "It was *so* romantic."

Evan shifted in his seat, weirdly uncomfortable at the thoughts of romance and engagements around Mary. He'd seen the commercials for Singleton's Jewelers, and they always showcased some sort of proposal involving one of the store's engagement rings.

"A couple was riding in a chair lift," she went on. "At Hopedale Valley Springs Ski Resort. And the guy got up his nerve to pop the—"

"Yes. Yes, I've seen it."

"You don't seem too impressed."

"Sure, I am," he said. "It's just not my thing."

"Skiing, or marriage proposals?"

He was quiet a moment, pushing the painful memory aside. If Cathy had waited for him during his deployment like she'd promised she would, he'd have become engaged once himself.

"Neither one," he said, sipping from his coffee.

She blanched, clearly realizing she'd made a misstep. "Evan, I'm sorry if I said something I shouldn't—"

"You didn't." He didn't want her pity, or anybody else's. Cathy was a long time ago, and he was over her.

He preferred to focus on other things. Like protecting the budgetary interests of his town.

"Mary, I think it's great about the sponsors you're bringing in, but we need to be reasonable here and start setting some limits before this parade runs away from us."

"Limits?" She unbuttoned her coat and shrugged out of it. Under it, she wore a dark green sweater over a starched white collar. She had on dark slacks too, and those totally impractical boots. "Can't you see? The sky could be the limit with all the support we're getting."

"Yeah, but there's the danger of outspending that support. You can't tell me you haven't made cash outlays already. For printing…advertising. And who knows what else."

Her cheeks colored. "We may have had to overextend some resources initially, on credit, but we'll make any expenditures back in spades."

"Then there are trash considerations."

She gaped at him. "Trash?"

"We have the Public Works Department to think of, and sanitation. The streets will be a wreck after such a big event."

She pressed her lips together and sat perfectly still. After a beat, she said, "We've been sitting here ten minutes and you haven't said one positive thing." She didn't sound angry about it—more like he'd hurt her feelings. Which he hadn't meant to do.

"You haven't given me any credit," she said. "Not one little bit, and I've accomplished so much in less than a week. I barely had any time at all in Richmond to come up with a proposal, but I did. I've been in Clark Creek for three days. *Three days*, Evan. And just look at what's happened. People are lining up. Happy to help out with the parade, and do you want to know why? It's because they love this town, I'm sure as much as you do. Only they're showing it differently."

Evan stared at her, dumbfounded. "So it's credit you

want?" Mary didn't strike him as the sort of woman who'd need this sort of reassurance. Then again, she was human.

"A little bit of acknowledgement would be good."

Evan felt like a jerk. Of course he should have acknowledged her accomplishments, way before now. That didn't negate the fact that the parade still faced problems, though.

"Hey, look, I'm sorry. I agree that you've made progress, amazing progress, in such a short time. Still, as the sheriff, it's my duty to acknowledge the challenges that a large Christmas parade will present to this town. Christmas Eve is just over a week away, and we still haven't solved—"

She groaned like she hadn't been able to stop herself. "Evan," she said, this time pleading. "I could honestly use your help, and not your resistance."

"I thought I was helping by…never mind." He hung his head, realizing that whatever he'd thought, he'd gotten it wrong. He sat silent a moment, thinking. Then he finally looked up. "All right," he said calmly. "What would you like me to do?"

"Help me plan the parade route, for starters."

At last. A task he was happy to tackle, because it would give him a chance to keep things contained. If they could limit the parade to one or two streets, that would be better than having mountains of floats meander all over town. Privately, he conceded this would also give him more time to spend around Mary, which he was itching to do. Assuming he could keep from disappointing her again. He hadn't enjoyed how that felt *at all*, and he meant to do better. "Do you have any ideas?"

"Yes." She took a town map from her satchel and unfolded it. "I'd like to start at the courthouse and end at the fairgrounds by Nash's farm."

Evan examined the yellow line she'd drawn with a

highlighter, tracing Main Street from one end to the next. That was much more favorable than he'd imagined. "I like the fact that the route's restricted to one street," he admitted, admiring her for making this suggestion.

Her eyebrows rose, like she couldn't believe he'd actually complimented her. "I thought that would make things more streamlined."

"Agreed."

She gave him a suspicious look. "So, you *can* be agreeable."

"I'm not disagreeable, generally. Just cautious."

"Hmm."

"And caution is a wise thing to exercise in coordinating a big event."

"I agree."

"There you have it!" he said. "You can be agreeable too."

"Ha ha." She drummed her fingers on the table, thinking. "Yes, I can be agreeable. And also…" Her eyes glimmered impishly. "I have a really fun idea."

*Uh-oh.* She was having another *inspiration.* One that would lead to more outlays of cash. "What is it?"

"Well. On Christmas Eve, I was thinking we could convert Main Street…into *Christmas Avenue.*"

Her voice rose in a lilting squeal on that last part and Evan's head spun. What in the world was she talking about?

She reached into her bag and pulled out a red and white street sign—sure enough, it said *Christmas Avenue.* "It's magnetic," she said, evidently pleased with herself. "Isn't it fantastic? I've ordered one for every street corner along the route. I'll point them out when we walk it."

"So, that fits over the signs saying Main Street?"

"Yes, but only temporarily. Since those signs are metal, these overlays will stick. When we remove them, they'll leave no marks and do no damage."

*Christmas Avenue.* Evan sighed. What would she think of next?

"We're also going to have signs pointing to the North Pole, so when Santa takes off from the courthouse square, it will look like he's headed that way."

Evan couldn't imagine what would be at the so-called North Pole. Besides those porta-potties.

"Then, when Santa reaches Nash's farm, he'll greet his reindeer!"

*Reindeer?*

She nodded at his blank expression. "Nash has volunteered to suit up a team of his horses with fake antlers and such, and Leroy and Austin have offered to dress up as elves."

Now Evan had heard everything. Mary must have done some ultra-sweet talking to get those two to go along with her plan. "You're kidding."

She sat back in her chair. "Nope."

"Who's playing Santa?"

"Your dad."

"Of course."

"And Marshall's opening up his inn as a cider and hot chocolate stop along the route, since the Clark Creek B&B is right around the corner from Main Street. People wanting a breather from the crowds can pop over to his place for refreshments. Andrea and Jeremy will have a table on the front porch. They'll be selling gingerbread and other goodies, too. Drinks and snacks will only be a dollar, with the majority of proceeds going toward the parade."

Evan watched her, gobsmacked. He could barely keep up.

"This parade's going to be amazing, Evan. Totally

wonderful. You'll see."

"What about those tickets you mentioned?"

"Designated volunteers will sell them from the gazebo. Tickets won't be mandatory, so there will be no cordoning off any areas or anything like that. Their purchase will only be encouraged for those wanting to support the parade—and Clark Creek. Apart from receiving a ticket to the "Parade on Christmas Avenue," anyone who pays the five-dollar voluntary ticket fee will receive their choice of souvenir."

She pulled a few more items from her bag: a cork drink coaster, a refrigerator magnet, and a small flag. They all depicted the gazebo decorated to the hilt for the holidays, and they were stamped with the words *Christmas in Clark Creek*. "These each cost less than a dollar to produce, so the town will be making a huge profit per ticket, even after allocating the prorated payments to parade participant groups. They'll all stand to benefit, too."

She handed Evan a drink coaster and he turned it over to study its underside. It appeared functional enough. The magnet could come in handy, too. And, okay, the flag could make a nice decoration for someone to stick in their pen holder at work, for example. Or maybe a child could wave one during the parade. He saw a bunch of kiddos waving tiny flags in his mind's eye… and then leaving them all behind after dropping them on the sidewalks.

It wasn't his fault that he could always see the flip side. That's what he'd been trained to do, both as a sheriff and in the Army beforehand. He was paid to be analytical, examine an equation from every angle. And, when there were pitfalls, it was his obligation to point them out. Only no amount of reasoning seemed to appeal to Mary. She was endlessly focused on the bright side. Exactly like she was now, getting all stoked up on her parade ideas.

"We'll also be selling these," she said with a contagious grin.

He pursed his lips to avoid smiling along with her. He was tough and used to holding his ground. He'd never been a guy who was easily swayed. But when Mary's big brown eyes shone with excitement, it was hard not to admire the time and energy she'd put into her efforts and get swept up in her enthusiasm. That's probably what had happened to his brothers. And to Leroy. And Austin. *Dressing up as elves?* Unbelievable.

She took a final item from her satchel and unfolded it: a long-sleeved T-shirt with the same gazebo design. "Twenty dollars! What do you think? Too much? Hmm. Maybe fifteen?"

"When did you do all this?"

"Last Friday in Richmond. I got these samples by rush order so I could present them to the town council for their approval. They arrived at the inn yesterday and I did an emergency Zoom with everyone to fill them in."

Evan didn't have to ask. He was sure the council members had loved the souvenirs, especially his mom.

"I'll place the bulk orders for everything after I have a better sense of parade numbers," she continued. "With expedited delivery, they'll arrive a day or two before the parade."

Evan knew what "expedited delivery" meant. More money. But he decided not to comment on that aspect. Instead, he asked a question. "How did you make the gazebo look decorated in the design?" To his knowledge, that hadn't been done yet.

She shared a sunny grin. "I improvised and used the online design program from the giftware manufacturer."

He kept his expression as neutral as possible, deciding

to reserve judgment until he saw what she came up with next. "It seems you've thought of everything."

"Almost." She finished up her peppermint mocha and slipped back into her coat. "We need to talk about parking and that traffic control you keep mentioning. I think I've worked out the parking part with the mayor. We can talk about traffic along the way. Come on."

Evan downed the last bit of his coffee and zipped up his uniform jacket. "Where are we headed?" he asked, putting on his hat, because the snow outdoors had started up again.

"To take a stroll down Christmas Avenue."

She shot him a winning smile and he was taken in. Mary was so unfailingly positive. She didn't even let his reasonable objections get her down. Instead of tossing in the towel when he cited complications, she always came back armed with her solutions.

They still had complications to address. Parking, traffic, trash, and lodging were among them. But against his better judgment, Evan was starting to wonder if Mary could really pull this parade fundraiser off.

Evan held open the door for Mary to exit the café ahead of him. It was nice, she thought, that he had a gentlemanly side. It helped offset his persistent negativity. It bugged her that all Evan did was point out problems with the parade. While she didn't need his approval, it would be nice to have it.

He could have at least pretended to be impressed by her cool souvenirs or her creative idea about converting Main Street into Christmas Avenue. At least he was pleased with her proposed parade route, so that was something. She had a feeling that, if she and Evan could only put their heads together instead of being at odds with each other, they could accomplish so much more.

Heavy snow pelted them from above as they stepped onto the sidewalk. The Whistle Stop Café stood at the end of Main Street where it met Three-Notched Pass across from Nash's farm. An old set of railroad tracks ran behind it, but Mary's research had told her they hadn't been used in years. She intended to take Evan to the fairgrounds, where parade patrons would park their vehicles, and show him the spot for Santa's workshop, before walking the parade route in reverse order, ending at the gazebo in the town square.

That would be convenient for him, since they'd wind up close to his office, and it wasn't honestly much of a walk for her to go back for her SUV at Marshall's inn. After learning how short distances were in Clark Creek, Mary realized she'd be better off walking most places. Unless she had supplies or decorations to lug with her, of course.

The storm had picked up and strong winds raged. It was far too gusty for her umbrella, so she tugged down her hat while Evan hung onto his. Then—*wham*—a big white ball slammed into Evan's uniform jacket sleeve and he halted.

"Gotcha, Sheriff Clark!" a young boy called. Mary spied a kid, about ten or eleven, standing by the corner with a friend, who held another snowball in his hands. Evan glared in their direction and the boys darted behind a street planter, giggling as they went.

Before he could do or say anything, another frozen orb collided with her shoulder. It didn't really hurt. More like surprised her. "Oh!" she cried laughing. "Hey!"

"Boys!" Evan hollered when they ducked back behind the planter. "You cut that out." They scooted around the corner, but Mary could hear them whispering, so they hadn't gone far.

"Oh yeah?" Mary wasn't sure what he would do. The kids were watching him too, stealing peeks in his direction when Evan wasn't looking.

Then he stunned her by bending down and sweeping a bunch of snow into his hands. There was a wicked gleam in his eyes that looked almost—playful. He winked at Mary and little tingles raced down her spine.

*Oh no.* What was *that* about?

"Let's see how they like having me join in the game," he said in a husky whisper. Next, he called around the corner. "Boys, come out here a second. I'd like to have a word."

There was no movement for a moment as more snow-flakes pounded the pavement and covered their coats. Then, slowly, the first of the two boys emerged.

"We're sorry," he said. "We're not in any kind of trouble?"

"Nope. Not yet..." Evan held two fully formed snow-balls behind his back, one in each hand, and Mary had an inkling what he intended to do. "Where's your brother?"

Mary hadn't realized that Evan knew them, but of course he must know everyone in this small town.

The first kid motioned to another, who sheepishly appeared, and Mary now noted the second child looked a little younger than the first.

"Setting a bad example for Spencer, are you, Joe?" he asked the first kid, whose shoulders sagged.

"We were just having a little fun."

"Well, the next time you decide pick a snowball fight," Evan said. "You need to play by the rules of engagement."

"Engagement?" Spencer asked. "What's that?"

"It's like when somebody's going to get married," Joe said.

Evan cleared his throat. "That's not exactly what I meant."

Mary smiled. "I think the sheriff is saying you need to ask people if they want to play before pelting them full-throttle."

"Ohhh," the children said together.

"Well?" Evan waited, but they were clearly confused. "Aren't you going to ask me?"

The younger boy grinned. "Are you serious, Sheriff Clark?"

"I think he's serious," Joe whispered in his ear. "He's got something behind his back."

The two kids scooped fresh snow into their gloves and grinned excitedly. "Okay!" the bigger one said. "You're on."

But before they could let loose, Evan surprised them with a one-two punch, nailing the kids on their coat sleeves as they shielded their faces with their arms.

"Hey!" the kids hollered, but they were laughing, ducking back behind the planter and loading up again.

"What do you say?" Evan asked Mary. "Want to engage?"

She stared down at her high-heeled boots. "Um."

"You be on their team," he whispered and nodded toward a street planter. "Go on—take your time and take cover."

She bit her bottom lip, unable to resist the challenge. "Sure!" She set her satchel on the covered stoop of the café and formed a hefty snowball of her own. Then on impulse she turned and lobbed it at Evan.

The kids cackled at the stunned look on Evan's face

and Mary couldn't help giggling as well. Evan shook a scolding finger, but she could tell he wasn't seriously mad. "You're asking for it."

"Who, me?"

He reached down to grab more snow, then waited patiently as she teetered across the icy sidewalk and got behind the planter with the kids. "All right if I join you?"

"You betcha, lady," the bigger kid, Joe, said. Then he handed her a well-formed snowball and she tossed it over the bench toward Evan. Rather than hitting him, it landed just shy of his feet.

"You're going to have to work on your aim," Evan said, his eyes gleaming. "Sort of like—this!" He hurled his snowball toward Mary. She ducked her head just in time.

"He's good," Spencer said in warning tones. "We'd better be careful."

Mary laughed. "Yeah," she told him confidentially. "I think you're right." Then she made another snowball and this time hit a bulls-eye—right in the middle of Evan's chest.

"Woo-hoo!" Spencer yelped, while Joe shouted, "*Score*."

"I was only warming up before," she called to Evan.

To her amazement, he actually chuckled. "I'll need to be more careful around you."

More snowballs flew between them, interspersed with yelps of glee and laughter.

Mary landed several good hits on Evan, but he was great at returning fire, getting her and the boys back with snowball slugs, causing them all to chortle or groan at the outcome, depending on who was giving or receiving.

Twenty minutes later, they were all snowballed out. Plus, the café manager kept shooting them glances out the window, like he wasn't thrilled about their blocking access to the front stoop of his café.

"See ya later, Sheriff Clark!" the two boys shouted, dashing away down Main Street. Mary suspected they couldn't wait to tell their friends they'd had a full-fledged snowball fight with the sheriff. She still couldn't believe she'd been part of one herself.

"See ya, lady!" Joe said. "Thanks for playing!"

"My name's Mary!" she called after them, and the younger boy shot her a grin.

"Bye, Miss Mary," he said with a happy wave.

Evan clutched his middle, breathing hard. He'd done a lot of running around and maneuvering while single-handedly combating Mary's team, and she'd worn herself out as well.

"That was awesome," she said, catching her breath. "I haven't played in the snow in years." She'd forgotten how much fun it was. Or what it was like to think about nothing but goofing off in the beautiful wintry weather for a while. The chilly air felt crisp in her lungs and her cheeks burned from the cold, but she'd had the best time. It still startled her a little that she'd had it with Evan. Then she remembered her wish in the gazebo, understanding that it had come true.

"You know something?" he said. "Neither have I."

Another couple stepped around them to enter the café, and then it was just the two of them alone on the sidewalk, standing face to face in the falling snow. He searched her eyes and Mary's heart skipped a beat. His countenance seemed different somehow. Not as hard-edged as before. More relaxed and accepting. It was almost like seeing another person. A person she wanted to know better.

He was close enough to hold her, to take her in his arms and kiss her right here on Main Street. And, deep in her heart, a part of her wanted him to.

*Ridiculous.* Besides, Evan would never do something like that. The Evan she knew was walled-off, and careful…

Yet the man she'd seen today had been happy and carefree. What life experiences had caused him to become bottled up, robbing him of his joy?

When she'd teased him about skiing and engagements, he'd paused and become distant. There'd been a sadness in his eyes. Evan was in his thirties, so presumably he'd dated people, maybe lots of people, over the years. She didn't get the impression he was seeing anyone now, though.

Mary wanted to see him, on casual terms like they'd experienced today, and not just for business reasons. "We'll have to do it again sometime," she said. She was thinking of a friendly outing, not a date. Still, he might have read it as forward, judging by his surprised look.

He tilted down his hat and shoved his hands into his jacket pockets, his tough veneer returning. But she knew it was an act, because she'd already caught a glimpse of the fun-loving guy beneath his stoic façade. "Don't push your luck," he said in a joking way, and Mary didn't mind the mild admonishment, because she understood what it meant. She wasn't the only one who knew she'd seen a different side of Evan.

He was *completely* aware of it, too.

Evan's phone rang and he pulled it from his uniform jacket pocket. "Sorry," he said. "It's Helen on dispatch. I'd better take this." He took the call. "Yeah? Oh no. He okay?" His brow creased. Was it bad news? "Whereabouts? What part of the highway? Yeah, yeah. I know it. I'll be there."

He hung up and said, "There's been a traffic accident on the outskirts of town."

Mary's heart seized up. "I hope nobody's hurt?"

"No, fortunately not. Jeb Wilson's truck slid off the

road, but he's all right."

She exhaled in relief. "Well, that part's a blessing."

"Yeah." Evan tucked away his phone. "So maybe we can take a raincheck on the parade route walk?"

"I'm heading over to Hopedale tomorrow. I need to get a lot of sponsorship forms signed."

"Friday, then?"

"Friday's good. Want to say Friday late afternoon?"

He nodded. "Just tell me where to meet you."

And when his gaze met hers, she felt those little tingles again.

# *Chapter Ten*

ARY'S DAY TRIP TO HOPEDALE was a lot of fun.
She met up with Ken at the Holly and the Ivy
Nursery, and he showed her around the picturesque
downtown area which bordered a mountain ridge. The
Hopedale Valley Springs Ski Resort was just outside
town, and many of its tourists frequented Hopedale for
dining and shopping, especially during the busy winter
ski season. Unlike in Clark Creek, its streets were packed
with holiday shoppers.

One of their first stops was at Singleton's Jewelers.
An attractive man with dark hair and light eyes shook
her hand. "Hey there, I'm Sam Singleton." He nodded
toward the brunette beside him with long wavy hair.
"This is my wife, Angie."

She shook Mary's hand too, and Mary couldn't
help but notice the gorgeous diamond ring on Angie's
hand. She scanned the store, seeing a jewelry case
display beneath a gorgeous Christmas wreath that
appeared to be dotted with mistletoe berries. A sign
above the case said: *Singleton Signature Diamond
Collection*.

"This is an incredible store," she told the Singletons.

"Thanks!" Sam said. "We like it."

They seemed like a happy couple, and there was a warm tenderness between them. "How long have you owned the shop?"

Angie nodded toward her husband. "Sam, for quite some time. When we got married a few years ago, I took joint ownership with him."

"Nice." Mary thought about how working relationships sometimes brought couples together.

That wouldn't be happening with her and Evan, though. Even if she had started seeing his warmer, fun-loving side. And even if he had gazed at her in that dreamy way when they'd been standing on the sidewalk outside the Whistle Stop Café, when he'd made her heart pound and her knees melt like butter...

"We were so happy to hear about your parade," Sam snapping her out of her reverie. "What a great idea at this time of year."

"Pepe's especially excited about it," Angie said. "He's our eight-year-old son."

"We've got a daughter too," Sam offered. "Magdalena. She's two."

"How sweet." Mary smiled, imagining their adorable children. "Thank you both for being one of our sponsors. So generous of you." She pulled some papers from her satchel. "I have a few forms for you to sign, if you don't mind?"

After they'd filled out their paperwork, Mary thanked them with a smile. "I hope you'll be able to make the parade and bring your family."

Angie shared a grin. "We'll bring all of them."

"All?"

"We're sort of a crowd when we're together," Sam said. "Especially now that my dad is seeing someone."

"You'll love meeting Sam's dad, David," Ken said. "And his girlfriend, Mabel Lee. She runs the flower shop across the way. We can stop in and see her next."

"Wonderful!"

"The Lopezes are special, too," Sam informed Mary. "Angie's grandmother lives with us. Angie's mom and her new husband also live nearby."

Mary loved how friendly and connected everyone seemed in these small towns.

"Then, by all means," she said. "Bring everyone. The more the merrier!"

It was a very successful day, and Ken took Mary to lunch at a bookstore café where she met his girlfriend, Dusty. Dusty was blonde-haired and blue eyed, with a bubbly personality.

"Ken's very excited about this parade of yours," Dusty said. "All of us at the Chamber of Commerce are, too. I'm so glad you reached out when you did."

"I can't thank you enough for your help. Everyone in Clark Creek is really grateful."

"That's what neighbors do," Ken said. "They help each other."

"Yeah." Dusty reached out and took his hand, looking all dreamy-eyed, and Mary suspected there wouldn't be *any* problem when Ken made his marriage proposal.

Evan was at his desk filing reports on his computer when Dennis walked in and asked, "What happened on the highway yesterday?"

"Jeb's going to need a new truck, but he's okay."

"How about the other guy?"

"The other guy was a guardrail," Evan said.

"Icy roads?"

"Yeah."

"You don't think that will be a problem during the parade?"

That's all Evan needed. One more headache caused by the weather. "Hope not. Public Works is going to treat the roads, and we'll keep a close eye on the forecast."

"Forecast looks good," Dennis said. "Supposed to be mostly sunny with a chance of flurries."

Evan shut his laptop. "Nothing like a white Christmas in Clark Creek."

Dennis laughed. "We always have snow."

Evan found himself having mixed emotions about the holiday. He hadn't really enjoyed it in years—not since his breakup with Cathy. While he'd gone through the motions of engaging in routine celebrations for the sake of his family, he'd been left feeling hollow inside.

He'd only been eighteen, and still in high school, when he fell for his vivacious blond classmate, Cathy Jennings. He'd enlisted in the Army because he wanted to get started on a career, so they could marry and start a family.

Boot camp training was brutal, but worth it, because he'd done well enough to catch his commander's eye. Promotion came quickly, and then he'd had his first deployment. He'd returned right before Christmas with a shiny new ring in his pocket. But by that time, Cathy had already said yes to somebody else.

Evan had thought she'd been stressed by their separation. She'd been stressed, all right. Right into somebody else's arms.

Evan motioned for Dennis to have a seat, mentally shaking off the bad memories. He didn't know why he was dwelling on them now. Maybe because he felt a special kinship with Dennis since they'd both served in Infantry. Dennis had what he might've had. A woman who'd stayed loyal to him while he'd been deployed, and who'd married him after his return.

"How are things going with Linda and the baby?"

"Really well. The doc says we're right on schedule for the twenty-ninth."

"Bet your other kids are getting excited."

Dennis grinned. "We all are."

"You sure you're okay working the parade so close to the delivery date?"

"Sure, I'm sure. Just tell me what you need me to do."

"I'm meeting with Mary tomorrow to talk about traffic. She says she has some ideas."

"She's a traffic cop now, too?" Dennis laughed. "No, seriously. I like her."

"You and half the town."

Dennis's eyebrows rose. "You mean, you don't?"

"She's all right."

"Only all right?" Dennis read his face, like he didn't believe him.

Evan thought back to their snowball fight and the fun time they'd had. He hadn't let himself relax like that since…he wasn't sure when. When he'd looked in her eyes, he'd felt a tug at his heartstrings. She'd had that effect on him before, and it was unnerving. He was fighting not to go there, but something misguided in his soul wanted to, anyway.

"Yep," he said, not wanting to admit his interest in Mary to Dennis, because he had trouble making sense of it himself. "Only all right."

Back at the inn, Mary had work to do with ordering those souvenirs. She'd been trying to wait until she had an accurate prediction for parade attendance before placing her order, but she had a good enough idea now, and really couldn't wait much longer if the merchandise was going to arrive on time.

Using the number of locals predicted to attend by the town council, and also her estimate of out-of-towners who might come, she'd done her best to arrive at accurate calculations, and she didn't want to mess things up. If she under-ordered, folks would be disappointed by supplies running out. If she over-ordered, though, that could bring a costly mistake down on Clark Creek.

She logged into the merchandise website she frequently used and pulled up the spreadsheet she'd made for the parade in a separate window on her computer. The spreadsheet had grown so large she had to shrink down some of the columns to be able to view it in a single frame.

The lights in her room blinked off and on, and then completely went out. Her computer froze up, too.

*What? Oh no!* Mary gathered her wits, reaching for her emergency flashlight and flicking it on. She heard Marshall knocking on doors, and then he got to hers.

"Sorry," he said, when she cracked her door open. He held a flashlight, too. "Old house issues. Only temporary. We'll be back in business in a flash."

Sure enough, in another five minutes, the lights came back on and Mary rebooted her computer. *Now, where was I? Right. Ordering the T-shirts.*

She completed her order and entered her company

credit card information, then pressed *Submit*. This amount would be filled in on the expense report she provided to the town council, along with her final bill. They'd have more than enough to pay it by then. After the parade, Clark Creek would be enjoying a hearty surplus.

The screen froze, and a small colorful wheel spun around and around on her desktop. *Oh, brother.* She resubmitted her order, but the electricity faltered a second time, and then a third—each time, just as she was complete her T-shirt order and sign off. *Ugh!*

She tried a couple more times with the lights flickering, eager to get this done. She was about to shut her laptop and give up for a while, when—*ta-dahh*! Her order went through.

*Whew. It's about time. I'm done!*

She sat back against the headboard and sighed with satisfaction. Only one week until the parade, but she was checking off those boxes on her to-do list. *Yes.* She looked forward to seeing Evan again, and—she hoped—finally winning his support. He did seem to be loosening up and becoming more open-minded about the parade's potential. It was hard for him not to be, she supposed, since she'd addressed most of his concerns. Maybe tomorrow, he'd come around a little more.

# Chapter Eleven

HE NEXT DAY, EVAN STOOD beside Mary by the split-rail fence alongside the fairground. Shadows hugged the mountains as daylight faded, and snow continued to fall.

She pointed to the large field his mom had suggested for a parking venue, and then to another section leading off a gravel road. "We thought the floats could pull in over there after the parade to disassemble. We'll have plenty of trash receptacles in place, so folks who want to "undecorate" their floats can do that right away."

Evan couldn't deny that would help keep the streets clean.

"I talked to the sanitation department about delivering the trash containers, and about removal, and they said their crews could handle that, no problem. Here's the best part of this plan." She shared a sunny grin. "I found a way to eliminate your traffic problem."

This he had to hear.

"Main Street traffic will only go one way!"

"What?"

"During the parade times, plus one hour before and one after."

He liked where Mary was going with this. If they kept the flow of traffic moving in one direction, it would be less likely to snarl up. "I'd suggest two, to play it safe."

"I was thinking we could put signs out near the highway," she said, "directing visitors to arrive in Clark Creek by coming down Three-Notched Pass. Then we can ask them to park at the fairgrounds, leave their vehicles there and walk down to the gazebo to buy their parade tickets and get souvenirs. After that, they can position themselves anywhere they'd like along the route. Only, when it's time to leave, they'll head back to the fairgrounds and pick up their vehicles, leaving on Three-Notched Pass. Ingress and egress from the parking area will all be one-way too, to keep things moving smoothly."

"So, out-of-towners will never even drive through Clark Creek?" Evan was impressed she'd thought of this.

"Nope. Not at all. I mean, they'll be *in* Clark Creek, but they'll park on its outskirts. I've lined up several volunteers to direct parking at the fairgrounds, and Main Street should be blocked off so nobody can enter that way."

Evan nodded. "The other streets leading to the town square probably should be closed off, too."

"Yes! Keeping things nice and clear for foot traffic." She beamed. "And those floats."

She spread out her hands in front of her while turning toward Nash's property. "This is where the pet adoptions station will go. Santa's workshop will be beside it, in case any child asks Santa for a new dog or kitty."

"Clever."

"The reindeer will be in this adjacent pasture," she continued. "Austin and Leroy are handling the rides."

"There'll be rides now?"

"Not just any ol' rides," she told him. "Reindeer rides."

Evan couldn't help but laugh, because she was so very

good at this. "You're not bad for a Christmas Consultant, you know."

Her eyes widened. "Wait a minute. Did I just hear a compliment?"

Evan lifted a shoulder. "Might have."

It was her turn to laugh. "Well, I'd like to compliment you too, for listening to my ideas."

"Truthfully," he told her, "they're pretty good ones."

She preened in the snow, little white flakes dotting her hair and eyelashes. "Shall we head toward the gazebo?"

"Sure."

Dusk had settled on Main Street and each of its streetlamps had turned on. Evan tipped his hat at the occasional passerby, issuing his greetings to the familiar faces. Mary shared friendly hellos and waves, too. Even though she didn't know everyone, it was clear she'd already made several acquaintances in Clark Creek.

"Hello, Mr. Parker!" she said to the band director, as he exited the music shop.

"Ms. Ward," he said. "Good to see you! The marching band is shaping up. We've already selected our pieces for the parade and will begin practicing tomorrow."

"Oh, how fantastic." She flushed happily and Evan couldn't help but think that her expression made her look sweet. And she *was* sweet, through and through. A goodhearted woman. About as goodhearted as they come. He was well aware of that now.

Making this parade a success wasn't just a job for Mary. It was a mission. She really did care about Clark Creek and its people.

She cheerily greeted Vivi Torres and the librarian next. "Mrs. Watson. Good evening!"

"Well, hello, Mary," Mrs. Watson said. "Looking forward to your parade."

Vivi Torres walked beside Mrs. Watson, and they'd both apparently been doing some Christmas shopping. "We all are," Vivi said with a warm grin.

As Evan and Mary strolled along Main Street, a light snow sifted through the air. White flakes danced beneath the streetlamps' glow, and colorful Christmas lights shone in store windows. The setting was scenic, almost romantic, and it occurred to Evan that he hadn't been out with a woman in a while. After his big letdown with Cathy, he hadn't been in mood for female company for months. He'd slowly gotten back into dating, but nothing ever seemed to click. He guessed whatever vibes he was sending out were not the sort to keep a woman interested for long.

The truth was, his heart hadn't been in it. He'd been just going through the motions because it seemed like the thing to do. He was the right age to settle down and raise a family. He'd finally realized that a family was a useless goal to have unless he found somebody he loved enough to want to marry. Nobody had come along like that so far.

He thought of that snowball fight he and Mary had engaged in with those kids when they'd come out of the Whistle Stop Café. For the smallest sliver of time, he'd let himself go and had enjoyed living in the moment. It wasn't something he intended to do often, but it had been nice while it lasted. It had been especially nice since it had happened with Mary.

"I love this town," she said, as they passed the Blue Heron Bookshop. "I'm sure that all those paradegoers will too."

He realized that he'd never thanked her, at least not sincerely and with a smidgen of humility. "I have to say you've impressed me," he said. "You're an unbearably sharp woman."

She shot him a cockeyed grin. "Unbearably?"

"Yeah. It's been kind of…overwhelming…how you've been able to accomplish so much in so little time. I mean, not overwhelming so much as impressive." He met her eyes. "Mary Ward, I'm very impressed by you."

Her eyebrows arched. "Why, thank you, Sheriff." She added playfully, "You're not too terrible yourself."

His back of his neck warmed, and he rubbed it. The effect she had on him wasn't an unpleasant one. It was actually kind of nice, and he was getting used to it. "So," he said, then he cleared his throat because his voice had embarrassingly gone husky. "The ticket-selling will take place over there?"

"Yes," she said. "In the gazebo."

They approached the square and walked toward the gazebo. Strings of lights circled the ice skating rink, and couples and families were out on the ice. It occurred to Evan that it was a Friday, so a typical date night. He wondered if Mary was seeing anybody, but she didn't act like she was. She hadn't mentioned a boyfriend or a significant other.

She noticed the skating rink too. "Ooh, fun! I've always wanted to try ice skating."

"Have you?" He observed her curiously. "Why?"

"Because, Evan." She rolled her eyes in an adorable manner. "It looks like such a cool thing to do."

"Cold is more like it. Especially if you fall and land on the ice."

"Ha ha." She leaned against one of the railings on the gazebo and crossed her arms. "How about you? Skate much?"

"Haven't in years. I mean, when I was a kid, sure. Who doesn't?"

"Me," she quipped. "I just told you."

Something weird was happening between them—it felt like their situation was morphing from a business relationship into some kind of friendship. The funny thing was, Evan didn't mind being friends with Mary. The truth was, he liked being in her company.

"On account of the hotel thing?"

"On account of lots of things." She shrugged. "Some of the kids had skating parties, but I was never invited."

He frowned at this. "That's terrible."

"It was okay." She sighed. "I was always the new kid. Not around for very long. Also, kind of geeky, in that I lived in hotels."

"I'm sorry, Mary."

"Don't be! My life had its good parts."

That was so like her. Always trying to look at the positives. But, deep in her heart, that had to have hurt. Evan guessed it had been hard being a kid on the outside looking in on so many childhood activities, while feeling excluded.

"What about your mom? Didn't she try to arrange playdates?"

"Lila? No." Mary waved this aside. "Her schedule was always really booked."

"I see."

"I knew some cool doormen, though. Charlie was especially sweet. He's the one who taught me how to ride a bike."

"How old was this Charlie?"

She giggled at his expression. "Very old. Like a grand-pa's age. He was really kind to me. Other people were too, at the various hotels. Only…"

She looked away.

"What is it?" he asked gently.

"I guess I learned to be self-sufficient." She shrugged. "You know. Not rely too much on anyone."

Evan's throat felt raw. That's how he thought of himself, too. Tough. Independent. Only, hearing it coming from her, it made him wonder if *independent* was sometimes more like *lonely*. He swallowed hard. "You said you've got no brothers or sisters. How about close friends?"

"I've got Judy." Her face brightened. "She and I are super tight. She's also, weirdly, my boss at work."

"How did that happen?"

"Judy's really smart and ambitious."

"So are you."

She blushed. "Thanks, Evan. What I mean is, she went for the supervisory position, and I didn't, until…" She stopped talking.

"Until?"

"Doesn't matter. What matters is how *spectacular* this place is going to look tomorrow." She swept her arms around the gazebo, her dark eyes sparkling. "Ken's bringing all his decorations *and* the town tree."

"How tall?"

"Twenty-six feet."

Evan whistled. "That's big."

"It won't look so huge in this setting."

"Where are you going to put it?"

"Over there," she nodded in the opposite direction. On the courthouse side. She stared up at the building's second floor. "How's that reindeer team holding up? And your coat rack?"

Evan shoved his hands in his jacket pockets, because he knew what she was asking. She wanted to know how he was enjoying her decorations. He couldn't tell her he'd removed them. "Oh well, I suspect they're just fine."

"Suspect? What do you mean?"

"Mary." He decided to change the subject, focusing one critical problem they hadn't solved. "You've done a great job with everything, and things seem to be coming along. Except for one thing."

Her smile faltered. "Yeah. Lodging."

Folks didn't have to stay over. They could come and be gone in the same day. But it would be so much better if they had the option to stay, and he and Mary both knew it.

"How's it going over at Marshall's place?" he asked.

"Really well. As soon as word started circulating about the parade, he got more bookings. The Clark Creek B&B is full up for several days leading up to Christmas."

"That's excellent. For Marshall."

"Yeah, but his inn's kind of small."

"Nothing like the size of the places you grew up in, I'm sure."

"True." Mary gazed around the town square. "I keep feeling like I'm missing something. Something obvious."

"You don't seem to miss much to me."

"Well, I'm missing this, and it bugs me." She turned to him suddenly. "What are you doing tomorrow?"

He blinked, caught off guard. "Uh. It's my day off, but I've promised to help Nash with something at his farm. Did you need—?"

"No, not really." She gave a soft smile. "I just wondered if you'd like to be here when the town tree gets installed."

"When will that be?"

"I don't have an exact time yet, so don't worry about it. As long as you're here for the tree lighting." She saw the question written on his face. "Sunday at five."

"I'll put it on my calendar."

"I know it's not the same as putting up your personal tree at home," she said. "But a community tree is really special in its own way."

"Well, since I don't put one up at home—"

"What?" Her eyes widened.

"No need. My Mom and Dad decorate their place, and that's where everyone goes for Christmas dinner. So."

"Marshall decorates his inn," she told him.

"Sure, it's a business establishment and in his interest."

"What about Nash?"

"He decorates too. He also has a kid, my niece Chloe, so it's natural for him—"

"Wait a minute." She looked amazed, and not necessarily in a good way. "You mean you've never decorated—ever?"

"My own place? No."

"Evan." She playfully pushed his arm, and he experienced a small spark when she did. "Come on. Get in the spirit."

"I am in the spirit. I'm helping you with your Christmas parade."

"And I appreciate that. I really do." She looked him over again. "I just can't believe you don't decorate for the holidays."

"I don't have any decorations," he said—and then he bit his tongue. Saying something like that around Mary might be seen as a plea for her to come on over to his place and decorate it herself.

"Well, that's too bad." Then her face lit up. "I've got some extras in my SUV."

"Thank you, but no."

She frowned at his consternation. "Suit yourself."

"It's getting late." Evan checked his watch and saw it was almost six. "I don't mean to keep you."

"Oh, right! I need to get back to my room and phone Judy before she leaves the office. Then I'm going to order dinner in and put my feet up and relax."

"What? Relax?" he teased. "You?"

"I know how to relax," she said. "You're the one who doesn't."

"Not so."

Her eyes glimmered. "Then take me ice skating."

His heart pounded at her invitation, and now he was almost sure she didn't have a boyfriend. He forced himself to say, "I don't think that's such a good idea."

"Why not?"

"We're working together."

"I'm not asking you to marry me, Evan. Gosh."

His ears burned hot. "Never thought that you were."

"So then, what's the problem?"

"I haven't done it in years."

"You said the same about the snowball fight, and you enjoyed that."

"Yeah, but that was different," he hedged.

"Different how?"

"It was—unplanned."

She rolled her eyes. "So you only do impromptu fun, huh? No planning."

"That sums it up," he said, sensing he was walking into a trap.

"So, if I just showed up and surprised you last minute and said, 'Hey, take me skating!' then you would?"

"Wait. What? No." She was moving awfully fast, and he had no clue where she was leading.

Mary thoughtfully pursed her lips. "If I could only solve that lodging thing."

"Now, *that* would surprise me."

"Would it?" He could practically hear her mental wheels turning. She was preparing to outfox him. He could feel it.

"So," she said slowly. "If you considered yourself sur-prised, because I'd solved our lodging issues...*then* you'd take me skating?"

Why was she being so bull-headed about this? "Uh, yeah. I guess." He knew full well that her achieving this goal was impossible. Unless she pulled a genie from a bottle and had him snap his fingers and create an enor-mous luxury hotel on Main Street.

"Okay." She grinned brightly. "It's a deal."

He'd just agreed to a pseudo-date that was never going to happen. Which sounded all right to him. "So, yeah. Um. Okay."

"Great." She shifted her satchel strap on her shoulder and moved to get past him. "I guess I'd better g—"

"Uh-huh, same," he said, stepping the other way. They nearly collided with him almost trampling her toes.

"Wow, sorry!" He jumped back.

She did too and her chin jerked up. "I'd better, er..."

She licked her lips and Evan's mouth went sandpaper dry.

"Right," he said hoarsely. "Me too." Then he skedad-dled around her and got out of there, striding toward the courthouse.

"See you on Sunday!" she called, as she walked away through the shadows. "At the tree lighting, if not before!"

He waved goodbye. "See you then!"

# *Chapter Twelve*

"I CAN'T BELIEVE IT, JUDY," MARY squealed with into the phone. "I actually asked him out."

"Who? Not the sheriff?"

"Well, yeah. In a roundabout manner, you could call it."

"What? How did he take that?"

Mary laughed, settling back against the headboard in her room. "I guess you could say he was confused."

"Mare-y. What's going on?"

"I wanted to go ice skating," she stated rationally. "So, I asked him to take me."

"Why not just take yourself?"

"Because I've never done it before, and it honestly looks like the kind of thing you do with someone else." Mary frowned, thinking of all those kids' skating parties she'd missed. Then she told herself not to be silly. She wasn't a kid anymore. And it hadn't been *that* big a deal. She was a grownup now, anyway.

"There's something else going on, too," she told Judy. "With Evan. Something I can't put my finger on." She wrapped a lock of her hair around her finger. "It's like he's all of a sudden become supportive of the parade."

"Well, that's *good*. And about time."

"I know." Mary sighed. "He *is* handsome, to tell you the truth. Very handsome underneath all that scruffy pragmatism. But there's more to it than that. It's about...I'm not sure. The way that he cares about the town, and his family. Evan's the honorable sort, you know?"

"Sounds like a principled guy."

"He is, but he's challenging," Mary said.

"You knew that from the start."

"Yeah."

A short silence hung between them.

Judy said, "So! When are you going out?"

"We're not. Yet. We sort of made a bet about me solving the lodging problem."

"Still haven't figured that out?"

"No, and I need to. If I don't, Evan won't take me skating. That's the deal we made."

"Well, when you put your mind to it, you can solve just about anything."

"I wish." Mary adjusted the comfy blankets around her. She'd finished some takeout Chinese in bed and was going to stream some of her favorite shows when she got off the phone.

"Just don't get too involved," Judy cautioned.

"What?"

"With Evan. This is only a short-term job. And *when*— not if—it all goes well, you'll be moving to Seattle."

"Yeah, yeah, of course. I know that, but that doesn't mean I can't have the tiniest bit of fun while I'm here."

"Just be careful, all right? I'd hate to see you setting yourself up for disappointment like you did the last time."

Mary gulped past the lump in her throat, which felt awfully sore. "Ben was another story."

"So were Caleb and Will." Judy sighed. "You can't keep

doing this, Mary. Forming attachments and dropping them."

"I don't do that."

"With me, no. But with men, um, yeah."

"Ouch. Way to be harsh."

"I'm just trying to protect you, you know," Judy said. "From yourself."

"Well, maybe I don't need protecting."

"Maybe not." Judy sounded weary.

Mary hated stressing her best friend. And maybe Judy was right. All that stuff she alluded to about her fear of commitment. But why was that even relevant here? She clearly wasn't committing to anybody in the town of Clark Creek.

"Hey, listen," Judy said, "I know that at the end of the day, you're going to do what you want to do. I'm not trying to butt in, just advising. You know it's because I care."

Mary's heart swelled with affection for her best friend. "Yeah, I know. I appreciate you looking out for me."

"Good luck solving that lodging problem." This time Mary would take Judy's good luck wishes, because she truthfully had no idea how she was going to pull this rabbit out of a hat.

After Mary signed off, she stewed over the conversation. Judy had good intentions and had only spoken out of concern, but she'd really hoped her best friend on earth would be happy for her. She'd made a bold move in asking Evan to go ice skating with her, and Judy had shot her assertiveness down. So okay, maybe she wasn't *seriously* interested in Evan. Because, yeah, Judy was right. Seriousness and romance didn't exactly match up in Mary's world.

She did have difficulty sticking with relationships,

because she definitely wasn't ready to settle down with a life partner. She liked staying on the move. Experiencing new places and things. She'd only wanted to go ice skating with Evan on friendly terms, so both of them could have fun. Just like they had during their snowball fight. There was obviously nothing wrong with that. It was okay to be congenial with someone you worked with. In most cases, that sort of professional camaraderie was seen as a plus.

Mary snuggled under the covers with her laptop, checking her streaming watchlist. Romantic comedies perfectly fit her mood tonight. She needed something lighthearted and entertaining, with a happy ending guaranteed. Mary scanned through the choices and selected a new release, which had recently been in theaters and which she'd heard was good.

What she needed was a brief escape to feed her soul and clear her head. Tomorrow, she'd focus on finalizing details for the parade and decide how she wanted to handle things with Evan. Maybe Judy was right. Maybe deepening her connection with him at this point in time was a bad move. Particularly in light of her pending relocation to Seattle.

Mary suddenly felt exhausted. The past week's cumulative pressures were taking their toll. Yawning, she started the movie.

She woke a 3:00 a.m., after sleeping more soundly than she had in months, to find the that her movie had ended hours before. The lights in her room still blazed and she rubbed her eyes, trying to recall the dream she'd had. It was something about the parade and—yes—lodging.

*Oh wow.* She'd had an inspiration. And it was… *brilliant.*

Homeowners renting out rooms had been a growing trend for years. With so many people in Clark Creek invested in the parade, maybe at least a few of them would be willing to offer lodging temporarily?

She set her laptop on her nightstand, knowing exactly how she was going to proceed. She'd call Judy first thing in the morning to see if Davenport Development Associates could lend home office support to any townsfolk interested in participating.

Mary reached for her phone on the nightstand and set its alarm.

*Yep. This is perfect.*

*Things are going to be good.*

The next morning, Evan opened his door to find his mom standing on his front steps holding a brown grocery bag.

"Mom? What are you doing here?"

He owned a Craftsman-style home behind the courthouse, which he'd bought and refurbished when he returned to Clark Creek to be the sheriff. As many renovations as he'd done, there was always more work to do.

His mom handed him the bag. He peeked inside and saw two food storage containers. She said, "Your dad and I had Brunswick stew for supper last night and there was a ton left over."

"Thanks." Evan wasn't much of a cook, but he did have a hearty appetite, which he'd inherited from his dad. Luckily, he was also in the habit of regular exercise thanks to his time in the Army. He could eat what he wanted, as long as he didn't go crazy about it.

His mom stepped inside, removing her gloves. "Brrr. Why is it so chilly in here?" A swirl of snowflakes blasted toward her and she gawked at the opening at the back of the living room. "Evan! You're missing a wall!"

He chuckled at her horrified expression. "Nope. Just installing a French door to lead out to the deck."

She eyed his jeans, sweatshirt, and work boots. "You're not dressed warmly enough for letting Old Man Winter indoors."

"I'll have it done by later today." He set the bag down on the small table in his dining area and strode to the gaping hole, taping down the heavy plastic sheeting that had been blown out of place.

She frowned and then said, "I was almost hoping not to catch you at home. I was thinking you might be with Mary."

His eyebrows rose. "Why?"

"I got a call from Vivi Torres…" Her light eyes twinkled. "She and Shirley Watson saw the two of you together on Main Street yesterday evening."

"We were walking the parade route."

"Oh? Is that all that it was? Business? Because Vivi said the two of you were looking very couple-y—almost date-like."

Evan raked a hand through his hair. "Mom."

"I wouldn't be opposed if it happens. I mean, it's not like you work together permanently in the same office. You can't tell me you haven't noticed she's pretty? And very smart. And she's talented—"

"And she's only here until Christmas," he reminded her pointedly.

"Maybe she'll decide to stay?"

"Big-city gal like her?" Evan shook his head. "Don't think so."

His mom wore a glum expression. "Maybe you're right." The next instant, she appeared perky again. "In the meantime, I'm glad to know you're getting along better."

"Yeah, we're getting along great."

Evan recalled the moment in the gazebo when he'd nearly bumped into Mary, and his heart beat harder. There'd been a tension between them—chemistry, even. It wasn't the first time he'd noticed it, either, although he'd tried to pretend that he hadn't.

"We're getting our town tree delivered today," his mom told him.

"That's what I hear."

"Are you going to come and see it?"

"Yeah, but it will have to be later," he said. "I'm going over to Nash's to help him move some stuff."

"Stuff?"

Evan's shoulders sagged because he knew this was painful for his big brother. "Becca's stuff."

There was a sad glimmer in her eyes. "Yes, I remember."

"Anyway, with Christmas coming, he decided maybe he should donate some of her things to charity. There are a few special items he's saving for Chloe, but other than those…"

"You're very good to help him. I can come too, if—"

"I don't think he wants too many people underfoot. He only tagged me because of my brawn," he joked.

His mom smiled softly. "What about Chloe?"

"Itzel's taking her ice skating."

"How sweet! You know what I think?" There was a knowing look in her eyes. "I think she might have a thing for your brother."

"Marshall?" Evan said, playing purposely obtuse, and his mom swatted his arm.

"You know which one I mean."

Evan laughed. "Yeah, I dunno. Maybe."

His mom cocked her chin. "But I don't think he's ready."

"Probably not," Evan agreed.

# Chapter Thirteen

"Y ES! THAT'S PERFECT!" MARY GRINNED at Ken as he and his buddy, Wayne, steadied the tall Fraser fir in its designated spot in the town square facing the courthouse.

Ken gave a thumbs up, and then he and Wayne got busy anchoring the tree in place. Another man, Ed, and a woman, Janie, hauled items from the bed of a pickup truck, carrying them toward the gazebo. Mary went to thank them for their efforts, and to help direct where everything went. The square already looked magical in the lightly drifting snow. It was going to appear even more spectacular once it was all decorated.

There were built-in benches hugging the inside perimeter of the gazebo, and Ed and Janie had laid out several strands of greenery there to use as garlands. They began carting over more Christmas trees. Two. Four... Wait a minute. And two more? Mary was almost sure she'd only asked for five to fit in the spaces between the gazebo benches.

As she strolled over to talk to Ken, her gaze trailed to the skating rink, which was busy on Saturday morning. A woman skating with a little girl looked familiar. She thought it was Itzel. But who was the elfin kid in pigtails?

Ken wiped his brow with a bandana. "Looking good," he said, nodding toward the big community tree.

"It's really beautiful, Ken. Thank you."

"They're all pre-strung with lights." He shoved his bandanna back in his pocket. "That's kind of a tricky job once a tree that tall is standing." He motioned to Wayne, who plugged a sturdy outdoor extension cord into the receptacle box near the skating rink, and the tree came to life. Even in daylight, its sparkling lights looked amazing. Mary was so happy to get this sneak preview of the tree-lighting ceremony tomorrow.

"I love it." She grinned at Ken and his helpers. "Thanks, guys. You're the best."

"We brought outdoor tree decorations too," Ken said. "And our ladder. It's probably safest if you let us hang those before we go."

"If you don't mind, that would be terrific." She glanced back at the gazebo, and at Janie who was standing there leaning the excess Christmas tree against a gazebo railing while peering around, like she was trying to decide what she was supposed to do with it. "So, I wanted to ask you about the extra tree."

"Extra? What do you mean?"

"When we talked about it, I thought we discussed five for the gazebo, but now—" She shrugged. "There seem to be six?"

He laughed. "I couldn't remember if we said five or six, so I erred on the side of caution. Didn't want to come up short."

"No. Well. Thank you!" Mary frowned. What should they do with the extra tree? "Would you like to take it back to the nursery?"

"Not when it's already here. Tell you what," he said

kindly. "Why don't you keep it?"

Well, she certainly couldn't keep it in her room at the inn, which was already decorated for Christmas very nicely. Then another thought occurred to her. *Evan.* She needed to see him, anyway.

Ken added, "Surely, a Christmas Consultant can't have too many Christmas trees?"

"That's true," she said, smiling. "Thanks, Ken. I'll find a good home for it."

An hour later, Mary waved Ken and his team goodbye, thanking them again for their generosity. The town tree was gorgeous, and the decorated gazebo looked so pretty with tiny strands of lights woven through its garlands. Ken had explained how the gazebo lights and town tree lights were scheduled to go on each evening at dusk using a preset timer. All she had to do during the tree-lighting ceremony was flip the switch.

Mary called to Ken as he sat in his truck with his driver's window partially down. "Good luck with everything in Colorado."

"Thank you," he said. "I'm hoping to make it a very merry Christmas."

He was such a nice guy. From their brief meeting, she believed Dusty was a great person too. She had to be, for someone as good-hearted as Ken to like her so much. No. Not like. *Love.* He was planning to propose, after all.

Her heart felt light as she turned toward the gazebo, studying that extra tree. She'd need to get her SUV from the inn to pick it up. It was a good thing she'd unloaded so many of those decorations at the courthouse, clearing more space in her vehicle. She still had a handful of decorations left. They'd be enough for decking somebody's halls and trimming this tree.

The one minor flaw in her plan was that she didn't know where Evan lived.

She glanced back at the skating rink. The little girl and the woman she'd spotted earlier were stepping off the ice. They sat down on a bench to remove their skates, and Mary was now sure that the petite brunette was Itzel. She wore a trim white coat with a scarf. Her wispy dark bangs and short hair poked out beneath her matching white hat. She looked up when she saw Mary approaching.

"Itzel, hi! I thought that was you."

"The gazebo looks fantastic. The big tree too." Itzel winked at the child beside her. The darling kid wore a puffy purple jacket and a fuzzy pink hat with a big white pompon on it. "We were watching all the activity from the skating rink."

The little girl grinned at Mary. "Hi, I'm Chloe."

Mary leaned toward her. "Hi, Chloe. It's so nice to meet you. Are you Nash's little girl?"

The child's grin widened, exposing two missing front teeth. "Uh-huh."

"I've heard about you from your Uncle Marshall. He says you're a very fine ballerina."

Chloe held up her arms in a partial pirouette. "We're doing *The Nutcracker*!"

"How cool," Mary said. "I'd love to see it."

"You should come," Itzel told her. "It's next Tuesday."

That was only two days before the parade, but Mary could scarcely say no to the precious look on Chloe's face. "I would love to come to your ballet."

"Yay!"

"I can buy you a ticket," Itzel said. "I'll get yours

when I buy mine." Her dark eyes lit up. "We can even go together, if you'd like."

"Oh, uh. Sure." Mary was touched. "That would be really nice. Just let me know about the ticket and I'll reimburse you."

As Itzel helped Chloe lace up her snow boots, Mary wondered how to approach this without making her interest in Evan obvious. Her friendship-type interest, she reminded herself. That's all that it was. There'd be no reason for Itzel to think any different. Besides that, she and Evan were working together.

"Itzel," she said. "I know you know that Evan's helping me with the parade."

"Yeah. How's that going?"

"Really well."

"I love the whole Christmas Avenue plan." She nodded with approval. "My mom told me about it. Your souvenirs too. This parade is going to rock it."

"Rock it, rock it!" Chloe swayed from side to side, pumping her small fists, and Mary and Itzel laughed at her energy. She was an adorable little girl, and Itzel seemed to do so well with her. Mary was curious about Itzel's relationship with Nash. Was it romantic?

"Thanks." Mary grinned at Chloe and Itzel. "I think so too. Only, there are a few details I need to run by Evan. Some new developments. But it's Saturday, and his day off."

"Oh, I'm sure he won't mind if you stop by his house," Itzel said. "Evan's very chill about that kind of stuff."

"Fantastic. Only…I'm not sure where he lives."

"No worries," Itzel said, taking out her cell phone. "Give me your number and I'll text you his address."

Evan loaded the last box of Becca's things in his truck. He kept his official vehicle at the courthouse and used that while he was on duty. This was family business, and he was glad that he could be here.

"You sure you don't mind dropping that off?" Nash asked.

Evan read Nash's long face. They hadn't spent much time going through things. Mostly, Nash had said, "Yeah, take it," in regard to clothing and personal items like Becca's books. She'd been a schoolteacher and had a ton of them. The jewelry had consumed more time. He'd agonized over her wedding band and engagement ring, ultimately deciding to set them aside for Chloe. Maybe Chloe would have a son one day, and he'd like to use the diamond. Or maybe she'd like to reset the gem in another piece of jewelry. Nash didn't know, but he couldn't give the set away, or sell it.

"It's not that much," Evan told him. "And I don't mind. I'll drop things off during my morning rounds on Monday." He braced his hand on Nash's shoulder. "You're doing the right thing."

Nash hung his head. "Probably should have done it a long time ago."

"We all heal in our own time."

"Women." Nash gave a melancholy smile. "You love them, then they leave you."

"Yeah."

Nash's neck colored. "I'm sorry, man. I didn't mean… about Cathy."

"I know what you meant." Evan shoved Nash's arm.

"She was a fool, you know."

"Seems happy enough now. Two point five kids."

Nash gave him a quizzical look. "Point five?"

"A couple of toddlers and she's pregnant."

"You need to stay off social media."

Evan sighed. "Doesn't matter anyway. Time's gone by."

Nash eyed Becca's things in Evan's truck. "It does march along."

"Ever going to get back in the game?" Evan asked.

"Not sure. Maybe someday." He met Evan's eyes. "You?"

Evan blew out a breath. "Hard to say."

"Mary's awfully nice."

"That's what folks keep telling me."

"Folks like who? Mom?"

Evan laughed. "Yeah."

"She's always been a decent judge of character. What do you think?" When Evan gave him a blank stare, Nash continued. "Of Mary?"

"I think she's…very good at her job. And that she's leaving at the end of next week."

"Richmond's not that far away."

"No, but you're way off base."

Nash chuckled, and Evan was heartened to see his mood lightening. "Okay. I'll lay off."

"Thank you." As Evan climbed into his truck, Nash said, "Hey, I heard the old Miller place sold."

"Did it?"

"Dad mentioned something about it. He heard from Fred," Nash said, referencing one of the real estate agents in town.

"I hope the new owners are handy." Evan knew that the rundown Victorian on Maple Street, across from Marshall's inn, was badly in need of fixing up. The fact

129

that it had sold held promise. It would be nice to see Evaline Miller's old place restored. It had stood empty for a couple of years, ever since the elderly Miss Miller moved out of state to live with her niece.

"The house does need work," Nash agreed.

"Any idea who bought it?"

"Dad wasn't sure. Only knew that they weren't local."

"Always nice having newcomers in Clark Creek," Evan said.

"Kind of like Mary Ward?" Nash ribbed.

Evan wryly twisted his lips. "You, Dr. Nash, are a very funny guy."

Nash shot him a smug look. "I do have my charms."

*Chapter Fourteen*

W HEN EVAN RETURNED TO HIS place, Mary was waiting on his front porch, a vision in the snow. She was also holding a Christmas tree upright in one hand while the base of its trunk rested on the stoop. She held an enormous canvas bag in her other hand, and it was stuffed to the brim. She couldn't have…but she had. She'd arrived to decorate his house.

He laughed and shook his head. Maybe he should have been perturbed, because he'd expressly asked her not to do this. But it was hard for him to be mad at Mary. Especially since he'd been thinking about her during his whole drive home from Nash's farm. Nash had teased him about liking her, and so had his mom. While he'd blown off their comments, he admitted to himself that there was something intriguing about her. Lots of somethings. Her persistence was one of them.

She watched him park his truck and pop his door open. "Evan!" Her face lit up and his pulse pounded. Yep, she was intriguing, all right. And his ticker knew it. "I was just about to leave you a note."

*And what?* he wondered, *drop off a Christmas tree?* He doubted he would have felt inclined to decorate it himself. With her here, he might be tempted. "Mary," he said. "I'm surprised to see you. How did you know where I live?"

She smiled her dimpled smile and Evan felt himself melt. Sort of like when a marshmallow gets roasted over a campfire. Which was definitely not like him, and also one hundred percent disgusting. *Get a grip, man. She's only a lady trying to help you overcome your holiday decor deficit. She's not tacking up any mistletoe.* Or was she?

"Itzel gave me directions," she said.

She must've seen Itzel at the town square, since Itzel had taken Chloe ice skating. "How did the tree installation go?" He climbed out of his truck and headed for his front door.

"There were several trees," she told him. "Including this bonus one here."

"Ah," he said. "A little lan-yap."

She laughed at his stab at humor and he like the way it sounded. Heartfelt and musical. "Yeah, I guess you could say so. I asked for five for the gazebo, but Ken got mixed up and brought six. He said not to worry about the extra tree—to just keep it. So."

Evan unlocked his door and peered over his shoulder. "You thought of me?"

Her cheeks colored. "You're not mad?"

"At you, Mary? Never."

She exhaled as he held open the door for her. "Whew. I guess I was a little worried. You know, after what you said."

"I didn't know you were planning to bring a Christmas tree." He took it from her and carried it over the threshold, making room for her to enter his foyer.

"You know what?" she said. "I didn't either." She stared around his living room, and Evan was glad he'd finished up with those French doors. Everything looked tidy now. "This is a sweet place. I like it!"

Maybe it was a small compliment, but he enjoyed that she liked his house. "Thanks. I've been working on it for a while."

"Well, everything looks great. Very—bachelor-like."

He laughed. "What's that supposed to mean?"

"Streamlined," she explained. "A sofa, two end tables and a recliner. Flatscreen TV over the fireplace. A dining table for two, and oh…" she peered into the kitchen, "a small galley kitchen, which is compact yet functional."

"You haven't examined the bedrooms."

Her blush deepened. "Don't intend to." She set her canvas bag on the floor, then asked, "How many are there?"

"Just two. A master and a nursery." He regretted sharing that last part. "What I mean is, the second room is much smaller so it was used as a nursery by the last people here."

"And now?"

"It's my study."

"Sounds perfect for you, except…" She leaned toward him. "Evan. There's nothing on the walls."

He surveyed the room, conceding she was right. Not that he'd really thought about it. "Not true," he said, noting the hearth. "There's my TV."

She giggled. "I'm not sure that counts. I was thinking of artwork. Photos. Things like that." He pointed to a couple of framed pictures on an end table. One was a group shot of his family that looked like it had been taken at Christmas, because there was a decorated tree in the background. The other was a pic of him with his two brothers on a boat, wearing sunglasses. They held fishing poles and wore big grins.

"Where was that one taken?" she asked about the

brothers shot.

"Outer Banks."

"North Carolina?"

"Yeah. Marshall, Nash, and I do a fishing trip every year in October."

"No girls allowed?" she asked lightly.

"It's an equal-opportunity adventure." Evan stroked his chin. "Becca used to join us."

"She was…?"

"Nash's late wife."

Her face fell. "Oh, wow. I'm sorry. How long has it been?"

"Three years now."

"That has to be tough."

"Can be. That's what I was doing at Nash's. Helping him clear out some of Becca's stuff."

She viewed him with admiration, and it made his heart full. He enjoyed it when she looked at him that way. Like she saw and appreciated who he was. "You were very good to help him." She thought a moment. "Is that why Chloe was with Itzel?"

"Yes."

"Are Nash and Itzel—?"

"No."

"Oh well." She studied his living room again, then pointed to a spot to the left of the French doors. "That looks like a good place for our tree. What do you think?"

His necked warmed because she'd said "our" like the tree belonged to both of them, and he found the thought of joint ownership appealing. "I think it's the perfect spot for our tree. Did you bring a stand with it?"

"I did. It's in my SUV. Ken provided those as well."

"Thoughtful guy."

"Yeah."

She turned toward the door but Evan held out his hand. "Toss me your keys and I'll grab it."

"You sure?"

"Of course."

"As long as you're grabbing the stand, there are a few more boxes of decorations, if you don't mind."

"Nope. Why don't you take off your coat and sit down?" He found he liked the idea of her making herself at home.

"I can't stay long."

"Come on," he urged. "You can't leave me all alone to deck my own halls."

She blushed again. "Okay. I'm glad to help."

Evan went outside and Mary removed her coat. She hadn't intended to stay. She did need to tell Evan about her lodging breakthrough, though. He should be very happy about that, and she wasn't honestly going to insist he take her skating. She was a little embarrassed she'd made that silly bet.

If Evan didn't want to go skating with her, that was fine. Maybe she could go with Itzel sometime before she left Clark Creek. Itzel was so warm and friendly, and Mary had really appreciated her invitation to go with her to the ballet. She knew life would be different in Seattle, but she found herself yearning to make friends there, too.

Friendships had never been a high priority for her, since she'd always poured herself into her work and had moved around so frequently. Plus, she always had Judy to rely on. But being in Clark Creek had made her see things differently. There was such a sense of community here, and she found that comforting.

She looked around the living room and spied a door near the dining area. Peeking inside, she saw it was the coat closet, so she hung up her coat after jamming her gloves and hat into the pockets.

Evan had leaned the Christmas tree against the wall near the corner. He really did have a sweet house, but it definitely lacked something. A homey feel, she guessed. Maybe her decorations would help liven things up?

Evan returned with the tree stand and two more boxes. "You really weren't kidding at the courthouse when you said you keep a lot of decorations in your cargo area."

She shrugged. "Old habits."

"So, how long have you been a Christmas hoarder?" he joked.

"Ever since college."

He set down the stand and the boxes. "What happened there?"

"I was the president of the Christmas Club! A club that I started."

He gave her an admiring look. "I might have known. What did you do at this Christmas Club?"

"We helped those less fortunate deck their halls."

"So, I'm less fortunate now?"

She smirked. "No, I'd say you're a very lucky guy, judging by what I've seen of Clark Creek and your family."

"True." As he took off his coat and hung it up, he asked, "Would you like coffee?"

"I don't want to put you to any trouble."

"No trouble. I was already planning to make some when I got home."

"Well, in that case…" She followed him into his kitchen, where he set up his coffee pot.

"How do you take yours?

"With a little bit of milk, if you got it."

"Half and half okay?"

"Great."

He started the coffee and took two mugs from the cupboard. Through the window above his sink, she saw more snowflakes drifting down. "It snows a lot in Clark Creek."

"That's because we're close to the mountains." His smile warmed Mary through and through.

"Where is the creek?" She been curious about where it was in relation to the town.

"On the other side of town. You turn left at the Whistle Stop Café onto Three-Notched Pass, cross over the railroad tracks and it's down a ways. It's got a swimming hole and folks go tubing there in summertime."

That sounded idyllic to Mary. "I've never been tubing."

"No?" His eyebrows rose. "You've led a deprived life."

"Ha ha, yeah."

The coffee finished and he poured her some, handing her a mug and spoon. Then he took a small carton of half and half from his refrigerator, which Mary saw was nearly empty, except for a couple of large soup containers. He poured her some half and half. "Just say when."

"When!" she said, when he'd given her a smidgen. She stirred and sipped from her coffee, which was tasty and hot.

"Get much of the white stuff over in Richmond?"

"Some."

"Bet they do tubing over there, somewhere on the James. It's a long river. Mountains to the coast."

"They might. I'll have to ask Judy."

"Your boss, and also your friend," he said, recalling what she'd told him.

Mary nodded. "She's very outdoorsy."

"What do you like to do?"

"Yoga," she answered. "And decorate."

"Might have guessed that second one." He toasted her with his coffee. "Thanks for bringing the tree, by the way."

"Ready to decorate it?"

"Any time you are."

They returned to the living room together and got busy setting up the tree. It was a nice full one with a good shape. Ken's nursery delivered really fine trees. Mary thought the ones in the gazebo were awesome too, and the town tree was super amazing.

"I think this will work." Evan tightened the screws on the tree stand, then scooted back from his crouched position, standing up. He set his hands on his hips. "Nice. What shall we name him?"

Her eyebrows rose. "Him?"

"I'm thinking it's a male tree, seeing as how it's in a bachelor pad and all."

Mary giggled at his assertion. "I don't think you really name trees."

"What? Why not? People name their pets."

"Yeah, but—"

"And bodies of water…and constellations."

"How about Polaris?" she asked him.

"As in, the North Star?"

"It…sorry…*he* might like it," she giggled again, not having realized Evan had this goofy side. "It is a Christmas tree, after all, and Polaris is the brightest star we've got."

"Ah, but it's not the Christmas Star."

"Who says?"

"Astronomers think it might have been the conjunction of Jupiter and Saturn."

"Or a miracle," she said sassily.

"Not discounting that." He turned to study the tree,

rubbing his chin. "Polaris. Hmm." His eyes twinkled. "I *like* it."

"Then Polaris it is!" She grabbed her canvas bag and carried it over. "We should have something in this bag to suit him."

"No bows," Evan teased. "Nothing too girly."

"I don't think you should put judgey gender limitations on your tree."

He smirked, and she could tell he was enjoying her humor. "Fair point. I'll keep an open mind."

She held up two boxes of strings of lights. "First the lights?"

He nodded. "Always."

"I thought you'd never done this before?"

"Never at my own place, but I've helped at my folks' place."

"Ooh, so you have experience."

He made a pinching motion between this thumb and forefinger. "Just a tad."

Mary smiled. She was enjoying this. Having a really good time with Evan. If he'd only been this amenable before, he wouldn't have proved nearly as difficult to work with. Maybe he was feeling better about the parade, since she'd come up with solutions to so many of his problems. Which reminded her: She needed to tell him about the Airbnbs.

She passed him one box of lights and held onto the other, opening it up. "I have some good news."

"Oh yeah? What's that? You've solved our lodging problem?" He laughed like it was impossible.

Mary grinned. "Yep. I've solved our lodging problem."

Evan nearly dropped his box of lights, but he caught it, and a gnarly tangle of cord with tiny attached bulbs spilled toward the floor. Fortunately, nothing broke.

"What? How?" He wound the light string back up while wrapping it between his splayed hand and elbow.

"I had another inspiration," she said brightly.

Evan's eyebrows arched. "Don't keep me in suspense." He began draping the lights around the tree by starting at the tippy top, which he was tall enough to reach without a ladder.

Mary set her own box of lights down and went to help him, positioning each string of lights on the tree as he continued unwinding, walking a few paces ahead of her. "I thought that some of the townsfolk could open up their homes as Airbnbs." When he opened his mouth to speak, she added, "Only temporarily. Davenport Development Associates is helping with the business setup."

"Wow. That's innovative. Do you think you'll get any takers?"

"I already have," she told him. "Several."

They finished stringing the lights and she handed him some colorful balls to hang on the three, while she did the same. "I'm afraid I don't have too many tree decorations left. Just these tree balls and some candy canes."

"That's okay. Polaris is a minimalist."

She gaped at him. "You really are funny."

"Why is that such a surprise?"

"I don't know. It just is." She thought back to his earlier comment about the town council robbing a bank, realizing he'd always had this side to him. He'd just kept it hidden away, like so many other interesting things about him.

"You just have to get to know me."

"I see."

"What's your innermost secret?" He scanned her eyes and butterflies flitted around in her belly.

"Um. I'm not sure I've got one." Her face heated.

"What you see is what you get."

He smiled and half of his mouth lifted up higher than the other, which made her heart pound harder. "Nothing wrong with that."

She handed him a box of candy canes, but it slipped from her hands. "Oops!"

He bent to catch it, and they nearly bumped heads.

Evan backed away and picked up the box of candy canes off the floor. This time they weren't so lucky. Each candy cane had cracked, a few of them in more than one place.

"Looks like Polaris is going to be even more of a minimalist than we thought," Mary said.

Evan shrugged. "What else have you got in that bag?"

"Well…" She grinned, enjoying the moment. Loving being here with him. Even if it was only in friendship, it felt good being in his company. Evan made her feel happy. "We have…garlands…and more lights! And, oh!" She spied a sprig of mistletoe attached to a silky white ribbon in the bottom of her bag, but decided not to mention it. He might think she was hinting, or even thinking of kissing him. The thought did cross her mind—briefly. But she quickly swept it away. "Um… also an advent calendar."

She unfurled the felt calendar, which hung from a small horizontal wooden pole with a ribbon attached so you could suspend it from a nail. Below a Christmas tree, twenty-five small pockets contained tiny ornaments, with Velcro on the back so you could adhere them.

"I think this will look splendid over your sofa," she told him.

He stroked his chin. "Doesn't look very bachelor-y."

"Ah! No judgments."

He laughed. "Right."

A short time later they'd finished with the garlands and the lights, and Evan had even allowed Mary to hang up her advent calendar. He'd participated too, by getting his hammer and driving in the nail in to hold it.

"You're right." He set his hammer on the coffee table and stepped back to view the calendar. "It does add color."

She grabbed her coat from the coat closet and put it on. "Don't forget to put up a new ornament every day!"

He shook his head, and there was a mischievous gleam in his eye. "Not going to promise you that."

"Evan."

"Why don't you put the first ones up?"

"What? Me?"

"It will only take a minute. Besides…" His blue eyes sparkled. "You're the Christmas Consultant."

"Ha ha. Yeah."

She had to get on her knees on the sofa to dig the small ornaments out of their pockets and stick them to the felt tree. She put up nineteen, then gasped. "Do you know what this means?" She peered at him over her shoulder. "Just five more days until the parade."

"Then it's a great thing you're so organized."

Mary stood to tug on her hat and gloves, trying to ignore the sudden feelings of worry. "Yeah, but there's still a lot to do." She wrapped her scarf around her neck and found her canvas tote next. She'd mostly emptied it of decorations, except for a garland and that buried mistletoe. "I've to got to oversee the Airbnb setup and put together a list of available accommodations to post on the town website and in newsletters advertising the parade…finalize the floats, my volunteer roster, the parade lineup, and—"

Evan crossed his arms in front of him. "When does the ice skating get penciled in?"

She looked up and met his eyes, and was immediately lost in their swoony blue depths. "What?"

He grinned, and her pulse quickened. "Wasn't that part of our deal? You work out lodging and I take you ice skating?" He cocked an eyebrow. "Still want to go?"

They stood in the small foyer inside his front door, and Mary tightened her grip on her bag. She kept telling herself this was all about friendship, but Evan's gaze was more than friendly. He appeared interested in her. Her heart skipped a beat.

"I...do."

"Great. How about tomorrow?"

She licked her lips. "It's Sunday, and the tree-lighting—"

"Right. You'll be busy." He frowned, and she worried that he thought she was blowing him off.

"But—Monday works! I mean, Monday evening? If that works for you?"

"How does seven sound?"

"Seven sounds good."

"Great! Meet you there?"

"Uh-huh!" She turned toward the door and accidentally dropped her bag. It hit the floor and spilled sideways. The sprig of mistletoe bounced out onto the carpet.

Mary wanted to facepalm. So hard.

Evan bent to retrieve it, then slowly stood up. "You didn't tell me you had this," he said, pinching it between his thumb and forefinger.

Her face burned extra hot. "I, er...wasn't sure you'd want...um...need it?"

"You never know." His eyes danced and her heart beat harder. "Want to help me put it up?"

"Uh..." Her mind raced with desire and confusion. Yeah, she wanted to kiss Evan. But no, she really couldn't.

And, maybe he was just joking around, and not hinting at that at all? "Maybe next time?"

He grinned, seeming satisfied with her answer. "All right. See you Monday, then."

"Yep." She scooped up her bag and hustled out the door. "See you then!"

Mary backed out of Evan's drive, nearly sideswiping his truck with her SUV as she went. Thank goodness he wasn't on the front porch watching her. Or had she seen his silhouette in the window? No. She'd probably imagined that.

She had plans with Evan! And somehow it felt very, very, very much like a date. Especially after all that business with the mistletoe. Whether he'd been joking or not, Evan had definitely been flirting with her. There was no mistaking that. Even if he wasn't seriously interested in being any more than friends, she couldn't help the way he made her feel inside. All tingly and like she was floating on the clouds, practically walking on air.

She pulled up to the corner far away from Evan's house, and before she turned on her turn signal, she gleefully pounded her steering wheel, taking care not to honk the horn. Which she almost accidentally did.

*Ye-es. Yes! Woo-hoo!*

*I'm going ice skating with Evan.*

# Chapter Fifteen

$\mathcal{M}$ ARY RETURNED TO THE CLARK Creek B&B to answer some emails that had come in from more potential sponsors about the parade. She'd seen the barrage of new messages loading on her phone, but needed her computer notes in front of her before responding. She'd also had more groups apply to enter floats in the parade, which was fantastic. She'd started a second spreadsheet to help keep all the information straight.

Once she'd taken care of that bit of work, she'd head into town for dinner. Several restaurants on Main Street were within walking distance, and she'd seen a cool-looking place, Taverna Italiana, that looked fun. Mary was in the mood for pasta. Something hearty like lasagna would be excellent.

She parked behind the inn and came in the back door, like Marshall had instructed her to do. She passed him in the downstairs hall, which had two large suites behind the common living areas. Marshall's private quarters were upstairs, overlooking the backyard.

He carried a chilled champagne bucket, wrapped in a towel and loaded with a corked bottle of bubbly. He'd secured a box of designer chocolate truffles between his side and his elbow. He could barely reach the knob on the guest room door, so Mary opened it for him. She'd seen Jeremy making up the suite earlier, and he'd said new guests were coming in this evening.

"Thanks, Mary," Marshall said.

She smiled at her gregarious host, happy to help. "Champagne," she said. "Ooh-la-la."

But the champagne and chocolates were only the half of it. The huge gas fireplace on the far side of the four-poster bed had been turned on, its flames flickering softly. A small table sat in front of the hearth, covered with a linen tablecloth and complemented by two carved wooden chairs with cushiony seats. On the table sat a gorgeous vase of dark red roses, two champagne flutes, and a carafe of ice water, as well as a bottle of red wine and a delicious-looking fruit and cheese platter. A separate plate of crackers sat off to one side.

"Whoa," she said, impressed. "Fancy."

"The Taylors are arriving shortly," Marshall said. "Gerald texted from the road. I asked him to give me a twenty-minute warning, so I could get everything set up."

"This is fabulous! Is it a surprise, or do they know?"

"I wanted to surprise them. It's their golden anniversary. Fifty years."

"Oh my. That's something."

"They have dinner reservations later, but I thought they might enjoy a snack when they arrive."

"How thoughtful." From her vantage point, she could see through the open bathroom door. A wicker shelf held an array of plush towels, a candle and some matches. It stood next to an antique clawfoot tub. *Most Romantic Getaway*, for sure.

Marshall set the champagne bucket down on the table and placed the chocolate box on the bed with an envelope.

"Anniversary card?"

He smiled. "Gift certificate. For a horse-drawn sleigh ride at Nash's farm."

Mary caught her breath. That sounded fantastic and fabulously romantic. "He does those?"

"Not generally," Marshall said. "Only for special occasions when I ask him. Leroy sets it up and does the driving."

"Five decades is really special, all right," Mary said.

"Yeah." Marshall crossed his arms in front of him. "I love seeing people in love."

She wondered about his background. "What did you do before running the inn?"

"I taught literature."

*Huh.* "University level?"

"Yeah."

"Ever think about writing?"

"No, I'd much rather read." She wasn't really surprised, given his large library. Guests were encouraged to peruse it and pick out a book or two to read by the library's fireplace or in their rooms.

"What made you come back to Clark Creek?"

"I heard about this place being for sale." He shifted on his feet. "And, well. There was someone."

Mary didn't know what to say. She felt like she'd trodden into invasive territory. He continued without her prompting.

"She was going to come with me." He gestured around. "Help me run this place, but then..." He shrugged. "I guess she got cold feet. Said she had her doubts about being in the hospitality business."

"Oh no."

"It's all right." He smiled warmly. "Sometimes things work out the way they're meant to. That's what I like to believe."

"Yeah," Mary said. "Me too."

"Anyway," he said. "It's been good being back and around my family."

"I think it's cool how you're all so close."

"You said you don't have brothers and sisters? How about your folks?"

"My parents divorced when I was little, and my mom lives in Portland now."

"Portland, Oregon? Do you see her much?"

"Not really, to tell you the truth. I might see more of her once I…" She trailed off. For some reason she felt weird mentioning her potential move to Marshall, or to anyone in Clark Creek, really. It wasn't set in stone, anyway. She still had to earn that promotion. "I mean, after the holidays."

"It's a shame you can't see her for Christmas," he said.

"I'll be all right."

"Will you stay here?"

Mary hadn't even considered the idea. She'd always assumed she'd leave after wrapping up the parade. "Probably not. I'll need to head back to Richmond."

She thought she saw sympathy in his eyes. "My mom and dad always have an extra place at their table."

"Thanks, Marshall. You're very kind."

The inn's front door chime sounded, and an older woman called out. "Hel-lo! Is anybody home?"

Marshall said, "That would be Geraldine."

"Taylor? And her husband is Gerald?" Their similar-sounding names were super cute.

He grinned. "It seems they're a great match."

The next day, Mary was thrilled to see the town square so packed for the tree-lighting ceremony. She stood in the gazebo with Connie and Jesse observing the crowd.

"It's just outstanding what you've done," Connie said. "So fab, Mary."

"And in one short week," Jesse added from beside her.

"I did have a few days in Richmond before that," Mary said modestly.

The were bundled up in their winter coats against the evening chill, but Mary felt warm inside. The parade hadn't happened yet, but everything had worked out well so far, including with Evan. She scanned the faces by the skating rink and those of others milling about near the town tree. They hadn't agreed to meet here or anything, but she still hoped to see him. He was on duty today, so his uniform should be easy to spot in the crowd.

She'd had a busy day. She'd spent her morning hours preparing an update for the mayor and the town council on the parade. There was so much to share and she'd wanted to provide some graphics with her presentation. When she'd delivered it at the courthouse this afternoon, the council members had stood and applauded. She'd cautioned them that her job wasn't finished yet, but they'd indicated they had faith in her.

Mary felt happy that Evan was starting to share that faith, because—no matter what she'd tried to tell herself earlier—his opinion did matter to her. She wanted him to be as happy and excited about her parade on Christmas Avenue as she was. Okay, so maybe asking Evan to show "excitement" was a bit of a stretch, since he was a more subdued guy. But he was warming to the idea of her parade, as well as to her. There'd been no mistaking the look in his eyes when he'd asked her about going ice skating. Or putting up that mistletoe.

Itzel entered the gazebo, giving everyone a friendly smile. "Mary," she said, "this is fantastic. Look at all the people here."

"Yes, and these are only the locals," Connie said.

Jesse nodded. "There will be more at the parade."

"That's going to be a lot of folks in Clark Creek," Itzel commented.

"Yeah," Mary said. "But we're prepared."

Marshall and Nash walked up next. Nash held Chloe's hand, and the kid's cheeks glowed as she glanced around. "Look at that big tree, Daddy," she said, pointing.

"Yeah, I know," he said. "I see it."

"Evening, folks," Marshall said when he, Nash and Chloe joined the group. Mary scanned the crowd again, but still didn't see Evan.

Nash addressed his parents and Mary. "Quite a crowd. Kudos. When do the tree lights go on?"

Mary checked her watch, hoping the timer worked as well as Ken had promised it would. Dusk had fallen and shadows stretched across the town square in the lightly falling snow. "Ten minutes." That's when the gazebo lights would turn on, too.

Marshall spoke to Itzel. "Nice haircut," he said, noticing the wispy short layers beneath her hat. "Suits you."

"Thanks." She fiddled with her hat, casting a sidelong glance at Nash, who gave her a puzzled look.

"You cut your hair?"

"Yeah, last week."

Nash observed her carefully. "Oh. Looks nice."

Chloe tugged at his hand. "Can Itzel take me skating

again? It was fun."

Nash smiled at his daughter. "Maybe some time." His words didn't sound like a commitment, and Itzel appeared as if she was trying hard not to frown. "Thanks for taking her, by the way," Nash told Itzel. "That was really helpful."

"No problem," she said. "Always happy to help out." Poor Itzel was desperately into Nash, and he hadn't a clue. Connie, Jesse, and Marshall all picked up on the vibe and raised their eyebrows at each other.

Nash gestured around the gazebo and out across the snowy lawn. "Your mom would have loved all this," he told Chloe. "She loved everything about winter and the holidays."

"Mommy was a teacher!" Chloe reported proudly.

The adults smiled at her innocence. She had to have been so small when her mom passed, Mary wondered if she remembered much about her at all. It was good of Nash to keep her memory alive by bringing her up to his daughter.

"She liked to ride horses, too," Chloe said. "She's an angel now." She smiled contentedly like she thought this was cool, and Itzel sniffed, digging a tissue from her pocket to wipe her eye.

Connie laid her hand on Itzel's arm, and Itzel shook her head. "Allergies."

Marshall met Mary's eyes with a sad look, and she knew that he saw what was going on. While Nash was oblivious, nobody seemed more in tune with love than Marshall.

"You're going to have a new neighbor soon," Connie told Marshall, thankfully changing the subject.

"Yeah," he said. "I saw the *Sold* sign on Miss Miller's place. Do you have any notion who's moving in?"

"In fact, I do." She cast a look at Jesse and he nodded for her to continue. Connie apparently knew some sort of secret and Jesse was in on it. "She came down to the courthouse on Friday to take out a business license."

"Business?" Nash questioned. "On Maple?"

Marshall stroked his beard.

"She's opening another B&B," Connie told her youngest son.

Beneath all that facial hair of his, Mary could have sworn Marshall paled. "What?"

"Probably not bad to have another lodging establishment in town," Nash said.

"Especially at times like these, with a big parade coming," Itzel chimed in, trying to back him up.

"She won't be operational before the parade," Jesse offered. "Not until after the first of the year."

"Who is this woman?" Marshall asked. "Does she have experience?" Mary hadn't thought Marshall would have a competitive nature, then she recalled his extreme pride in winning those three awards.

"Don't know about the experience part," Connie said, "but her name is Karen Johnson. She's a little quiet but very nice, and on the younger side. Roughly your age." She got a twinkle in her eye. "And *single*."

Marshall furrowed his brow, and Mary could tell he wasn't at all focused on the single part. Itzel noticed this too, and shot Mary a look.

"It's fine to have another inn in town, of course," Marshall said. "I only wish she wasn't opening one right across the street from my place."

"It's a prime location," Connie said.

Jesse concurred. "Close to dining and shopping."

"Maybe your two businesses will be good for each other?" Itzel added hopefully.

Marshalled seemed lost in his private thoughts. "Yeah, maybe."

Based on her worries about lodging and the parade, Mary conceded that Clark Creek probably could use at least one more inn, but she decided to keep her opinion to herself out of respect for Marshall, who was obviously still stewing about it.

"Look!" Chloe shouted, and the adults glanced around as the gazebo lights came on and the town tree lights shone out in the darkness, its decorations shimmering in the falling snow.

"Oh wow," Itzel said. "Gorgeous."

Those were Mary's thoughts exactly, because that's when she saw Evan standing beside Dennis and the town tree, his handsome face bathed in its glow as he stared up at the star on top. Then, slowly, as if he could feel her watching him, he turned his eyes to Mary, picking her out among the people in the illuminated gazebo.

He smiled and Mary's heart took a happy leap. Evan was so kind and caring. Strong and capable. Dedicated to his family and to Clark Creek. The tiniest part of her couldn't help but wish he felt an ounce of dedication toward her. She was going to be in so much trouble ice skating with him tomorrow, because there was no mistaking what was happening here.

She was falling for Evan Clark, and falling hard.

# Chapter Sixteen

*E*VAN RETURNED TO HIS OFFICE Monday morning after completing his early-morning patrols. Everything was peaceful in Clark Creek. He'd seen no one else on the streets except for the Public Works employees. When Evan was growing up, his dad had driven a snowplow, and he and his brothers had thought that was so cool. They'd even taken turns riding with him a couple of times. Later, Jesse had moved into management, where he still worked part-time. Jesse's main job was farming. He raised silage corn and soybeans. Of the three brothers, only Nash had been bitten by the farming bug. His crop was hay, which fit in with his love of horses.

Evan hadn't been on a horse in a long time, and he wondered what Mary would think about riding. Not that he was mentally setting up a second date, or anything like that. They hadn't even had a first one, and he wasn't sure how Mary considered their ice skating outing. While it was true that they were colleagues working together on the parade, something more had transpired between them recently. Her showing up at his house with that Christmas tree had been a big surprise. He had to admit that he'd liked it. He'd also enjoyed her company while she was there and had been sorry to see her leave.

His house did seem homier with all her Christmas decorations in place. He'd even followed her instructions and put up a Velcro ornament on that advent calendar yesterday and today. Though it was a bit of an embarrassing thing for a grown man to do, the simple action had made him feel like a kid again. In a way that made him think about Christmas as a fun time, and something to look forward to, the way he used to.

All yesterday evening during the tree-lighting ceremony, he'd been hoping to run into her. Then he'd seen her standing in the gazebo. When she'd seen him, she'd smiled her dimpled smile, and she'd looked more than pretty. She'd been absolutely beautiful, causing all sorts of crazy thoughts to brew in Evan's head. Like what it would be like to hold her and kiss those incredible lips of hers. And whether it was possible for her to come to care for him, like he was beginning to care for her.

He glanced around his office, thinking it looked barren in here compared to how his decorated house did now. His old coat rack stood in the corner, but it seemed to be missing something. Evan slid open his bottom desk drawer and extracted the string of lights and garland he'd stowed away. Yep. It was that garland with the threaded tinsel. All shimmery and over-the-top-looking, but he didn't mind. Somehow it just seemed right.

He set the garland and lights on his office sofa and walked to the coat rack, moving it in front of the window. Then he wound it with the garland and the lights and turned them on. Their cheery glow reminded him of Mary, and his heart warmed. He was sorry he'd give those reindeer to Itzel, but he couldn't very well take them back, so he'd have to be content with this minor dose of holiday cheer.

Someone knocked on his door and he looked up to find his mom ushering along a couple of delivery people with dollies. Each dolly held a stack of three large boxes. "I hope you don't mind," she said. "I was wondering if we could keep these in here temporarily? Mary will be using the conference room later as her operations center, but we'll be needing it for meetings in the meantime." She glanced at the empty spot where the coat rack had been. "Oh, look! You have room in the corner."

He greeted the delivery guys with a polite hello, then spoke to his mom. "What is all that?"

"Some of the supplies Mary ordered for the parade. Souvenirs."

"Right." Evan recalled the tiny flags, coasters, and magnets. There had to be a ton of them to fill up so many huge boxes.

"Do you mind?" his mom said. "My office barely has any room."

He knew why, too. It was on account of all her Christmas decorations. Evan chuckled. What was a few boxes in the scheme of things? He had plenty of extra space in here, anyway. "Sure. No problem."

He directed the delivery people to stack the boxes in the corner, then one of them said, "We've got a few more in the truck."

"Is that right?" Evan shook his head, amazed there were more. Maybe there was a lot of packaging material in each box? Either that, or he had no decent sense of numbers when it came to ordering materials like this. Mary clearly did. She was the expert in these matters, so he trusted her judgment.

After six more boxes piled up in the corner, he still believed in Mary. Even when there were six more after that. And, wow. Yet another load. Soon the box piles started encroaching on his coat rack in front of the window, and then on his sofa and desk. That was one heck of a lot of magnets and flags. But whatever she'd ordered, she'd obviously done so with his mom's and the town council's approval.

He felt a little ashamed of the way he'd questioned her capabilities at the outset, but she'd persistently allayed his concerns. Mary Ward was on top of this parade. And if she had anything to say about it—which she certainly did, as the town's Christmas Consultant—she was going to make it a raging success.

Mary exited the print shop behind the courthouse after checking on her tickets. They'd be all printed up and ready by tomorrow. She'd have to bring her SUV around because the boxes would be heavy. At the moment she was on foot. One of the things she enjoyed about Clark Creek was the fact that you could walk almost everywhere. It was a very sweet town, which seemed to keep getting sweeter. She thought of Evan standing in the snow by the town tree and her face warmed when she recalled his handsome grin. It was apparent he'd been happy to see her, and she'd been *oh, so happy* to see him.

They were meeting tonight at the skating rink and she couldn't wait. At the same time, she felt slightly nervous about it, like she was going on a first date. But it wasn't a date—or was it? In her heart and head, she felt so confused. All she knew for certain was that she wanted to see Evan again. Alone. Just the two of them. So they could talk and have fun, and maybe not focus on the parade for once.

There was so much she was curious about. His background, and what it had been like for him growing up in

Clark Creek. He'd mentioned the river and tubing and that had sounded like so much fun. She wondered what had made him decide to leave Clark Creek and join the Army. And, ultimately, why he'd decided to come back again. Ironically, she already knew more about Marshall's and Nash's stories, both from what they'd told and from what she'd gathered from being in town.

Evan was much more guarded about everything. He had a tough exterior, and she had the sense he didn't let many people through those emotional walls he'd set up. She was pleased that he'd grown comfortable enough to let his guard down around her, because she liked the man he was underneath a lot. Someone caring and with a great sense of humor. Of course, the image he presented to the public was admirable too. And adorable, she couldn't help but think with a sigh.

Her phone rang and she pulled it from the purse that she'd tucked in her satchel. "Hello?"

"Mary, hi! It's Judy. How are things going?"

"Really moving along."

"That's great, because it's countdown time," Judy said.

"I know! Only three days until the parade. Can you believe it?"

"Yeah, it will be here before we know it." Judy paused and her voice took on a strange tone. "Mary. I wanted to ask you about that order you placed?"

"Order?" She thought back to Thursday. "Oh yes! My parade supplies! All taken care of. Should be arriving soon."

"Upper management in Seattle has a question." She drew in a breath and Mary wondered why she sounded so serious. Judy was starting to worry her. "It's about the T-shirts?"

"T-shirts? Well, um. They're fantastic. Long-sleeved

with 'Christmas in Clark Creek' on them."

"It's not about the design," Judy said coolly, and Mary's heart hammered, because Judy had never sounded so serious. "It's about the number of them you ordered."

Mary rushed to defend her actions. "They're only ten dollars each! And we're selling them for at least fifteen, maybe twenty. The town council approved the purchase."

Judy sounded incredulous. "For thirty thousand dollars?"

Mary stopped walking and bile rose in her throat. "What...what did you say?" she asked, feeling suddenly ill. "No, that can't be right. I only ordered three hundred."

"No, Mary," Judy said. "You ordered three *thousand*."

Mary's head felt light. "No. I'm very sure. I double-checked the number." She'd ordered three thousand of the smaller dollar items, but definitely not the ten-dollar T-shirts.

Then she remembered the computer glitch and the lights going out, and how when her computer rebooted, it took multiple tries before the T-shirt order went through. She thought she'd re-entered her information three or four times, but...surely not ten? She'd kind of lost count in the midst of her frustration.

*Oh no. No, no, no. No.*

If she'd honestly ordered three thousand T-shirts, in addition to their purchase price, they'd incur an enormous delivery fee. *Expedited delivery. Yikes.*

"Mary?" Judy asked. "Are you still there?"

"Um-hmm." Mary's head spun furiously. What was she going to do? If the order hadn't been processed yet, maybe it wasn't too late to change it. The rush delivery window was between today and Wednesday.

*Thirty thousand dollars.* That was a brand-new car. A nice one.

Or maybe, Clark Creek's entire future.

"I thought your budget for parade incidentals was ten thousand dollars? I'm talking, all in. Programs, souvenirs, shipping…"

"It was a mistake, Judy," she said, her pulse racing. "I can fix it."

"I really hope so, because that's a lot of cash for the company to absorb if Clark Creek can't come up with repayment."

"I understand. I really do." Sweat beaded Mary's hairline and her face burned hot. "Don't worry. I'll call the merchandiser right away."

She ended the call and dashed through the town square, heading back to the inn. She passed by the gazebo on her way and glanced up at Evan's courthouse office on the second floor. Tiny Christmas lights twinkled in his window.

Mary's heart sank. Everyone in Clark Creek had come to rely on her expertise, even—finally—Evan, and now she was letting everybody down. If she couldn't amend this error with her order, she actually *could* bankrupt the town.

Mary scurried down Main Street then turned right on Maple, taking care not to slip on the slick sidewalks in her high-heeled boots. It was snowing again, but this time the snow felt like prickly frozen tears raining down from the sky. Even the heavens were crying.

How had this disaster happened to her? *How, how, how. How?*

"Morning, Mary," Marshall said when she entered the inn through the front door. "How did everything go at the printer's?"

She pasted on her brightest smile. "Ah, just great!" she said, unable to admit her world was crashing apart.

Marshall was just another person in Clark Creek who'd placed faith in her and who would be hurt by her ineptness. Nash and Chloe would suffer, too, as well as Itzel and Dennis, Leroy and Austin…and all of the other wonderful people she'd met.

With an extra thirty-thousand-dollar expenditure, it would be nearly impossible for Clark Creek to break even, much less turn a profit. Even with all those generous sponsorships, the town wouldn't earn a penny from the parade. It would go into debt.

Mary couldn't wait to get to her room and log onto her computer. She dropped her satchel on the bed and sat down still wearing her coat. She logged into the merchandise website and pulled up her order history. Her orders for the magnets, flags, and coasters had gone through simultaneously, and looked accurate. Good. But that had been before the power outage, after which her internet connection had been spotty for several minutes.

She'd had to start over a few times with her order for the T-shirts, but she'd seriously thought it had only gone through once. She viewed the page with her previous orders listed and all were marked completed and delivered. Mary bit her lip so hard it pinched. Sure enough, the same T-shirt order had been placed *ten* times.

She found the customer service number and called it from her cell.

"I'm sorry, ma'am," the customer service rep told her after she explained the situation. "Those T-shirts normally sell for twelve dollars. When you purchased them for ten you agreed to our nonrefundable sale conditions. Items like that are hard to take back. Because they're custom-designed, nobody else can use them."

"But it was a *mistake*," Mary practically wailed into her mouthpiece. Then she reined herself in, assuming a more professional tone. "I mean, this is a corporate account. I can't just—"

"You can put in a refund request if you wish, but there are no guarantees. We're basically shutting down for the holidays starting tomorrow, so nobody will get a chance to look at your ticket until after New Year's."

Great. Just great. She guessed late was better than never. Maybe she could salvage things retroactively. She could only hope.

"Okay, I'd like to do that. Thank you." Then she asked where she could find the form on their website and ended the call, her heart pounding.

# Chapter Seventeen

W HEN IT GOT TO BE ten past seven, Evan began worrying that Mary wasn't going to show. But then she arrived, looking all fresh-faced and pretty, dressed in her coat, scarf and hat, and jeans.

"I'm sorry I'm late!" she said, out of breath because she'd been hurrying along. "I had a little…uh…internet issue to deal with."

"Reception can be spotty in those old houses," Evan said, understanding. "Hope you got everything worked out?"

"Working on it." She appeared tense about something. Evan hoped it wasn't him. He'd been looking forward to seeing Mary all day, but now something about her mood seemed off.

"You got a delivery at the courthouse today," he told her. "A very large delivery of boxes."

She bit her bottom lip. "Must be those supplies I ordered."

"There seem to be a whole lot of them."

"Ha ha! Yeah, well. It's going to be quite a parade."

"Really big moneymaker," he said, so proud of her accomplishments.

"For *sure*. So!" she said, smiling her brightest smile—though it seemed a little forced. "Should we go and get our skates?"

He gently laid his hand on her arm. "Hey." She peered over her shoulder, and if he didn't know better he'd think there was worry in her big brown eyes. "Is everything okay?"

"Yeah, I'm sorry, Evan." She sighed. "It's not about you—really. I've been looking forward to tonight, and to forgetting about the parade for a while."

If it was a break she wanted, she'd certainly earned it. "You've been working awfully hard." He let his glove drop from her coat sleeve. "Too hard, maybe?"

She set her chin. "I needed to get it all done."

"Seems mostly done to me. I passed my mom at the courthouse and she told me the Airbnb option has been executed."

"Yes. Nearly a hundred families have offered to open up their homes."

"That's amazing." He smiled softly and said it because he believed it. "You're amazing."

She pursed her lips. "Parade hasn't happened yet."

"But it will, and it will be great." He searched her eyes. "I believe in you, Mary Ward. You're—"

"Unbearably sharp?" she cut in, teasing, and Evan laughed at her reference to what he'd called her earlier. Then she laughed, too. He was glad that she'd made at stab at humor, because their mingled laughter lightened the mood.

"Yep." He scrutinized the square and its festive holiday decorations, which were there fully on account of Mary. "The town square looks great. The tree, the gazebo…" His gaze fell on her, and Evan swallowed hard. "Everything."

"I couldn't have done it without you," she said.

"Oh yes, you could."

Mary dropped her chin to hide her blush, then she nodded toward the rental hut for ice skates. "So," she said. "How about it?"

"Ready when you are," he said.

They picked out their skates and, when it was time to pay, Evan insisted it was his treat.

"I can't let you," she protested.

Evan stared down into her eyes. "Oh yes, you can. We made a bet and you won." He arched an eyebrow. "Remember?"

"But the deal was for you to go."

"No. The deal was for me to take you ice skating. And so—" He withdrew his wallet while the rental hut attendant watched with an amused smirk. "We'd like these two sets of skates, please." He addressed Mary. "What do you say, for an hour?"

"An hour should be fine." Then she couldn't resist throwing in a playful jab. "Beats thirty minutes."

He paid and placed his wallet back in his jacket, and they walked to a nearby bench, each holding their own set of skates. "You're never going to let me live that down, huh?"

"You *did* stay for longer," she told him. "Probably forty-five minutes."

"How do you know I wouldn't have stayed an hour?"

Her jaw dropped. "Would you really? If I hadn't gotten that call from your mom?"

He shrugged and glanced at her playfully. "Guess you'll never know."

She nudged him as they sat on the bench, and he liked it when her warmth brushed his shoulder. "You really are a big tease."

"No. I'm totally serious."

Mary giggled. "See. That's just what I mean." She crossed one of her legs over the other and tugged on her left boot. She was wearing that impractical pair with the super high heels. Evan was surprised she hadn't fallen and hurt herself, but he was glad she'd hadn't. "Argh. These things go on so easily, but they're murder to get off."

"Would you like my help?" In the time she'd been wrestling with that single piece of footwear, Evan had already put on both his skates and laced them up.

She glanced at him uncertainly and he dropped down off the bench, crouching in front of her. "Come on," he said, extending his hands. "Give me your foot."

She complied and her color deepened. "This is a little embarrassing."

He settled his grip along her calf with one hand and cupped the heel of her boot with the other. In one sharp tug he had it off. "Nope. What would have been embarrassing is if a big strong dude like me couldn't have gotten it off."

Her dark eyes shone. "Thank you."

He passed her the boot, then held out his hands again and removed her second boot.

His eyebrows rose. "Do you need me to lace up your skates?"

"No, thanks." She sassily swished her hair. "I think I can handle that part."

After she did, Evan took their regular boots and stashed them in a locker by the rental desk. "Okay," he said striding back over to her. "Ready to rock and roll?"

She tried to stand up from the bench, but her skates got away from her, scooting toward the rink first. "Ahh!" She grabbed onto the back of the bench to steady herself, her knees wobbly.

"Easy does it, there." He stomped through the snow,

angling his blades in a way so he wouldn't slide, and supported her under her elbow.

"It's slippery!"

He winked. "Going to be even more slippery on the ice."

"Oh." She looked like she was having doubts, but he encouraged her with a grin.

"Just hang onto me and we'll go slow. You'll do fine."

She nodded and they moved at a snail's pace toward the rink gate. At this speed they'd use up their entire hour just getting there. But Evan honestly didn't mind. He liked having Mary on his arm. Even if she was clinging to him for dear life.

"Oh, oohhh!" she shouted, as each of her skates started traveling in a different direction.

"Here, I have an idea," he said. Then he stepped out in front of her.

"Wait! Don't leave!"

He had no intention of doing that. He still held onto one of her hands. Evan reached the rink entrance, then backed onto the ice, spinning to face Mary. He took her second hand and now held both her hands in his. He stared at her reassuringly. "Better?"

She nodded, because she could look in his eyes, and seemed to find that reassuring.

"Good," he said. "Then we'll do it this way."

He started to move in a practiced glide, using his skates to propel him backward while he guided her along, peering periodically over his shoulder to ensure the coast was clear. There were a few other people on the ice, but not a ton, since it was Monday. They'd picked a good night to come.

"Wait! You're going backwards?"

"Seems that way, doesn't it?" Though Evan hadn't ice

skated in years, it was kind of like riding a bike, in that everything came back to him. Including, fortunately, his balance. Mary seemed to better maintain hers with their hands linked and by continually moving forward.

"I'm doing it," she cried with amazement. "I'm really skating!" She was radiant with happiness and surprise.

"Yes, you are." They approached their first turn and he took it slowly, bringing her along as she swung out wide at the curve.

"Wheee! Oh Evan, this is crazy."

He grinned at her sweetness. "Crazy good, right?"

"Crazy *great*," she said, laughing when they rounded the second turn. He increased their speed, moving them faster, but still keeping their movements steady. A couple of kids passed them, racing after each other.

"I'm going to get you, goober!"

"No, you, fool!"

Mary laughed at their playful banter. "Kids!" She rolled her eyes, and Evan's heart thudded. *Kids,* he thought, and suddenly he could imagine having them with Mary.

Without meaning to, he slowed his pace, but she kept coming on the fast trajectory he'd caused her to take. "Whoa! Evan!" He released her hands and held out his arms, catching her as she slammed into him—hard. "Oh no!" she fretted, gazing up at him. Then she dropped his hold, nearly slipping through his grasp. Evan caught her, shoring her up.

"Mary!" He scanned her eyes. "Are you all right?"

She placed her palms on his cheeks, her breath ragged. "Yeah. Yeah, I think so."

But Evan wasn't all right. He knew he'd never be all right unless he kissed her. His heart pounded harder, and all he could think of was bringing his mouth to hers. She was so kind and wonderful. Amazingly talented, and always gave everything her best. He felt the tug of a tide in her eyes that he couldn't resist. She tilted up her chin, tiny puffs of air escaping her kissable lips and warming the chilly space between them. Which grew smaller, and smaller…Mary's lips parted. She wanted this too.

"Look out! Coming through!" a shrill voice called. Evan spied a woman, who appeared to be in her seventies, barreling straight for them on the ice.

"Geraldine!" an older man shouted. "Stop! Come back here!" He tottered along on his skates, not as much skating as ice-walking, while swaying precipitously.

"I can't, Gerald! I can't!" She held up her arms, waving them and shouting, "Geronimo!"

Evan had to intervene or the older woman was going to seriously hurt herself. Mary was nervous on skates, but decently fit. Plus, she was practiced at something that would help her. Evan had a split-second to think all this through, but he was used to analyzing emergency situations and making fast decisions.

He steadied Mary's shoulders in his hands until he was certain she had her balance. "Remember that yoga thing you do?"

She stared up at him, terrified.

"Find your center," he instructed huskily. "Don't move."

He let her go and reached out his arm, nabbing the freaked-out Geraldine by her coat sleeve as she zoomed by. "Ack!" She shouted in surprise and nearly fell, but Evan pivoted quickly, catching her beneath her elbows. She stood there panting, wild-eyed, while plodding Gerald worked to arrive by her side.

"Dear," he said. "I think it's time we call it a day."

Geraldine blinked at Evan in gratitude. "Thank you."

Evan nodded, returning his attention to Mary, who

stood in the middle of the rink in mountain pose, her palms pressed together at heart-level and her eyes closed. She'd evidently found her center and was staying completely still. She had her palms pressed together in front of her at heart level, and lowered them slowly as he skated back over to her. "Oh, Evan. Wow. You're a hero." She sounded a little breathy.

"Don't know about that," he joked. He peered into her eyes. "You okay?"

"I know those two," she said, as Geraldine and Gerald carefully exited through the gate. "They're staying at the Clark Creek B&B." She gazed at him, wide-eyed. "Fiftieth anniversary! Can you imagine that?"

"Fiftieth? Huh." He smiled down at her, surprised to find himself able to imagine fifty years of wedded bliss very well. "How about that?"

"Evan?" she asked him. "How did you know about yoga and finding my center?"

He was amused by the question in her eyes. "I saw something about it in a movie."

"I see."

"You're apparently very good at it." He pressed his palms together and shot her a teasing grin. "*Namaste.*"

Her dimples deepened when she bowed her head and answered him. "*Namaste.*"

Evan brought Mary a cup of hot chocolate from the stand near the rink. He'd offered to get them some and she'd thanked him, not trusting her sore legs to hold her steady at the moment. She'd had her knees locked so tight on the ice for fear of falling down that her joints actually ached. And still, she'd had the best time. Evan had been so tender and caring, trying to make sure she was okay every step of the way.

When she'd slipped and he'd held her in his arms, she could have sworn for a moment that they were going to share a kiss. She would have welcomed one, too. Even if that did mean getting more deeply involved with Evan. At this point, it was hard for her not to want to be. She pushed thoughts of Seattle aside, wondering if a promotion could still happen. It probably wouldn't if she couldn't recoup that huge expenditure on the T-shirts. Worst case scenario, she'd be out of a job.

"Here you are," he said, handing her a cup and sitting beside her. "So, what did you think of your first time ice skating?"

She laughed, relieved to have something to focus on other than her messed-up handling of the parade. "I'm not sure we should call it skating. It was more like *you* were skating and I was just tagging along."

"I didn't mind you tagging along." His eyes twinkled and her heart warmed. It felt so good making him happy, and when he looked at her that way, she could tell he was.

She sipped from her cup. The hot chocolate was delicious. "Nice save with Geraldine."

"Poor woman. I don't think she knew what she was getting into."

"I give her an A plus for her sense of adventure, though," Mary said. "She and her husband are very good sports to still be trying new things after fifty years of marriage."

"How do you know it was a new thing?"

"Educated observation."

He chuckled and she loved the warm rumbling sound it made. "Maybe you should have been a schoolteacher."

"What makes you say that?"

"You talk like one. Giving people grades. Being educational."

She elbowed him. "I said educated."

He wryly twisted his lips. "You also enjoy correcting people."

"Yeah. Well. I'm not the only one." Her eyebrows rose until that sank in.

Evan belly laughed. "Touché."

Mary grinning and sipped from her hot chocolate, thinking this was so much better than sitting back in her room and dwelling on her mistake. She'd find a way to work that out, surely. Wasn't that what she was? A problem solver? Just look at all the problems she'd solved relating to the parade already. She drew in a deep breath of the refreshing evening air, feeling better. Being around Evan always made her feel better. His presence was calming somehow. Like how he'd been able to reassure her when she'd been petrified on the ice.

"I can't believe you haven't ice skated since you were a kid," she told him. "You're very good at it. All those jazzy moves."

He leaned back against the bench and draped his arm over the back of it, so his arm rested behind her. The gesture felt protective and caring, even if he'd done it subconsciously.

"Jazzy moves, ah yes," he said, staring up into the night sky. The snow had stopped for a bit, but it still blanketed just about everything in the town square, making the scenery so pretty. "I'm really good at those."

The fingers of his right glove lightly strummed her shoulder. Her heart pitter-pattered when she realized she wished his arm would drop lower and that he'd wrap it around her. "Nice out here," he said.

"Yeah." She instinctively scooted toward him, drawn to his warmth in the freezing cold.

He apparently took that as a cue to lower his arm around her shoulders, hugging her gently with one arm. Mary sighed happily, feeling so connected to Evan. Being with him just felt right.

"What kinds of things did you do as a kid?" he asked her.

"I used my imagination a lot."

"What do you mean?"

"You know how kids have tea parties?"

"Yeah."

"Well, I did a lot of that. But instead of tea parties, we had executive lunches."

"Executive—wow. Impressive."

She giggled. "I always had a briefcase."

"Where did you get that?"

"From the lost and found. Charlie, you remember I told you about him?"

"The older doorman, right."

"He used to take me to the lost and found and let me pick out gifts. This was only after the requisite period when nobody had claimed things."

"Somebody lost a briefcase?"

She nodded. "A brand-new one. They found it in the elevator. It was empty with a price tag attached."

"I see. So, you held executive lunches." He wrinkled his brow, apparently trying to picture this. "How old were you then?"

"Nine or ten. My stuffed animals were my board of directors."

He laughed. "Did they have briefcases, too?"

"No. Only agendas."

He smiled like he was charmed by her. "Where did you

get the idea? I thought your mom was a chef?"

"Not from her," Mary said. "From other people I saw coming and going from the hotel. Their lives looked so glamorous. I decided one day I'd like to have that kind of life too."

"In business?"

"Yes. That's what I studied in school and how I met Judy."

He gave her shoulder a squeeze. "Well I think you make a really great businessperson, even without the briefcase."

Would he think that if he knew about the ordering mistake? Putting it out of her head, she changed the subject. "What about you? Growing up?"

"Oh, the usual. Baseball with my brothers and kick the can. We played a lot outdoors. There was work to do on our parents' farm too. Daily chores."

"What were yours?"

"Feeding the chickens and goats."

"You had chickens and goats?" she asked, amazed.

"My parents still do."

"But you never wanted animals?"

"I live within the city limits, so farm animals aren't allowed." He shrugged. "Wouldn't mind getting a dog one day."

"What kind?"

"Dunno."

"What about a rescue?" She grinned up at him. "There will be lots of those in the parade."

He shook his finger at her in a teasing way. "Now, don't you go convincing me to get a dog on top of everything else. You've already convinced me to decorate my house as well as my office, and to help Clark Creek host a humongous parade."

She snuggled up against him. "I can be very convincing

then, huh?"

He stared down into her eyes and affection was written in his. "Yes. You can."

"Is Clark Creek named after your family?"

"It is. My great-great-*great*-Grandpa discovered the body of water during one of his hiking and camping expeditions when he was mapping out this section of the mountains."

"So, he was an explorer, then?"

"Not by trade, by passion. He sold crop insurance for his day job."

"How fascinating." She thought on this, remembering another question she had. "Your roots here are so deep. What made you ever want to leave this town?"

He shifted his position, removing his arm from around her, and Mary worried that she'd inadvertently popped the romantic bubble that had engulfed them.

"I wanted to join the Army," he said, his voice scratchy. "There was a girl." Evan cleared his throat. "Young woman, and it looked serious. We thought…No, it was more like *I* thought enlisting was a good way to guarantee a stable career. Benefits. All those things that matter when you're considering a family."

"What happened?" she asked softly.

"She wasn't so thrilled with the necessary separation. During my first deployment, she bolted and married somebody else."

"Oh, Evan." Her heart ached for him. "I'm sorry. Did she have the guts to tell you at least?"

"Nope. Let me find out for myself when I returned."

"That must have been an awful thing to come home to."

He sighed, viewing the town tree and then the gazebo. "It was right before Christmas."

Understanding filled her heart and she suddenly knew why Evan had been so prickly about Christmas. He had such painful memories associated with the season, it was no wonder.

"And the crazy thing was?" He raked a hand through his hair. "I was going to ask her to marry me. Had a ring picked out and everything." His shoulders sagged and he hung his head. "I'm sorry. I don't know why I'm telling you this."

"No, it's okay." She touched his arm. "I'm glad that you shared, but not happy about what happened. I'm sure that was devastating."

"Anyway." He leaned back against the bench. "I did a few more tours. You know, served my time. But there were things I missed about Clark Creek, and after a while I found myself longing to come home."

"Was she from here?"

"Initially, but she moved away to get married. Wyoming."

"Wow. That's far."

"Yeah." He glanced at her in the soft light streaming down from the rink lights, and his profile cut a rugged picture. "How about you? Any long-lost almost-fiancés floating around?"

She laughed sadly. "Not even close."

"That's a little surprising."

"Not to me, it isn't. I've just never been big into commitment."

"I guess I get why."

She studied him with surprise. "What do you mean?"

"Well, your upbringing was different from a lot of folks. You moved around a lot. Lived in hotels. I can see where that might have felt unsettling."

She liked that he was being straight with her. Besides

Judy, not many other people were.

"So, maybe, just maybe. You've got a bit of wanderer in you. You're traveling, you're searching for the next best thing."

She held her breath, because it felt like he'd just taken a page from her soul and read it completely. How could he know her so well?

"Mary, it's okay to search. Okay to question." He scanned her eyes. "It's also okay to decide that you're tired of traveling."

"But I…" Her chin trembled. "Don't have any place to go home to. Not really."

"I know that's how you feel, and I'm sorry." He took her hand, and she let him, savoring the comfort of their connection, and his warm understanding of her. "Maybe someday. If you happened upon the right place…"

"I think I might be there soon."

He squeezed her hand. "Yeah?"

"I have a lot to sort through," she said. "A lot that I'm dealing with."

He sighed and released her hand. "Don't we all."

They sat a while watching the ice skaters go by while both of them finished their hot chocolate. He seemed like he was trying to get up the nerve to say something. Finally, he said, "Richmond's not that far away, you know." He winked. "Something to keep in mind for the future, once you've sorted everything out."

Mary's heart felt full to bursting, but then it broke a little, because she grasped what Evan was driving at. He was hinting that maybe someday they could have a relationship, and that he'd be willing to undertake it long-distance. But the long-distance he was contemplating didn't stretch all the way to Seattle. Evan was right about who she was, and how she saw herself. She couldn't possibly stay in one place. That was antithetical to who she was.

They both stood and tossed their empty cups in a trash bin. "This has been really great," she said meaning it. "Thank you."

"Thank you for coming up with the idea," he said. "I had a lot of fun."

"Me, too." This outing had been memorable. Special. A nice escape from the new pressures she was under. But now, she had to go back to the inn and face the music. She only had two more days to save Clark Creek.

He thought a moment, then said, "My niece, Chloe, is going to be in a ballet tomorrow. I know you have a lot going on with the parade—"

"Oh yeah, I know." She stepped back, preparing to leave. "I plan to be there."

"Do you?" He looked pleased. "That's great. So do I. So, I guess I'll see you there?"

"Yeah," she said with a wave. "See you there!"

Mary strolled back to the inn, her heart hurting. Evan was such a nice man and he was beginning to like her a lot. She returned those feelings. But where could any of this lead? If she bankrupted the town that would definitely change Evan's opinion of her. He'd never consider dating her then. And Seattle would be completely out of the picture. She'd likely be unemployed and needing to move on from Richmond, to some other place where she could start fresh.

She so wanted to believe that her fundraising efforts could still be successful. But for the first time in a long while, she felt anxious and afraid. She hated those feelings. They reminded her of when she was a kid and had no control over her circumstances. Just when she and her mom had made themselves at home in a new hotel, the rug would get yanked out from under them and they'd be sent to someplace new. That was a big reason she'd opted to take charge of her destiny, by deciding on her own terms when it was time for her to move on, before anyone else could dictate that for her.

If she ruined Clark Creek financially, things would be out of her hands again. As often as she'd changed jobs, Mary had never been fired from any of them…

She breathed deeply and tried to focus her energy on the tasks at hand. The best way to face her fears was for her to get up early in the morning, have some strong coffee, and figure out how to fix the mess she'd made with that thirty-thousand-dollar over-expenditure. Maybe it wasn't too late.

# Chapter Eighteen

THE NEXT DAY, MARY SAT at a breakfast table at the inn with her laptop on the table.

"More coffee?" Andrea asked, walking over. The younger woman with a ponytail was bright-eyed and cheerful, having risen even earlier than Mary to prepare the Clark Creek B&B's delicious bacon and egg breakfast with homemade buttermilk biscuits.

"Yes, thanks!"

A few couples had been eating in the breakfast area, which was set up with cozy tables and chairs. They finished their meals and said good morning to Mary as they passed her, leaving. One of the couples was Geraldine and Gerald. Both wore their coats like they were headed outdoors.

"Please thank your friend again for us for the heroic save," Geraldine said.

Gerald zipped up his jacket. "Yes, please do. I don't know what might have happened to my bunny if he hadn't stepped in."

"I'll be sure to pass your thanks along to Sheriff Clark," Mary said.

"Oh?" Geraldine smiled. "He's the sheriff? No wonder

he's so quick on his feet."

Gerald winked. "Probably lots of practice chasing after those bad guys."

Mary chuckled at his joke, doubting there were too many bad guys circulating around Clark Creek. At the moment, the only person here with destructive potential seemed to be her.

"You two headed out this morning?" Mary asked, as Geraldine and Gerald put on their hats.

"We're going on a sleigh ride," Geraldine said happily. "Marshall set it up."

"That sounds wonderful," Mary told them. "I hope you have the best time. And, if I haven't said so already, happy anniversary."

"Why, thank you," Gerald said.

Mary returned her gaze to her computer, scanning her budget. It was so last minute, there really wasn't anything she could cut, besides her consulting fee. She was certainly willing to do that, but Davenport wouldn't like it, since her earnings brought in revenue to the company. Her fee was actually more than she received in take-home pay, since a portion of it went into overhead and benefits. She could ask Davenport to waive a partial salary payment, but that would be a very unusual request. If she was going to do that, she might as well quit. That was assuming she didn't get fired first for ruining the reputation of the firm.

Her heart pounded in nervous anticipation as she went through the other parade expenses on her spreadsheet. Clark Creek's expenditures for policing and public works definitely couldn't be cut, and the rest of the support was down to volunteers. She'd budgeted ten thousand dollars for souvenirs and other parade supplies, like printing tickets and the programs.

Luckily, that one generous Santa's Circle donation

she'd received from the ski resort gentleman would be enough to cover that. She'd hoped for more higher-level donations, but at this late date it was unlikely she'd receive them. And, with that costly T-shirt purchase, she'd overrun her budget by—she gulped—twenty-seven thousand dollars.

Her palms felt damp as she clicked through her spreadsheet, examining each column with an eagle eye. The ticket and program printing expenses were already fixed, and she was scheduled to pick those up today. She'd ordered one thousand each of the one-dollar-per-item souvenirs, because she'd anticipated at least three thousand ticket sales at five dollars each. Given the size of the town and the number of visitors she expected from elsewhere, including those in Hopedale who'd promised to come, she thought she was mostly on target with that.

But, hoping that all of those voluntary ticket buyers would *also* purchase a fifteen-dollar T-shirt was a bit of a stretch. Since parade tickets were optional, not everyone attending would buy one, and in some cases, such as with couples or families, people might purchase fewer tickets than the actual number in their group, since ticket purchases were viewed as donations.

Mary rubbed her forehead. Even some folks not purchasing tickets might wind up buying T-shirts. Nobody was going to buy three *thousand* of them at fifteen dollars, though. Mary guessed she'd have to sell them at a lower price to be able to move as many as possible, in case she couldn't return them. Her heart clenched when she realized she might even need to sell them at—or below—cost.

She clicked to another section of her spreadsheet showing pledges in support of the various floats, but most of those proceeds were earmarked to go directly to those organizations. Just a small portion would go to the town. There certainly wasn't enough excess to make up for her enormous mistake. Mary set down her coffee, her stomach feeling sour.

She intended to go up to her room and start making phone calls, double-checking with all the donors to make sure they were on board. She could even try seeing if any of them would be willing to increase their already generous donations by giving a little more. Mary knew it was a lot to ask at the holidays, especially of people who'd already given so much. All of Clark Creek had come together in support of her parade, including those kind families who'd opened up their homes as temporary Airbnbs.

And now, it could all fall apart due to her ineptness. Though her mistake hadn't been intentional, she'd made it nonetheless. She'd come here to help the town get back on its feet. Instead, she felt just like the Grinch, about to steal Christmas right out from under Clark Creek. If there was any way humanly possible, Mary wasn't going to let Clark Creek's citizens down. She intended to keep working *this* problem until she found a solution. Somewhere. Somehow.

Maybe what she really needed was a miracle.

Evan finished his meeting with his staff in the second-floor conference room, after briefing everyone on the parade and how that would impact their offices. His dispatcher Helen normally worked from home, but she always attended staff meetings. Itzel had offered to direct the volunteers helping Mary with parade lineup. Dennis would assist Evan with crowd control by patrolling the parade route and ensuring everyone was watching at a safe distance while staying back from the road.

Helen was the last to leave, as it took her a little longer in her electric wheelchair. "I'd like to help too," she said, looking up. "Maybe with ticket or T-shirt sales?"

Evan smiled at the efficient middle-aged woman with graying red hair. She was incredibly smart and had nerves of steel. She could calm even the most frantic caller into providing her with critical information. "Having you available for dispatch will be a huge help. I'm hoping the day's uneventful, but you never know."

Her face fell, and he guessed why. If she was at home and on call with the equipment, she'd entirely miss the parade. He kicked himself for being so thoughtless and suggested an alternative.

"Tell you what," Evan said. "Why don't we have any incoming calls forwarded to your cell phone? That way you won't have to miss all the fun."

She beamed at him. "That would be great." She hesitated, then added, "Bernie would like to help out, too." Evan knew her husband Bernie had macular degeneration, so his eyesight had been compromised, but he could certainly assist in some way.

"Having more hands on deck would be amazing, Helen. Thank you. Please thank Bernie for me, too."

Helen left and Connie peeked in the room as Evan gathered his notes off the table.

"There you are," she said, her eyes shining. He could tell she was in a good mood. She always was around Christmas. "I wanted to ask you about Mary using this conference room for her operations center for the rest of this week. She requested a large table for her parade lineup planning, and she has other things to organize. She has all those boxes in your office to unpack, for one thing. I was thinking maybe you could help her?"

"Of course," he said, pleased by the opportunity. After their ice-skating outing, he'd been wondering when he'd see her again. He knew she'd be at the ballet tonight, but she was going with Itzel, so he could hardly ask her out for dinner afterwards. Not unless he wanted to invite the both of them, and he didn't want to intrude on their girl time since they'd already made plans.

It was hard to believe the parade was the day after tomorrow. The time had gone so quickly, and soon Mary's time in Clark Creek would be over. When she'd arrived here, all he'd been able to think of was getting rid of her. Now, he found himself regretting the fact that she had to go. He'd told her things he hadn't told to many people, and she'd shared private details about her life with him. Instead of satisfying his curiosity, their conversation had only piqued it, and Evan found himself wanting to learn more.

His mom cocked her head. "I heard you and Mary went ice skating last night."

Evan's ears warmed. "Who told you that?"

"Marshall."

"Marshall?"

"One of his guests was apparently singing your praises earlier today—something about the sheriff and his 'girl-friend' saving Geraldine from near disaster."

"Oh, uh…that."

His mom shot him a hopeful look. "Evan?"

"It's nothing, Mom. It's just that Mary's been working so hard, I thought it would be nice for her to take a break." He shoved his hands in his uniform pockets. "Plus, we made a bet."

"What kind of bet?"

"She bet me that, if she could solve our parade lodging

problems, I would take her skating."

His mom clapped her hands together. "Ooh, so it was her idea, was it?"

He shifted on his feet. "We both agreed to the wager."

She got a twinkle in her eye. "I see."

"I need to head back to my office and wrap up a few things, so I'm not late for Chloe's ballet."

"*The Nutcracker*, yes!" his mom said, like she'd suddenly remembered. "I'd better scoot along, too, and collect your dad."

Evan smiled, knowing they carpooled together since Public Works was located in the basement of this same building.

"I heard that Mary's going to be there," his mom said with a knowing grin. "Vivi Torres told me she and Itzel are going together."

Mary had been so busy with her phone calls she hadn't been able to check the slew of new text messaging coming in, or her emails. She hoped a lot of those messages brought good news in terms of increased sponsorship. She planned to read through them and respond before heading to the Children's Theater to meet Itzel for Chloe's ballet.

At the moment, she was loading the back of her SUV with boxes of programs and tickets from the printers. Snow cascaded from the sky, coating the tops of her boxes, and she wiped them clean with her gloves before sliding them into the back of her SUV. Connie had mentioned something about her using a conference room at the courthouse to organize her parade materials tomorrow, and that sounded like a fantastic idea.

She drove back to the inn to freshen up before going to the theater. She and Itzel had discussed grabbing a light dinner after the show, and she'd been really happy about Itzel suggesting it. She'd basically eaten all her meals alone since coming to Clark Creek, which was natural for a woman traveling on her own on business. Besides that, she was accustomed to it. Still, it would be fun to have the company, and Itzel seemed like such a good person.

While she hadn't shared a meal with anyone in Clark Creek, at least she'd had coffee and hot chocolate with the sheriff. Her mind started drifting into a fantasy about her and Evan enjoying a romantic candlelight dinner together at the Taverna Italiana. It was an intimate place with a cozy atmosphere and Chianti bottles holding candles on every table.

Mary nearly missed her turn on Maple Street, dreaming up what she and Evan might order and imagining them swapping tastes of their delicious food. She shook her head to clear it of the image, but the picture in her imagination hung on.

She envisioned the two of them drinking wine and toasting each other, while laughing at each other's jokes. Then the moment grew tender between them. He gazed into her eyes and leaned across the table to give her a kiss.

She pulled into the inn's driveway, knowing she really should stop thinking about Evan in such romantic terms. But it was hard not to think romantically about him, when she recalled the way he'd embraced her at the skating rink, and how he'd sweetly held her hand later during their intimate talk.

If she were a different sort of person, the kind who liked to stay in one place and put down roots, then Evan would definitely be somebody she'd consider putting down roots with. But Mary wasn't there yet. It wasn't who she was. *Who I am is that wanderer Evan talked about. A totally free spirit, somebody who feels happiest when she's on the go, and so...* She heaved a breath. *I need to keep going.*

Fingers crossed, all would turn out well with the parade and she'd be going to Seattle.

# Chapter Nineteen

*W*HEN EVAN ARRIVED AT THE Children's Theater, the auditorium was packed. Marshall saw him and waved him over. He was sitting next to Itzel, and Mary was on her other side. Nash was on the far side of Marshall, and there was one vacant seat beside him. Evan supposed that had been saved for him. He greeted the group, and Nash surprised him by moving over.

"I can take this seat," he said, "and we can all slide down one so you can sit on the other end next to Mary." He shot Evan a guileless look. "Thought that might be nice since you've been working together."

Evan's mom turned around from where she sat with his dad in front of the others. "Evening, Evan." The lights started to dim. "Looks like you made it just in time."

People moved over and Evan sidestepped down the row, being careful to avoid everyone's feet, and took the seat next to Mary. He felt awkward about it, but he couldn't very well decline Nash's offer. Something that Nash pointedly knew. The sneak.

Itzel greeted him with a wave of her program. "Long time no see."

He nodded and waved at everyone, then his gaze fell

on Mary. She said "Hi," but had her nose in the program and barely looked up.

"How did today go?" he asked her in a whisper.

"Fine," she said. "Really fine."

He wasn't sure if she seemed distant or distracted, but something was off. He hoped she wasn't regretting their ice-skating date, because he sure wasn't.

The Children's Theater director appeared to applause and she introduced the annual program. The Nutcracker was performed here every Christmas, but this was the first time Evan had ever had a family member in it. So, it was the first time he'd attended.

Before the curtain went up, Evan leaned toward Mary. "Just two days until the parade."

He'd said that in an effort to lend support and let her know he was thinking about it. Yet, instead of smiling, she frowned. "I know."

Evan peered at Itzel, but predictably her gaze was on Nash. Maybe Evan should have suggested the two of *them* sit together. But the truth was, he'd never do that to his brother. He counted himself the least meddlesome of the pack.

"Oh." Mary sighed happily as the music picked up and the first dancers came on stage.

It didn't take long for Evan to get sucked in by the production too, and soon he was chuckling at the kids' charm. When Chloe arrived on stage, tiptoeing along exquisitely with her tiny arms held high, she absolutely stole the show.

Evan peered at Nash, who beamed proudly, just like you'd expect a good dad to do. Chloe was lucky to have such a dedicated father, and he was blessed by her. Evan peeked at Mary, whose cheeks held a radiant glow, and he wondered if she was thinking what he was…about what being a parent would be like. Evan had an inkling that Mary would make a great mom. She would sure be organized about it. Professionally accomplished. Positive and upbeat, a really good role model for any young kid.

The show ended with a standing ovation by the appreciative relatives and friends of the performers. As the auditorium cleared, Mary turned to Itzel. "That was so great." She spoke next to Nash. "Chloe did an amazing job!"

Was he imagining it, or was she ignoring him? And why?

Evan ventured, "My mom mentioned you might need some help unpacking those boxes tomorrow?"

Her brow crinkled uncertainly. "Um, yeah. Sure!"

"Mary?" Itzel tugged on her elbow. "Hate to interrupt, but our reservation is at seven."

"Right," Mary said, before making her apologies. "I'm sorry, Evan. I'd better go."

"All right. So. You do want my help, then?"

"Tomorrow? Um-hmm. Yeah, that would be great. Thanks!" She waved to the others as Itzel led her away. "Bye, all! Fun ballet."

Evan watched her trail Itzel out of the auditorium following the press of others, and his heart sank. What had he imagined? That Mary was feeling just as into him as he was into her?

He felt Marshall's hand on his shoulder. His brother had observed Evan watching Mary walk away, and said cagily, "She's a very sweet woman."

"Yeah."

Apparently, Marshall couldn't resist the moment, because he leaned toward him and whispered. "You a little bit *sweet on her*?"

Evan shoved him in the chest. "Cut it out, will ya?

Marshall held up both hands. "Didn't mean to step on any toes."

Mary and Itzel ate at a diner-type place called the Dine N Dash. Both ordered a burger and fries. "You have to let me treat you to dinner," Mary said. "It's only fair, since you wouldn't let me reimburse you for my ticket."

"All right." Itzel grinned and took a bite of her burger. "I'll let you."

Mary heaped catsup on her fries, thinking they looked delicious. Sadly, she didn't have her normal appetite, and she knew why. She wasn't just worried about the parade; she was also stressing over how she'd treated Evan. Itzel had picked up on it too.

"So, um. Is there something going on with you and Evan?"

"What do you mean?"

"Things seemed a little tense at the theater."

Itzel was right, and that had been all on her.

"Did he say or do something?" Itzel continued. "I mean, I know sometimes he can come off as stern, but he's got a heart of gold underneath."

It was precisely that heart Mary was worried about breaking. She'd had other guys accuse her of being uncaring and reckless. She'd never seen it from anybody else's perspective before, maybe because she hadn't wanted to.

With Evan, she could guess his point of view, because she'd begun to be in tune with him. So much so that she understood that maybe she'd led him on. She'd been the one who suggested ice skating. Then she brought him that Christmas tree. He probably knew she'd been dying to kiss him at the skating rink, because the guy was not stupid. He was a highly intelligent and attractive man who knew his way around women.

"I really like Evan," she told Itzel honestly. "Like him a lot."

"He's got a ton to offer," Itzel said. "For a sheriff."

"I know that's true, but…" Mary shrugged.

"You live in Richmond. Yeah, I get that makes things complicated."

Mary had been carrying the secret about Seattle her whole time here, and she was burning to share it with someone. Itzel was so kind and sympathetic, maybe she'd understand.

"It's not about Richmond," she told Itzel. "If I do well with this assignment in Clark Creek, I'm going to get promoted."

"Go you."

"To Seattle."

Itzel frowned. "Seattle?"

"It's not only that," Mary confided. "I…oh." She sucked in a breath and held it when heat prickled her eyes.

Itzel reached out and squeezed her hand, only making her want to cry harder.

Mary took her napkin and dabbed at the small trickle of tears that had leaked from her eyes. "I think I've made a big mistake, Itzel. I mean, I know I have—huge. But please don't tell your mom until I fix it."

Itzel gasped. "Is this about the parade?"

Mary nodded.

"Can you fix it?"

Her voice shook. "I don't know."

"But you're going to try, right?"

"My absolute best," Mary said with conviction.

Itzel squeezed her hand. "Then, that's good enough for me."

Mary released Itzel's hand to wipe her cheeks.

"Mary," Itzel said softly. "We all make mistakes."

"I'll bet Evan doesn't."

Itzel thought on this, and then she laughed. "No, you're probably right."

"He is pretty perfect, isn't he?" Mary said.

Itzel's eyes lit up. "So then, what's the problem?"

"Apart from Seattle and my big mistake?" Mary winced. "I'm not very good with commitments."

Itzel rolled her eyes. "Those all sound like excuses to me."

"Maybe so. But you've got to admit that they're good ones."

Itzel laughed, sounding resigned, but Mary could tell that she understood.

"Want to know what I think?" Itzel said. "I think nothing is over until it's over."

"What do you mean?"

"There're two days left until the parade."

"That's only forty-eight hours."

"You never know."

Mary laughed, appreciative of this newfound friendship. If she were staying in Clark Creek, she'd definitely be seeing more of Itzel. While she was a few years younger than Mary, that didn't seem to make a difference. Itzel was almost like the little sister she'd never had.

"What about you and the country doctor?" Mary asked.

A hopeful look came into Itzel's eyes. "Like I say. It's not over until it's over."

"How long have you had a thing for him?"

"Almost two years."

"Oh, Itzel."

"It's all right," Itzel said. "I see other people."

"Well, that's good. You're young."

"Not that much younger than you."

"By at least five years," Mary guessed.

"So?"

"So." Mary shot her a look. "It's good for you to have a life."

Itzel smiled. "I think it's good for you to have one, too."

Later that night, Mary called Judy. She didn't know why she felt guilty about her dinner with Itzel, because she shouldn't. Judy had plenty of other friends.

"Hey," Judy said when she answered. "I was just about to call you."

"You were?"

"Yeah. It's like all day long I've been feeling this energy. Sensing that something was off."

Mary got a heavy feeling in her stomach. "You know what's off. It's got a thirty-thousand dollar price tag on it."

"No, I meant besides that. And Mary?"

"Hmm."

"I wanted to say I'm sorry. I apologize if I came off as harsh the other day."

"I understand," Mary said. "At Davenport, you're my boss. My failures are a reflection on you."

"You haven't failed yet."

"I'm on a downward spiral."

"This is not the woman I know and love," Judy said. "The woman I know and love is invincible. She can conquer anything. I know you'll find a way. Have you tried phoning the merchandiser about a refund?"

"That's one of the first things I tried. They're closed down until after the holidays. I put in a request for a refund, but things don't look good."

"What? Why not?"

"I bought the T-shirts on sale, so they're supposedly nonrefundable. Plus, they've got Clark Creek's gazebo on the front. What are they going to do with that?"

"I see what you mean. Well, here's a thought—maybe you'll sell them! It's possible."

"Maybe, but I don't think it's probable."

"How is the rest of the prep going?" Judy asked.

"That's going fine. I picked up the tickets and parade programs today."

"And the sheriff? Still being difficult, I'll bet."

"No, actually he's come around."

"Really?"

Mary paused and then she braved it. "He took me ice skating."

"Is this about that bet you made about the lodging?"

"Yeah."

"Come on then, don't make me pull it out of you."

Mary giggled. "Okay. We had a great time. He's kind, thoughtful, understanding, and oh, Judy," she said, her voice wavering. "I think I'm getting a thing for him."

"Uh-oh. Is it mutual?"

"I think so."

"That complicates things."

"Only if I let it," Mary said. "I've decided to take your advice and not get too involved."

"Sounds like you already *are* involved to me."

Mary paused, knowing Judy was right. Judy was always right. Except for when she was wrong, which was, like… never. "Only slightly."

"I don't think 'slightly' counts in romance."

"I never said it was a romance."

"You didn't have to."

"What are you?" Mary teased. "Clairvoyant?"

"Just call me Madam Crystal Ball."

Mary laughed again. "I really miss you."

"I miss you, too. How about the rest of the town? People friendly?"

"More than friendly. They're warm…accepting. You'll have to come and visit Clark Creek to see for yourself. Hopedale's really cool, too. It has a similar vibe."

"Oh yeah, that's the place with the ski resort where you found all those sponsors."

Mary decided to tell her about Itzel. "I think I made new friend."

"You're making friends now? That's great. I thought you only knew how to make boyfriends, and then dump them."

"Ha ha. You're so mean."

"Seriously though, I'm happy for you. Who is she, or he?"

"Itzel Torres. She works at Evan's office, and she's really sweet. Straight talker too."

"You probably can't have too many of those in your life."

"Shut. *Up.*"

Judy laughed.

"I'm glad you don't mind."

"Now, why would I mind?" Judy said. "You're expanding your horizons, which is what I've always said you should do. It's true I gave you that advice in college and it's taken you nearly twelve years…"

"I've had other friends before."

"Yeah, but have you kept them?"

"Not fair," Mary said. "I've moved around a lot."

"True. You have. And, hey. Who knows? Maybe this time with Itzel things will be different?"

Mary hoped so, because she really liked Itzel and found herself wanting to keep up with her. She was rooting for Itzel and Nash to have a happy ending, if that was in the cards for them.

"I'm going to try better this time," Mary told her friend, and she meant it. "So, what's going on in Richmond?"

"I thought you'd never ask." Judy giggled. "I've got a date."

"Woo! New guy?"

"It's a fourth date."

"*What*? Jud-y, and you didn't tell me?"

"I wanted to get past that awkward phase."

"Which awkward phase?"

"Where I decide if he can handle being introduced to my family." Both of Judy's parents had been born in the United States, but her dad's heritage was Filipino. The family was very tight-knit and her paternal grand-parents lived with them. Judy's Lolo and Lola, as she called them, made a habit of grilling her boyfriends on their intentions. She'd always kind of put up with it and didn't seem to mind. Some of the guys she'd gone out with were another story.

"You have an amazing family."

"Thanks. I just want to be sure that whoever I'm dating thinks so, too."

"So, wait. You've taken him home?"

"Not home. We met in a public place for coffee. I figured it was safer that way."

Mary howled with laughter. "Stop."

"No, seriously. It was fine. I made sure the shop had no utensils, only coffee stirrers. You never know about those plastic knives and sporks."

Judy was so funny. "Your family is not that menacing." While her grandparents asked a lot of questions, that was mainly because they were interested in Judy's friends, and they actually were very sweet.

"Maybe not to you."

"Well? How did he do?"

"Paul? He did all right."

"Ooh, I like the name. When are you seeing him again?"

"At Christmas. We'll see how he does with the menu."

"I'm sure he'll do fine."

"Hmm, maybe. Still early days. I'll keep you posted! You keep me posted on your progress, too—with that sheriff and your parade. You're in the eleventh hour now."

Mary gulped. "Yeah."

"I'll be sending you some work stuff tomorrow," Judy said in closing. "The accounting software and all that. Let me know if you have questions."

"All right, Judy. Talk soon."

# Chapter Twenty

$\mathscr{E}$ VAN COMPLETED HIS EARLY MORNING patrols and returned to the courthouse, thinking Mary might already be there working in the conference room, but she hadn't arrived yet. He decided to get a head start on those boxes by moving them into the conference room from his office before she got there. He was on his second haul when his mom entered the conference room and set an oblong box on the table. It looked like a shirt box, but bigger.

"I'm afraid I have some bad news." Her mouth puckered in a frown. "Your dad's got the stomach flu."

"Oh no. Did it just come on suddenly?"

"Yes, this morning," she said. "We were halfway in to work and he had me turn around and take him back home."

"I'm sorry to hear it."

"I'm hoping it's just a twenty-four-hour bug, or maybe something he ate that didn't agree with him."

"What did y'all have for dinner?"

"Jesse's favorite, turkey chili."

"Don't tell me he added jalapeños?"

"He always does."

Evan shook his head. "Nash has warned him about that with his ulcers."

"I know. That's why I made the chili extra mild and served it with sour cream. While I was tossing the salad, your dad sneaked in some chopped peppers. I'm guessing he also added a hefty dose of hot sauce, because the bottle was nearly empty. I didn't notice until later, and by then it was too late to scold him."

Evan smirked. "But you still did anyway."

His mom shrugged. "He said something about it being better to beg for forgiveness than to ask for permission." She shook her head. "In any case, Jesse and I talked about it and decided we're better erring on the side of caution." She patted the box she'd set on the table, which Evan now understood held his dad's Santa suit. "I tried calling Mary, but her voicemail box is full up, so I emailed. Can you give this to her when she comes in, along with your dad's apologies? I'm afraid he won't be playing Santa in this parade."

"Of course." Evan frowned, knowing how much his dad had been looking forward to the occasion. "I'm just sorry he'll have to miss it." Apart from feeling sorry for his dad, he also felt bad for Mary, since this would mean a last-minute kink in her parade, and everything else had gone smoothly so far.

"At least he'll get to see the video later," his mom said. "Mary's arranged for some kids from the high school's media class to record the whole thing."

Mary really did think of everything. She was more than a Christmas Consultant. She was a Christmas planning phenomenon. While their relationship had started off a little rocky, they'd made progress while coordinating the parade. Then lately, they'd gotten closer. On Monday night, he'd even believed dating-territory close. Then, last night at the ballet, she'd not seemed interested in talking to him at all.

Maybe he'd upset her by coming on too strong during their ice-skating outing. He probably shouldn't have put his arm around her or held her hand while they were talking. It hadn't been a date, no matter how much it might have felt like one. Though she didn't protest at the time, it was possible he'd misread her signals and that he'd made her uncomfortable. They were working together, and he was supposed to be her Clark Creek liaison, someone who kept his professional distance.

Just because they'd each shared a bit about their personal lives didn't mean that they'd taken things to the next level. Even if they had, the next level up from work colleagues was friendship, not romance. He wasn't looking for romance anyway. Which was exactly why he needed to apologize to Mary this morning and clear the air.

Mary arrived at the courthouse at a little past nine. She had a package of index cards in her satchel and each one had a parade participant's name on it. Her first order of business was to finalize the parade lineup so she could email the parade entries and advise them of their order number. She had volunteers slated to direct the lineup in the morning, and they would help parade participants get to the right place based on their number.

The parade was going to last for one hour and there were sixty-eight entries, including the marching band and other musical groups who'd signed on. The mayor would ride on the lead float, following the marching band playing Christmas tunes. The town council members would proceed on their float next, serving as parade marshals. Santa's sleigh was last, and the grand finale bringing up the rear of the parade. The order of everything in the middle still needed to be worked out.

Mary climbed the stairs to the second floor and headed down the hall. Connie had told her she'd be working in the conference room opposite the elevators, which she found easily. It had a long conference table, perfect for laying out her note cards and also great for organizing the souvenirs once she unpacked them. She thought the boxes had been delivered to Evan's office, but someone had apparently moved them here. She goggled at the huge stacks of boxes piled next to each other. They took up half the room.

*Don't panic. It will all be fine. Everybody loves T-shirts.*

"Morning!"

She turned to find Evan standing on the threshold and wearing his uniform. He'd left his hat in his office.

"Evan, hey."

He shot her a cockeyed grin. "Tomorrow's the big day."

"Yes, it is," she answered, trying to sound cheery.

"My mom said you might need my help unpacking some of those boxes?"

"Oh, well…" Her gaze trailed back across the room and she nervously counted the stacks. "That might go faster with your help."

"No worries." He strode to the pile and lifted a box, hauling it over to the table. Mary noted that a flatter oblong box was already there, and she wondered what it was.

"Uh, wait!" She stopped Evan from opening the big box, and he glanced over his shoulder. "Do you think we could start after lunch?"

"If that's better."

"Yeah. I need to finalize the lineup this morning and get an email out to all the entries."

"All right. Why don't you just come and get me when you're ready?" She nodded, but he hesitated in the doorway.

"Mary," he said, "about last night—"

"Amazing ballet! Your niece Chloe was just precious."

"Yeah." He leaned his shoulder against the doorjamb. "I actually wanted to talk to you about something else." She figured he had, which was why she'd tried to preempt it. And failed. She knew she'd behaved badly at the ballet, and he'd probably been thrown by her dismissive attitude. It was all because of the guilt that was eating her up. Guilt over disappointing Evan and letting down the town.

"It's about Monday," Evan said.

"You mean, the ice skating?" she asked, surprised. They'd had a super time, which—when she thought about it—probably made the way she'd acted last night seem doubly confusing.

"Yeah, that." He viewed her sincerely. "Look, I'm really sorry if I made you uncomfortable. That wasn't my intention. I know we're working together, as colleagues and all, but after you brought me that Christmas tree, I felt like things had changed between us. That we'd started forming a friendship, maybe something more. I really apologize if I was wrong."

Her heart pounded in a painful rhythm. He was trying so hard and was such a great guy. She couldn't lie to him. He didn't deserve it. "Evan," she said softly. "You weren't wrong."

The tense lines in his forehead eased, but his eyes glimmered with worry.

"I sensed the change between us, too," she said. "I'm sorry I was weird last night. I didn't mean to be rude. It's just that I've got a lot on my mind. There's tons going on with this parade that I've got to get organized." *And corrected, so I don't bankrupt Clark Creek. And anger the higher-ups at Davenport. And ultimately lose my job. And you.* She felt overheated in her coat, and removed it, hanging over one of the conference table chairs.

"Of course."

She set her satchel on the table next to the oblong box and pulled out her index cards.

"I hate to add one more stressor to your day," he said, "but my mom dropped by this morning with some bad news."

She stopped sifting through the cards and looked up. *What now?*

"My dad's come down ill."

Mary frowned. "Poor Jesse. Is it serious?"

"Mom thinks a twenty-four-hour thing, but they're not sure."

She blanched, then reached for the oblong box, very gingerly pulling up its lid on one side. Velvety red material greeted her, along with a bunch of fluffy white trim and a wide black belt. Her pulse spiked. "I've lost my Santa, haven't I?"

Of course she had. As if overrunning the town budget by tens of thousands of dollars wasn't enough. Now, she'd lost the star of the parade. She tried not to imagine anything else going wrong because she didn't want to invite trouble, and she'd always heard it came in threes.

"I'm sure you'll find another one," Evan said.

"By tomorrow? Who?"

"Maybe Marshall?"

"He's offering refreshments at his inn."

"How about Nash?"

"Then what will he do with Chloe? He's taking her

to the parade."

Her mind whirled in a panic, then her eyes locked on his. Given his buff frame and body, he wasn't the *best* fit for the job, but maybe with sufficient padding and a fake beard…

"Oh, no." He held up both hands, backing out of the room. "I'm sorry. Not me. I don't do jolly."

He was probably being honest there.

"Besides, I'm already on duty with crowd control."

She knew he was right. He was the sheriff, with sheriff-like duties to perform. Mary sank down in a chair, trying not to let tension overwhelm her. Still, her nerves felt raw and her emotions on edge. Maybe if she counted to ten and focused on clearing her mind, she'd feel calmer. She shut her eyes and tried some deep breathing, but that only made her lightheaded. Maybe she was drawing in too much air and hyperventilating.

"Are you all right?" he asked anxiously.

"Yeah, thanks. Fine."

After a few minutes she opened her eyes, and he was still there staring at her.

"Is there, um…something I can do? Maybe get you a glass of water?"

"No thanks." She pulled a water bottle from her satchel. "Got some, right here."

Evan walked back to his office, thinking he'd never seen Mary looking so stressed. Granted, losing her Santa last-minute wasn't ideal, but the situation wasn't insurmountable. Although it was kind of hard to know who would replace his dad. Anyone that Evan could think of who might fit the bill was already participating in the parade in some way, either as a parade entry or as one of the volunteers.

Itzel sat at her desk in the reception area typing on her computer. Mary's stand of reindeer was beside her. She apparently didn't mind the sculpture taking up a third of her desk—and maybe he shouldn't have minded, either. When he thought about it, he realized he'd been unappreciative of Mary's early gifts. He appreciated a lot more about her now, though. Including how upset she was about losing her Santa.

"I heard about your dad," Itzel said. "I'm sorry he's sick."

Evan poured himself some coffee from the pot on the counter. "Yeah, me too."

"Mary's got to be freaking with the parade happening tomorrow."

"It is a very last-minute change."

Itzel blinked like she'd had a brainstorm. "Maybe you should do it?"

"Me? Play Santa?" He shook his head. "Don't think so."

"Why not?"

Evan sipped from his coffee. "I'm on duty."

"Can't Dennis take over for you?"

"He's already serving as my deputy."

"So, promote him temporarily." She grinned broadly. "And deputize me!"

Evan set aside Itzel's crazy suggestion and carried his coffee back to his office, shutting his door. While he didn't often close it, he needed time to think.

Apart from his mom, he'd never seen anybody who loved Christmas as much as Mary. Maybe it had to do with the nomadic life she'd led as a kid. Christmas traditions are all about home and family, and it didn't seem like she'd grown up feeling like she'd had much of either. It made him sad to think she still didn't have any place she counted as home. And yet, she was all about giving that sense of hope and happiness to others. What other kind of person drove around with an excessive amount of holiday decorations in her SUV?

The kind of person who believes in the special magic of Christmas. A person determined to share that joy with others, just like she'd done when she was in college and ran that Christmas Club she'd told him about. She'd come to Clark Creek armed with optimism and an innovative proposal. Then, she'd worked hard to organize an incredible event in record time. Evan understood that the Santa float wasn't just about a big guy in a red suit. Santa Claus was a special emblem of the parade, an iconic figure reminding children of the true spirit of the holiday: its hope…its wonder…its undeniable magic. The parade couldn't go on without him.

Evan's gaze fell on his coat rack in front of the window, twinkling with Christmas lights. It wasn't the prettiest of pictures, but if he tried really, really hard, he *could* imagine himself dressed in a red suit and shiny black boots for a few short hours. If it would help Mary by reducing her stress about the parade, then the gesture would be worth it. She'd put too much into this parade to have something like this complicate it now. What would it cost him, anyway? Nobody in town would ever guess it was him.

# Chapter Twenty-One

MARY HAD JUST FINISHED SENDING her email to parade participants about the lineup tomorrow when Evan walked in the open conference room door.

"Mary," he said with a determined air. "I'm going to do it."

"It?"

"Be your Santa Claus."

She did a double-take, because she hadn't even gotten around to working on the replacement. That was next on her agenda. "But I thought you said you don't do jolly?"

"I don't." He strode over to the table and flipped the lid off the Santa suit box. "But I can probably fake it for an hour or two." He reached into the box and placed the Santa hat on his head. Then he grabbed the tunic holding it up against his uniform. "Ho. Ho. Ho," he said in the dullest, most mechanical fashion *ever*. "There! How's that?"

"Um."

He frowned at her expression. "Right. Maybe I can work on that."

While she was thrilled he'd volunteered, she was one hundred percent surprised, as well. And yeah, he definitely needed to work on those *ho-ho-hos*.

"What about your parade duties?" she asked.

"I've spoken to Dennis and he's taking over my role."

"What about his?"

"I'm deputizing Itzel."

"And she's okay with that?"

"It was her idea." He grinned and Mary's stomach twisted nervously. This was one problem solved, and so kind of Evan to step forward. Unfortunately, he wasn't a super great Santa Claus. "Are you sure about this?"

"Yep. I've thought it over. The Santa float is the grand finale of the parade, and then there's Santa's Workshop to consider. Don't want to let those kiddos down." He stretched the tunic out by his sides; it was much larger than he was.

"We might need to find a pillow."

Mary bit her lip. "Yeah." She stared at him in awe, surveying his Santa hat. That fit him well enough and he actually looked cute it in it, in an unexpected way.

"Want me to try again?"

"Er, sure."

"HO. HO. HO." This time it was no less stilted, only louder. He scrutinized her. She didn't think she'd winced, but she might have. "Not any better?"

Mary exhaled, considering her options. She couldn't very well refuse his generous offer. Who knew if she'd be able to find another Santa Claus at this late date? Christmas Eve—and the parade—was tomorrow.

She stood up next to him and placed her arms out in front of her in a semicircle like she was surrounding a huge imaginary belly. "Try it like this." She put on her jolliest deep baritone. "*Ho-ho-ho.*"

"Got it." He set the tunic aside and mimicked what she'd done with her arms. "Ho. Ho. Ho," he said, as he bounced on his heels.

He was trying so hard, she didn't want to hurt his feelings, but that sounded just the same as the first time. "That's good! Really good!" And also might scare off the youngest children. He didn't sound so much like Saint Nick as Ebenezer Scrooge playing Saint Nick.

Even though she'd considered Evan Scrooge-like in the beginning, now that she knew him better, she didn't at all. But that was because she had gotten to see his private side. Unfortunately, Mechanical Santa was the guy who showed up in public.

She shot him a sunny grin, appreciative of his efforts. "With all the parade noise, people might not even hear those ho-ho-hos anyway. Maybe you should just smile and wave?"

"But what about afterwards at Santa's Workshop?"

*Yeah, what about afterwards…* "Er, you should do the same!"

His forehead creased beneath that Santa hat, and she worried he'd read that as a criticism. "I mean, you've got such a nice smile. It's very, very jolly when you apply yourself. So, come on. Act natural! Smile!" She encouraged him, gesturing with her hands, and his smile did not look natural at all. It actually looked like he'd just swallowed a ton of fish oil.

"You know what?" she said. "We don't need to worry about that right now. Everything will come more easily to you tomorrow once you're dressed up and in character." She hoped. "In the meantime, I really would love your help with some of these boxes."

Evan folded the Santa tunic and placed it back in the box along with his hat. "Not breaking for lunch?"

Mary checked the time on her phone and saw that daylight was wasting. There was still a lot to do and organize. Apart from unpacking them from the boxes, the souvenirs needed to be taken out of their individual packaging and sorted into bins, so they'd be easy to hand out during ticket sales. Then she had her starter cash box to set up. She'd run by the bank this morning on the way here. "Do you think we could have something brought in?"

"The Whistle Stop delivers."

"Really? That would be perfect."

She didn't know how she was going to explain the huge number of T-shirts to Evan once they started going through boxes, but since he wasn't typically involved in fundraising, or parade organizing, maybe he wouldn't think that anything was off.

Mary still worried about running into a huge deficit with the parade. She didn't know how she'd sell all those T-shirts, but she really had to, since it sounded unlikely that they could be returned. Then, there was that other lingering feeling she had. That sense of doom hovering over her about bad things coming in threes. But she honestly couldn't think of one more thing that could go wrong. Thanks to Evan her Santa Claus crisis had been averted, and nothing could be as bad as her T-shirt ordering mistake.

"Thanks for playing Santa in the parade," she told him. "That really is above and beyond the call of duty, and very nice of you."

"I'm happy to help out," he said. "After all you've put into this parade, I want to do my part, too. I'll be honest: When you proposed the plan, I couldn't fathom how it would work. All I could imagine was this huge financial catastrophe affecting Clark Creek, with the parade costing the town more than it made. With all your excellent oversight, I can now see how wrong I was."

"Wrong." Mary swallowed hard, her nerves on edge. "Right."

Evan and Mary finished their sandwiches from the Whistle Stop Café, then he helped her open some boxes. One looked different from the others in that it was narrow, long, and flat. They opened that one first, finding the "Christmas Avenue" signs inside.

"Nice," he said, holding one up. "I can see it."

Mary appeared happy at his support of the parade. It had been a gradual process, but he'd finally gotten behind the idea. His playing Santa Claus was proof of that.

They moved onto the square boxes next. One was filled with little flags and the other with magnets. Mary suggested they get the boxes unloaded before doing any unwrapping, and he was game for that plan.

Evan cut into the third box with his scissors, opening its flaps. "We have—T-shirts!" He peered down into the box, seeing piles and piles of them. "Lots and lots of T-shirts."

"There are probably a few more." She grimaced, and he wondered why that was a problem. She grabbed handfuls of T-shirts, setting them on the table in stacks. "I was thinking we shouldn't open all the T-shirt boxes," she said. "Maybe just a couple, and have the others handy as backups."

"All right." Whatever her procedure, that was fine with him. "Should I open another box and see what's in it?"

"Sure!"

He did, and found the coasters. "Where do you want these?" They actually looked really good with the gazebo design on them. The magnets and the flags were nice, too.

She smiled but seemed preoccupied. "Can you just set those on the far end of the table until I finish with these T-shirts?"

He nodded and opened another box. "More T-shirts!"

"Um, yep."

A few minutes later he ripped into another. "And more." The next box revealed more of the same. "How many T-shirts did you order?" he asked, looking up.

She drew in a shaky breath. "Loads."

"Wow," he said, continuing to paw through them. "There have to be enough T-shirts here for everyone in town, including babies." He chuckled and held one up in front of him. "But this one's definitely not toddler size."

"Nope!" Mary stared at the design on the front of the T-shirt and then tried to gauge its size. "Looks like a medium." She seemed very tense, not like her normally upbeat self.

Evan flipped the shirt around and peered at the size tag inside its collar.

"Close," he said. "It's a large."

Mary looked like a deer caught in somebody's headlights. She wasn't moving. Wasn't talking. Only staring at the back of the shirt. He glanced down at it, then gazed at her, and her eyes watered. He'd didn't know why she was so upset. He got things wrong like that all the time. "Hey," he said gently. "Misjudging a size isn't such a huge—"

"It has a typo."

"What? Where?" He shook out the shirt and read what it said on the back: *Christmas is Clark Creek.*

"It's supposed to say *in*, Evan. In! *Christmas in Clark Creek.*" She darted to a box and yanked out another shirt. "Maybe that one's a fluke."

It wasn't.

"*No*," she murmured under her breath. "*No, no, no. No.*" She had the T-shirt balled up in her fists and was squeezing the daylights out of it, holding it to her chest.

"Mary—"

It was like she didn't hear him. She tore into another box and dug out more T-shirts. And then another box, and the ones he'd opened previously. All the T-shirts said the same thing: *Christmas is Clark Creek.*

"How could this happen?" She scanned the ceiling. "How, how, how. How?"

She was clearly panicking, going over the top. "Maybe people won't notice?" Evan suggested. "Or maybe you can get a refund from the company, since this was their mistake."

"Was it, though? I checked the design dozens of times! I didn't even create a new one for the order, just clicked on what I'd used for the sample." She gasped and raced for her satchel, extracting the sample items she'd shown Evan at the café. The T-shirt was among them, neatly rolled up. She unfurled it and shook it out. Her eyes widened. "Evan," she said, evidently remembering he was there. "It has the typo." She started to cry. Not a lot. Just a few random tears, and Evan broke a sweat.

"How many of these did you order, in total?"

He guessed he shouldn't have asked that, because now the tears came harder, streaking down her face. Great move. He had to regroup. "Hang on," he said, "it's not so bad. It's like I said, people probably won't even notice! You showed that to me at the Whistle Stop." When he thought about it, she hadn't shown him the back, but he decided not to mention that part. "And...and, before that to my mom and the town council."

"Yeah, but I showed them virtually—by computer.

So maybe the details didn't pop."

They were sure popping now, because ever since it had been called to his attention, all Evan could see was that typo.

She sank down into a chair, dazed. "The third thing."

"What do you mean 'the third thing'? What's that?"

"Bad things." She wiped her cheeks with the back of her hands, pulling herself together. "They come in threes."

"Not always."

"They sure did this time."

"Was losing your Santa Claus one of them?"

She nodded slowly.

"And the first was…?"

It all came out in a rush. "Oh Evan, I didn't mean to. There was this power outage thing going on at the inn and the lights flickered, and then they went off. Then on, then off again a whole bunch of times."

"When was this?"

"On Thursday, after I went to Hopedale. I was in the middle of putting in my order for souvenirs, and had already ordered the other things. Only the T-shirts were left."

"Okay," he said, not understanding.

"With the internet sketchy, I didn't know the order had gone through the first time. In fact, I didn't think it went through at all. So I tried again. And again."

He saw where this was headed. "How many times?"

Her eyebrows knitted together. "Ten."

"Oh wow, so there are…?" He looked around examining the boxes.

"A lot, a lot, a lot."

"How many?"

"Three thousand."

He sank down in a chair beside her. "That's a lot of

T-shirts."

"I *know*…" Her voice cracked but she didn't weep this time. Still, she looked on the verge.

"Do you think we can sell that many?"

She vehemently shook her head.

"How about at cost?"

She shrugged, and he could tell she was mortified.

"Mary," he said kindly. "Things like that happen to people. Everybody makes mistakes. Maybe you can send some back?"

"I asked about that, but it doesn't look likely."

"Okay. Well." He prepared himself for the damage. "How much did all these T-shirts cost?"

She stared at him and said nothing.

"Mary?"

She spoke so softly he scarcely heard her. "Thirty thousand dollars."

Evan rubbed his ears. "Thirty thousand…dollars?"

"*Plus taxes and shipping*," she wailed.

He stood and began pacing around the conference room in the limited space between boxes. That was a lot of money. A lot *a lot* of money. He'd seen her budget for the parade because she'd showed it to him in her proposal. Parade expenditures including printing and souvenirs were supposed to be capped at ten thousand dollars. For everything. It was a shoestring budget, but a small-town parade. Mary had given everybody her word she could make it work.

"I'm so sorry." She looked more miserable than he'd ever seen her, and his heart ached for her. "But if some sort of miracle doesn't happen tomorrow, it's going to be like you predicted. This parade could bankrupt Clark Creek. And nobody's going to want these now." She gestured to the T-shirts. "Not when they're imperfect."

Evan thought hard. He'd been in dicey situations and had always found a way to maneuver himself out of them. He considered the printed matter on the T-shirts. The front showed the gazebo design like the smaller souvenir items did, except the T-shirts carried the slogan on back—in really huge letters. Perhaps they could turn it to their advantage.

"All right," he said, still pacing. "Maybe we can spin it."

"Spin it?"

"Yeah." He glanced at her and she sat up a little straighter in her chair.

"How?"

"What if we act like the typo was intentional. In other words, not a typo at all?"

"I don't get it."

"We're making a statement about Clark Creek, Mary. Christmas *is* Clark Creek, as in the spirit of Christmas is represented by this town."

"Uh, I'm not sure who's going to buy that."

"Maybe lots of people."

She swept her hair off her forehead. "Maybe?"

He observed the mess on the table, understanding there was more work to do. But he also understood that Mary needed a break. He reflected on his earlier idea about taking her horseback riding, thinking the fresh air might do both of them good. If she really did bankrupt Clark Creek with this parade, he couldn't be mad at her. She'd worked like crazy to make it a success, and he'd meant what he'd said about everybody making mistakes.

Still, if her parade effort failed, he would be mightily disappointed and very concerned about the town's finances, which frankly couldn't take one more hit. But thinking negatively about the outcome of the parade wasn't going to do anybody any good. The die had been cast with Mary's mistake, and things were what they were. The best way for him to proceed was by adopting some of her endless optimism and being supportive.

"Come on," he said, nodding toward the door. "Let's get out of here."

"What? Now?"

"You look like you could use a breather from all this. Honestly, so could I."

"Where are we going?" Relief flooded her face, and he knew he'd made the right call.

"Nash keeps horses at his farm. I've got an open invitation to ride whenever I want to. What do you say?"

"Aren't you on duty this afternoon?"

"Was on duty this morning. Technically took the afternoon off. Figured I'd be spending it with you."

She looked happy for the first time all day, making Evan's heavy heart feel lighter. "Well, in that case, I say yes."

That was just what he'd been hoping she'd say.

He grinned, and she grinned back at him.

"I need to go home and change first," he said. He glanced down at her spiky-heeled boots. "You might want to, too. Got any flatter shoes?"

# Chapter Twenty-Two

I T WAS MIDAFTERNOON WHEN THEY reached Nash's farm, and still snowing. Mary saw that Santa's Workshop had been erected to the right of Nash's main gate. There was space beside it for the animal adoption tent, and a line of portable toilets had been installed in the area bordering the fairgrounds. She drew in a deep breath, feeling calmer about things. The parade was falling into place, and the whole town was getting ready. Maybe Evan was right. Maybe there was a way to spin her mistake on the T-shirts. The typo part. She still didn't know how on earth she'd sell three thousand of them.

Evan called Nash at his clinic to let him know they were coming, and his brother was all for them taking a ride. He suggested they use a couple of the horses who weren't working as reindeer during the parade, mentioning that Austin and Leroy had taken off early since they had a busy day tomorrow. Evan relayed all this to Mary after ending his call, but she'd been able to glean most of it from his end of the conversation.

"You were great to think of this," she said. "I've always wanted to ride horses."

"But never did?"

She shook her head. "Not that I didn't want to. I begged my mom for lessons for years."

"I can see where those might have been harder to come by in your situation."

"Oh, we lived in places where my schoolmates went riding."

"I'll say it again," he teased. "You've led a deprived life."

"Ha ha, yeah." She gazed out at the snowy landscape as they passed under the sign for Meadowmont Farm. "It's beautiful here."

He took his attention off the driveway a brief moment to study her. "Sure is."

Mary's face warmed because of the way he looked at her. Evan had a way of making her feel appreciated. Special. Beautiful, even. And she liked being all those things in Evan's eyes. She was so glad to be getting away from parade planning for a while. The parade in Clark Creek had completely consumed all her energy these past two weeks, and she'd taken very few breaks. Her stomach fluttered when she realized that she'd taken some of those breaks with Evan. While decorating his house, and then ice skating, which had been romantic and fun.

He pulled up to the barn and parked his truck, then they walked over to the stables. "I'll put you on one of the gentler horses."

Since she'd never done this before, that sounded safest. "Where will we ride?"

"There's a nice trail through the woods on the far side of the rear pasture." He checked the sky. "We've got plenty of time before it gets dark."

"Evan," she said. "Thank you for doing this."

"My pleasure," he said, like he meant it.

They entered the stables and the horses inched forward in their stalls to see who was coming. "Afternoon, Nellie,"

Evan said, stroking her on the nose. "Then he greeted the others in turn. Mary could tell he had an easy way with the animals. She could also sense that they liked him.

"We'll be riding Jumper and Trixie today."

"Jumper?" Mary's heart thumped. She hoped that wasn't her horse.

Evan read her look and chuckled. "Jumper's only called that because he won't jump. He's a very docile horse. You'll ride him. Trixie's a bit more spirited, so I'll take her."

Mary watched him grab the tackle and saddle up the horses like he was an expert at it, which he was, compared to her. "Did you and your brothers ride a lot as boys?"

"Yeah."

"Miss it?"

"Don't have to. I've got this place right here."

"Nice of Nash to let us ride."

"He's happy to have help exercising the horses. Gives Leroy and Austin a break."

Mary grinned, thinking of the two farmhands. "I like Leroy and Austin. They're sweet."

"Right." The corners of his mouth twitched. "Just don't let them hear you call 'em that."

Mary was glad she'd changed into jeans and her more casual coat. Evan wore jeans too, and looked rugged and handsome, just like some Western cowboy. He stared down at her brown leather boots.

"I see you've got a pair without heels on them."

"These are my play boots," she said lightly.

"It's a good thing you packed them. Those spiky heeled ones might have been a problem in these stirrups."

He led Jumper out of his stall and patted the saddle. "Ready to hop on?"

Mary stared up at the horse, who appeared way larger right up next to her. Chloe's horse, Nellie, hadn't stood this high when she'd met her face to face. "He's a big fella, huh?"

Evan laughed. "Changing your mind?"

"Absolutely not." She grabbed onto the saddle horn and, with some effort, wriggled her left boot into the left stirrup. Then she sort of hung there, overextended, with the toes of her right foot on the ground.

Evan noted her predicament. "Here," he said gallantly. "Let me give you a boost."

He centered his hands around her waist, then—*whoa*—she was up and over the saddle, plopping down on it.

Evan looked up at her. "All right?"

She nodded and he handed her the reins. She held them in one hand while still grasping the saddle horn with the other. "Then say giddy-up."

"Hang on. People actually say that?"

He nodded encouragingly. "Just take it nice and slow till we're outdoors. Once you're comfortable, you can go a little faster."

She stroked Jumper between his ears and they twitched. "Giddy-up, boy," she whispered, afraid of sounding too mean.

Evan mounted Trixie. "You might have to tell him a little louder and give him a nudge with your heels."

Mary nodded. She had this. It was just like she'd seen in the movies. She lifted the reins and commanded more firmly, "Giddy-up, Jumper!" She gave him two swift kicks with her heels, and he bolted.

"*Wha—ahhh! Jumper, no!*" She dug in her heels, hanging on for dear life, and Jumper went faster. Breaking from a trot into a canter. "Evan—help!"

Evan galloped up beside her on Trixie and leaned over, latching onto her reins as they raced along in tandem, the white landscape around them becoming a blur.

He tugged on her reins, but she couldn't let go. They were trapped between her tightly clenched gloves and the saddle horn.

"You've got to release the reins, Mary."

"What? No. *I'll fa…fall!*"

She kept bobbing up and down, up and down, in the saddle and—*ow*—her bum was starting to hurt. Her legs were throbbing, too, from their viselike grip on the horse's middle. *Wait. Oh no.* "Evan," she stammered, growing woozy. "My head feels really light."

"Easy." Evan yanked at the reins again with a steady downward tug. "Just keep hanging onto that saddle horn," he instructed.

Like she was about to let go of it. Sure.

Once he had Jumper's reins in hand, he pulled back on them at the same time he tugged on Trixie's. "Whoa, boy! *Whoa*," he said, bringing Jumper under control. He drew Trixie to a halt. Jumper stopped too, and snorted.

Mary's breath came in fits and starts, but at least she was still on Jumper and not on the ground. She stared down at it, deciding it looked very hard and cold, a lot like that skating rink.

"I think that's more excitement than this old boy has had in years," Evan told her.

Mary's heart pounded. "I thought you said he didn't jump?"

"He doesn't."

"He sure knows how to run."

Evan peered into her eyes. "Maybe we should head back."

"Already?"

He viewed her doubtfully. "You want to keep going?"

She bit her bottom lip. She'd always wanted to ride, but not exactly like that.

"I have a better idea," he said, turning both horses around. Mary still hung onto the saddle horn, but her posture had eased. With Evan leading her horse, there was far less of a chance of Jumper making another break for it. "How about you ride on Trixie with me?"

"You mean like with you doing all the work, and me just along for the ride?"

His eyes danced. "That's the general idea."

"Then I'm all for it," she said.

A short time later, Jumper had been returned to his stall and his saddle removed.

Evan helped hoist Mary onto Trixie. She asked him, "Should I scoot back?"

"No, forward." He grinned and her pulse skittered. "You'll get a better view."

She hadn't expected to be riding in front, but when Evan settled himself in and surrounded her with his arms, she was glad that she was. He made her feel safe and protected. This time, Mary had no fears that she'd fall off. They trotted out of the stable and toward the rear pasture. Snow drifted lightly, adding to the magical ambiance of the countryside.

"How ya doing?" he asked, leaning forward. His warm breath tickled her neck, and little tingles raced down her spine, and then back up again.

She smiled over her shoulder. "Better."

"Good." He snuggled her closer and gave a command to his horse by making a clicking sound with his tongue, and they began moving faster.

She still jostled in the saddle but there was a regular

rhythm to it, so she adjusted, keeping time with Evan's movements behind her. Brisk air nipped at her cheeks and snowflakes coated her hair and eyelashes. She laughed, feeling free and uninhibited. "I like this way better than riding on my own," she told him.

"Just takes practice," he said smoothly, and Mary realized she'd rather have more practice doing this. With him so close she could smell his outdoorsy cologne.

He leaned forward to guide Trixie into a turn and his beard stubble brushed her cheek. Mary's heart stuttered and then it beat faster. She'd never had an experience like this, and had never experienced anyone as wonderful as Evan.

When she'd told him about her ordering mistake, he hadn't scolded her or issued any well-deserved reprimands about her endangering the financial well-being of the town. It was true he'd seemed shocked at first, but then he'd reflected on the situation and tried to make her feel better about things. Even that infuriating typo. How had she missed it? She just didn't know. She hoped Evan was right and that they could *spin it*, so people would still buy the T-shirts anyway.

She also hoped for a really big turnout for the parade. All one hundred of the Airbnb rentals had been booked, so she knew they were counting on at least two hundred visitors from out of town, since most of those rooms were doubles, and some even offered lodging for entire families. She hoped for another couple of hundred visitors from Hopewell, and more from the surrounding area. In addition to out-of-towners, she expected roughly two thousand of Clark Creek's citizens to attend, not counting those participating in the parade. That barely reached twenty-eight hundred ticket sales, assuming everybody bought one, and she doubted most of those folks would buy T-shirts.

"Everything tomorrow will turn out fine," Evan said, like he'd known she'd been worrying about it. "You've worked hard on this parade."

She wished. "But what if—"

He embraced her from his position on the horse. "Positive thoughts, Mary."

Her face heated and suddenly her thoughts turned away from the parade and back into the moment. "Why are you being so good to me?"

His voice was a deep rumble. "Because you deserve it." The way he said it made her feel like she did. Like it was okay to make mistakes, because that was part of being human. She would do her best tomorrow to give Clark Creek the most spectacular Christmas parade ever, and maybe things would be all right.

If they weren't, and she failed, she'd deliver her heartfelt apologies to the town and to Davenport. Then she'd need to resign from her position and find a way to move on, like she'd always moved on before. Right now, it seemed impossible to envision being anywhere but here with Evan, and she found herself not wanting their time together to end.

They entered a clearing by the edge of the woods which led to a path. If she'd thought the scenery was magical in the pasture, it was even more spectacular under a canopy of snow-covered trees. It was like they were in their own private realm. So special and quiet. She could hear the sound of the snow softly pelting the trees as they made their way deeper into the forest.

The wind picked up, blowing snow from the under-brush, and some rained down on them from above. "Whoa!" Evan cried, sweeping the snow from Mary's hat and shoulders with his glove. "That was a surprise.

You okay?"

She giggled, because it hadn't been a bad one. Being pelted by nature with snow was just one more unexpected event that complemented this experience. "Yeah, I'm fine." She peered at him over her shoulder. "How about you?"

His eyes kindled with warmth. "Never been better."

He held her tighter and she eased back against him, enjoying his strength and warmth. He slowed Trixie's pace again, and the steady clip-clopping of her hooves matched Mary's pounding heartbeat. This was so special and romantic. They were in their very own world, her and Evan.

"I wish you didn't have to go," he said, his tone husky.

And, in the moment, she found herself wishing that very same thing. "Yeah."

"Maybe we can keep up?" he suggested. "You know, after the parade."

But Mary didn't know what would be happening after tomorrow. Everything depended on the outcome of the parade. She hadn't told Evan about Seattle, and she decided there was no point mentioning it now, since it might not happen anyway. So instead of making false promises, she spoke the truth she felt in her heart. "I'd like that."

Daylight started to fade so Evan returned them to the stables, his spirit soaring. He hadn't been this lighthearted in a while and it felt good. He'd broached the subject of him and Mary keeping up their relationship after she left Clark Creek, and she'd said she'd like that, too. Nothing would make him happier than continuing to see Mary. He'd drive to Richmond seven days a week just to buy her a coffee, if that's what it took.

He hopped down off Trixie, then helped Mary next. She put her hand on his shoulder, wearing a big grin. He could tell that she'd liked the horseback riding. He had, too.

Evan encouraged her to jump down, and she did, as he held out his arms to help her. She slipped but he instantly caught her. The next thing he knew, he held her in an embrace, as Trixie ambled away to munch on some hay in her open stall. There was no one else here besides the horses and the two of them. And suddenly, it felt like nothing else mattered in the world. Mary must have sensed that dynamic between them, too.

She gazed up at him and her cheeks tinged pink. He'd known she was good-looking before, but he'd never seen her this beautiful, and part of the attraction was the way she looked at him. Like she desperately wanted him to kiss her. He wanted that too.

"Evan, I…" She licked her lips. "Don't think that we should—"

He cupped her chin in his hand and stared deeply in her eyes. "Why not?"

"Because, the parade—"

"Is tomorrow."

"And, I'm leaving—"

"Yeah, but you won't be far."

"*Ohhh.*" She moaned, sounding enticed but conflicted.

He reached up and gently stroked her cheek. "I won't kiss you, if you don't want me to."

"I want you to," she whispered, and shut her eyes.

Evan's mouth hovered closer and his lips brushed over hers, then—*wham!* An icy cold shower of crystals clobbered them from above.

Mary yelped and jumped back, staring at him wide-eyed.

Evan slowly looked up, seeing that the pile of snow that had been wedged above the stables' doorframe had broken loose and cascaded down on them. "Sorry."

"Oh boy." She shook her head and started laughing. "Maybe it wasn't meant to be?"

He wasn't so sure about that.

She pushed up her coat sleeve to check her watch. "Oh gosh, almost five o'clock. We should probably get back to the courthouse."

Evan raked a hand through his hair, regretting the lost opportunity of that kiss. Then he told himself there were bound to be others. That's what he wanted to believe. "Yeah. Let me just take care of Trixie."

She nodded and offered to help as he removed Trixie's saddle and put other things away.

He was tempted to try to kiss her again, but this probably wasn't the time. The spell had already been broken. She gave him an impish smile, offering an alternate suggestion as they left the stables.

"Race you to your truck?"

Evan hadn't raced anybody on foot in years. Just like he hadn't been ice skating.

Or—he swallowed hard—fallen for a woman, like he was certain he was doing now.

"You're on!" he said, running after her. He paused to grab a fistful of snow off the ground and he hurled it at her.

"Evan!" she cried in mock offense, but she was giggling. She bent down and made her own snowball and lobbed it at him. They exchanged several more volleys, reminding Evan of the fun they'd had outside the Whistle

Stop Café with the boys.

They finally reached his truck, both of them laughing.

"I guess it was a tie?" he said.

"Nope!" she tagged his truck. "I won!" He laughed and her dark eyes sparkled. "Better luck next time."

Affection warmed his soul, and something deeper than that. Because he was really hoping there would be a next time with Mary. For footraces and snowball fights, horseback riding and skating, and well…a whole lot of other things.

"Thanks," he said, grinning happily as they climbed into his truck.

Evan dropped Mary off at the Clark Creek B&B so she could shower and change into something dry. He was going home to do the same, and they planned to meet back up at the courthouse shortly. It was after five and they still had tons of work to do to get ready for tomorrow morning. Mary entered the inn and passed Gerald and Geraldine coming down the hall. They were on their way out and dressed for an early dinner.

"Looks like someone's been playing in the snow!" Geraldine teased with a titter.

Mary self-consciously touched her damp hair and then the band of her hat, which had icy snow stuck to it. "Ha ha. Yeah. Went out for a horseback ride." She was amazed to hear herself say it so naturally, like she rode horses all the time. Which she clearly *did not* from her episode with Jumper. Evan had seen evidence of that.

"We went out with some horses," Gerald said. "At Marshall's brother's farm."

"We went sleigh riding," Geraldine's eyes twinkled. "It was so much fun."

"You all staying for the parade?" Mary asked them.

"Oh yes," Geraldine said.

Her husband nodded. "We'd planned to leave today, but when Marshall told us about it, we decided to stay on. Sounds like a fantastic time."

Mary was glad that the older couple would be there. She liked Gerald and Geraldine a lot.

"Were you out with your sheriff friend?" Geraldine asked her.

Mary's face warmed. "Actually, I was."

Geraldine's eyes held a knowing gleam. "He's very handsome."

"Yeah, well." Mary licked her lips, trying not to think about that at the moment, or about how he'd nearly kissed her, and how badly she'd wanted him to. "He and I are working together," she explained. "On the...the parade!" Which is why she needed to untangle herself from this conversation and get moving. "I'm sorry," she told them politely. "If you'll excuse me, I need to run upstairs and change. I have to get back to the courthouse to tend to some details."

"Of course," Geraldine said.

Mary hurried up the stairs and into her room, her heart hammering. If she'd thought ice skating with Evan had been fun and romantic, there was no topping that incredibly dreamy horseback ride through the snowy woods on Trixie. And then, afterwards, when he held her in his arms and his lips barely brushed hers, she'd nearly melted. She sighed, the sensory memory flooding her, and her body tingled from head to toe. She'd never met anyone as swoony as Evan, and yet she couldn't let crushing on him persist. She had to push all those feelings to the back of her mind and focus on coordinating the parade. That's where she had to center her energy.

She returned to the courthouse with renewed determination to complete her preparations and make the parade a success. Doubt and worry were her enemies in this situation. She needed to remain positive and hopeful. Being out in the country and away from the pressures of the parade had helped her regain her perspective. She strode into the conference room, her confidence renewed. Evan was already there opening up boxes.

"You cleaned up quickly," she told him.

He smiled but kept working. "Yeah, so did you."

She'd feared that things might be awkward between them because of what had happened at the stables, but Evan seemed to share her commitment to setting their personal relationship aside so they could concentrate on the task at hand. Glancing around the room, Mary saw that task was enormous. They had to streamline their efforts somehow.

"Where do you want me to put things when I take them out of the boxes?"

Mary considered their options, suggesting they set up an assembly line of sorts. He could open and unpack boxes, placing items on the table. Then she would unwrap any individual packaging and sort the souvenirs into bins. She sat down at the table to work while Evan stood at the other end.

"So I was thinking about where everyone should be during the parade," Evan told her as they worked. He opened a box of flags, placing them by fistfuls on the table. "I'd suggest Itzel cover the section of Main Street that runs from the fairgrounds' parking area to Maple. That's roughly the midpoint for the parade." He emptied a big box of magnets next. "Dennis can patrol the section between Maple and the town square, and I can keep a general eye on things."

"But you're riding on a float."

"Yeah, but mine is last." He winked at her and Mary tried to ignore the giddiness she felt inside, reminding herself to focus. "So I can walk around a bit at first."

"All right."

"Might even be able to help you with the lineup."

"Thanks, that would be super." Mary had been wondering how she was going to handle directing it on her own, with Itzel deputized and stationed near the fairgrounds, so she was grateful for his help. He probably knew more about the parade than anyone else in town by now, besides her.

She was about to ask him about communications when he volunteered. "I'll be carrying a walkie-talkie. It won't be visible beneath my Santa Suit. Itzel and Dennis will each have one too, and so will you."

"Perfect." Mary dropped several magnets into the magnet bin, mentally complimenting herself on the design. They were really cute.

"Also giving one to Helen," he added. "Since she's on dispatch and it's critical for her to get through if she can't reach us otherwise. Sometimes cell communications can get a little wonky during big gatherings."

Mary had experienced that firsthand. "Understood."

He hoisted another box onto a chair to open it and stared around the room. "Hey, I think this is the last one."

Mary scanned the area, seeing he was right. "Great. We might just get this done."

"We *will* get this done."

The glint of affection in his eyes made her heart flutter. Mary dropped her chin to hide her blush, removing the cellophane from another magnet. "Evan," she said after a pause. "Once we're finished with the boxes, you don't have to stay."

His brow furrowed. "I really don't mind. If there's something else I can do?"

She checked her watch and saw it was approaching seven. "You need to eat dinner," she said. "So, when you're done with that box—"

"You need to eat too." He thought for a moment. "How about pizza?"

But she'd had pizza earlier and had been thinking about picking up Thai on her way back to the inn. She'd seen a place on Main Street that did carry-out. Besides, she didn't want to keep him. "I'll pick up something later," she said. "In the meantime, once I'm done with these"—she gestured at her sorted souvenirs on the table—"I've got to go through paperwork and accounting stuff."

"Are you sure?" He actually looked disappointed, and Mary found herself being disappointed, too. She loved spending time with Evan, but tonight she had important things to accomplish.

"Yeah, but thanks for your offer."

"No problem." He cut the final box open. "You'll never guess," he said, pulling back its flaps.

Mary rolled her eyes and they both laughed together when they said, "T-shirts!"

# Chapter Twenty-Three

MARY WOKE UP ON CHRISTMAS Eve, a ball of nerves. This was it. Parade day was here, and she had so much to do. It was just before six a.m. and still pitch-black outside while she did her morning yoga. She needed to be focused and calm for the day's activities ahead. Marshall had thoughtfully offered to leave muffins and fruit outside her door, along with a carafe of hot coffee. When she checked after completing her yoga routine, it was there. Breakfast at the B&B didn't begin until seven-thirty, and Mary would be long gone by then.

The parade started at nine, but she had to coordinate the lineup an hour beforehand. She was excited to see all the different floats and knew that the music entries she'd interspersed among the others would be especially appreciated by the crowd. In addition to the high school marching band, she had the middle school jazz choir singing popular Christmas tunes, and the fourth-grade recorder players from Clark Creek elementary riding on the second-to-last float and playing "Santa Claus is Coming to Town."

The bell ringers from the Community Church would ride the church bus with its windows down, while chiming out the "Carol of the Bells," and their spot was somewhere in the middle. It was going to be a fabulous parade. The Paw Brigade, four pickup trucks sporting animal adoption banners and carrying rescue cats and dogs all snuggled in blankets and wearing animal sweaters, was Mary's favorite part. The clear weather was expected to hold, with only a few flurries predicted for later, but those wouldn't dampen the parade. If anything, a little light snow would lend the event extra Christmas charm.

Evan and Dennis had agreed to adhere the *Christmas Avenue* magnets to the street signs on Main Street before seven o'clock. Connie had solicited help from the maintenance crew at the courthouse to transport the tickets, programs, and souvenirs from the courthouse conference room to the gazebo, along with folding tables and chairs. They were to begin moving things over at seven, so as soon as Mary left the inn, she'd go to the gazebo to check on them. All volunteers had been asked to arrive by seven forty-five, and meet with Mary at "Christmas Central," meaning the gazebo.

Mary showered and dressed quickly, then passed Marshall in the lobby on her way out the door. "Good luck with everything today!" he said.

"Thanks! You too. I hope the refreshment sales go well. Will you be sneaking away to get a peek at the parade?"

"Most definitely," Marshall said. "Jeremy, Andrea and I are doing a rotation. That way none of us will have to miss it."

Mary left the B&B at the same time a woman across the street exited a dilapidated old Victorian. It was the house that had recently sold and that the Clarks had been talking about. When Mary reached the sidewalk, she saw that a brand-new sign had been erected in its front yard. It read *The Sweetheart Inn*.

The woman stood there admiring the sign for a moment and then walked to her car, which was parked on the street. "Oh, hello!" she said to Mary, noticing her.

"Good morning." Mary smiled at the stranger. "Are you the one who bought the house?"

"I *am*," the woman said proudly. She had dark brown eyes and a sunny smile and looked to be roughly Mary's age. Two short blond braids poked out from beneath her winter hat. "My name's Karen Johnson."

"Mary Ward. Nice to meet you."

"You too, Mary." She cast a glance at Marshall's place. "Are you one of the owners of the B&B?"

"Oh no. Just visiting."

"Clark Creek's a great place to visit," Karen said. "I'm sure it will attract even more tourists after today." Karen pressed her key fob to open her car door, and Mary wondered where she was headed so early.

"Aren't you staying for the parade?"

"I wish I could." Karen shrugged. "But I need to get back to Williamsburg for Christmas with my family."

It was such a simple statement, but it cut so deep. While Karen had only been replying to her question, her answer had underscored something important that Mary was missing: a family to go home to at Christmas.

"I'll be back for good after the first of the year," Karen said, getting into her car. "Hope to see more of you if you're around!"

"Oh, no, I'm not..." But Karen didn't hear her. "Staying." She'd already shut the door and was waving goodbye.

Mary strode toward the gazebo as muted daylight spread across the snowy town square. The ice rink was deserted at this hour, but the gazebo and its surrounding area buzzed with activity. A woman in a wheelchair stacked programs on a folding table beside a walkie-talkie. She smiled when she heard Mary approaching.

"Hi—I don't believe we've met," she said. "I'm Helen Hastings, the Sheriff's Office's dispatcher." Mary returned Helen's greeting, then Helen introduced her husband next. "This is Bernie," she said referring to the older Black gentleman beside her with short gray hair.

"Mary." Bernie uncertainly held out his hand in her direction before angling it right in front of her. When she shook hands with him, he said, "I'm afraid my eyesight's not as sharp as it used to be."

"Bernie's handing out programs," Helen said. "I'm selling tickets." Both of them wore one of the sticker badges that read *Parade Volunteer*.

"How great of you both to help out. Thank you."

Mary greeted several town council members, including Vivi Torres.

"Itzel is in the courthouse helping Evan with something," Vivi said to Mary. "Isn't it so exciting about her being deputized?"

"Yes, very!" Mary said. "I've got to go and grab my lineup cards from the conference room. I'll look for her inside." Mary wanted to touch base with Itzel and everyone on her team. She also needed to pick up her walkie-talkie.

Mary turned away and Connie caught her elbow. She stood next to an open box of T-shirts and Mary's heart stilled. "Mary," she said. "About these T-shirts…" Mary bit her lip.

"I think they're fab!" Connie held one up in front of

her, showcasing the back. "Christmas *is* Clark Creek, everybody!" she proclaimed, capturing the busy group's attention. People turned her way. "This was Mary's brainstorm," she told the others, latching onto the idea. "Clark Creek equals Christmas." She leaned toward Mary and whispered. "Evan told me all about your clever plan. Love it."

"Er, thanks." Sweat beaded Mary's hairline. Now she just had to hope two thousand nine-hundred and ninety-nine other folks loved it too. At least she had Evan to thank for helping her save face with his mom the mayor, and the other people in town.

"How's Jesse doing this morning?" she asked Connie.

"Still not one hundred percent," Connie said. "But he was feeling a little better when I left him. Not running a fever or anything, fortunately, so we're hoping he'll rebound by tomorrow. We always have the boys over for Christmas dinner. Little Chloe too, of course."

Mary nodded, considering what a fun family gathering that must be. "Well, when you speak with him, please tell him I hope he feels better soon."

"Thank you, Mary."

Mary glanced toward the street and spotted the band director approaching with his full marching band in uniform. The teenagers weren't in formation—more like meandering all over the place, while chatting and holding their instruments off to one side. "Excuse me," she said to Connie, "I'd better go and grab that lineup. The entries are starting to arrive."

Mary found Evan in the conference room with Itzel, who had a deputy's badge pinned to her unzipped jacket. Mary also noticed she was wearing a walkie-talkie. Itzel evidently had provided Evan with lots of padding for his Santa suit, and now helped him adjust the shoulders of his tunic. "There," she said in a motherly fashion. Itzel was the type to mother-hen everyone, including those older than she was. "Super Santa-like!"

Evan looked doubtful.

"Ah, you're missing your beard!" Mary said, spotting it on the table beside the Santa hat. Evan's eyes twinkled when he saw her.

"Morning, Mary."

"Morning, Evan."

Itzel scrutinized them both like she was trying to decide whether she detected an undercurrent between them. A *romantic undercurrent*, it was clear, from her interested gaze.

Evan picked up the fake beard and strapped it on, and then tugged on the Santa hat. "So?" he asked, posing for their approval.

"It's not *so*." Itzel rolled her eyes. "It's ho-ho-ho."

He grinned beneath his fake beard and shot a spirited glance at Mary. "*Ho-ho-ho!*"

Mary's jaw unhinged at his deep belly laugh. He actually sounded jolly. "You did it!"

Evan patted his huge round tummy. "I know." He reached for an extra walkie-talkie on the table and gave it to her. "This one's yours. Know how to work it?"

Mary nodded.

"Great."

Itzel zipped up her jacket and headed for the door. "I'd better get over to the fairgrounds. When I came through town this morning, people were already starting to arrive in the parking area." Mary passed her a page from the papers she'd placed in a manila folder, along with a small roll of stickers. "Here's the list of volunteers working parking this morning. They already have their wands and reflective vests." Those had been Evan's idea, and he'd had Dennis deliver them to the volunteer coordinator in that section. "Can you ask everyone to wear a sticker, including our reindeer handlers, Austin and Leroy?"

Itzel chuckled. "Sure thing."

Mary tucked the walkie-talkie in her largest coat pocket and grabbed her stash of index cards from the table. All she had to do was place a quick call to Judy, then she could get busy with the lineup.

She spoke to Evan once Itzel left, not wanting to mention the whole typo fiasco in front of her. Although she probably would have told Itzel later, if she were sticking around and meeting up with her again. Mary guessed her T-shirt mistakes might make a funny story in retrospect, but she wasn't laughing about them now. "Thanks for running interference with the mayor, by spinning the T-shirt typo."

"I was happy to do it. Sometimes it's better to get out ahead of things, before they catch up with you." His snowy white fake eyebrows arched and he did look like a jolly old elf. An incredibly adorable jolly old elf. She almost giggled because his appearance was so contrary to his regular demeanor.

"Mary," he said seriously. "I've had an inspiration."

She folded her arms in front of her, tickled by this. "What? You?"

"It's about selling those T-shirts."

She was all ears.

"I think we should toss them out."

Okay, now he'd lost his marbles. Maybe the stress of playing Santa and acting so jolly was taking its toll. He noticed her doubtful expression.

"Ho-ho-*ho*. You thought I meant throw them away."

"Didn't you?"

"No." His blue eyes glimmered. "I meant toss them out—from my sleigh."

242

"What?"

"You know how at sports games, and other events, gifts are tossed into the crowd?"

"Yeah, so?"

"So, what if we choose a certain number of T-shirts as giveaways, then those can serve as advertising. Say, for example, you're standing beside me and I catch a T-shirt, but you don't. I admire the T-shirt and tell my friends—or family—how cool it is. Suddenly, you want one too. Then, your kid wants one, and your husband says you should buy one for your mother-in-law."

"That's ingenious, Evan! How many should we give away?"

"At least a few dozen, maybe more."

"I like your idea. Like it a lot." She added her own marketing angle. "How about if we add a second-shirt discount as a sweetener? Supposing it works out like you say, and more than one person in a group wants to buy one? They could get one for twenty and—"

"Maybe you'd better start lower," he said. "We've got a lot of T-shirts to move."

"True. Fifteen?"

Evan nodded. "And two for twenty-five."

Mary pursed her lips. "That means selling the second one at cost."

"Yeah, but maybe you'll sell more that way."

Evan was right. She was much better off getting rid of the T-shirts by breaking even on some of them. That strategy beat facing the uncertainty of returning them, which was risky.

"What about the ones we're giving away? Those will be a loss."

"It takes money to make money."

"Right." *And, maybe with this plan we can make most of*

243

*that thirty thousand dollars back.* She was so pleased by his solution she wanted to kiss him, and so she did. Smack-dab in the center of his forehead. "Thank you, Santa!"

His neck reddened. "Ho-ho-ho!" he crooned with a cheery air.

Dennis walked into the room holding a large plastic container of carnation boutonnieres. "Hi, Mary," he said, "Happy Christmas Eve."

"Happy Christmas Eve to you."

"These were just delivered by the florist." He stared down the flowers. "Should I take them somewhere?"

"The gazebo would be great, thank you. They're for the mayor and the parade marshals to wear."

Evan adjusted his fake beard. "I'll go with him," he told Mary. He extended his hand. "Why don't you give me the first part of that parade lineup and I'll get things started."

She grinned, passing him half of her index cards. "Awesome. Thanks."

He left and her cell phone rang. It was Judy. Perfect timing.

"Hey, how are things going?" Judy asked. "Hectic?"

"A little, but basically under control."

"Great. Did you download that accounting program I sent you?"

"Yeah. I went through the tutorial a couple of times last night."

"Super. Everything's up and running here and will sync automatically with the data you enter on your end. Your parade expenses are all entered and there are individual columns for different types of revenue. Your pledge donations have already been added. Did you download the app to your phone?"

"Yeah."

"Good, then you can update data real-time. If you get

a number for ticket sales at the midpoint, say, you can go ahead and enter that number, then update it later. Same with merchandise sales. Not sure when you'll be hearing from Marshall about his refreshment total, but you can always add that in later."

"Got it," Mary said. "I've asked our cashiers to give me a running count when they're able. If things get busy, some of the information might be delayed, but we'll definitely get it all entered after the parade ends."

"How's the crowd looking?"

"It's early, so only parade workers on this end so far. Itzel saw a few vehicles headed towards parking."

"Things will pick up. Your announcements in the local area papers looked really good, and adding the parade as an Airbnb event to tie in with the lodging option was a real stroke of genius."

Mary was glad she'd thought of that, because every extra bit of exposure helped.

"The parade's running till ten?" Judy asked.

"The actual parade part, yes. We're keeping Santa's Workshop and the reindeer rides going for an additional hour or so. The animal adoption tent, too. Everything will be over by lunchtime, and local restaurants have all prepared themselves for a heavy rush."

"This could be a really good thing for Clark Creek."

Mary felt another twinge of nerves. "Hope so."

"So when are you coming home?"

"Maybe later today, or first thing in the morning. Haven't decided."

"Well, if you don't have any plans, you can come and have Christmas at my parents' house with me."

"*And* your new boyfriend?" Mary appreciated Judy's kindness, but demurred. "I don't think so."

"Come on. We'd love to have you. *I'd* love to have

you, and, hey! You can meet Paul, maybe even serve as a buffer between him and my grandparents."

"Funny," Mary said.

"I wasn't joking."

"I'll give you a call after the parade, all right?"

"Okay. I'm pulling for you, Mary."

"Thanks, Judy. I know you are."

She hung up the phone, missing her friend. Things had been so crazy, Mary hadn't had a chance to tell Judy about Evan playing Santa Claus or the romantic horseback ride they'd shared in the country. She hadn't confessed her totally messed up and conflicted emotions either. She was liking Evan so much, and her feelings for him kept deepening. Yet with her potential move to the West Coast, she couldn't envision a future for them. Long-distance relationships were hard. Maybe they worked out sometimes, but they'd never worked out for her.

Mary picked up her half of the notecards and left the conference room, turning out the light. What mattered now was the success of the parade. This wasn't about her promotion; she wanted it for the town. She needed the parade to be a big hit for Clark Creek, and if it was, that would mean getting reassigned to Seattle. The promotion still sounded exciting, but not nearly as much as it once had. Mary sighed, understanding that after she left here, she was going to really miss Clark Creek. Not just the town, but its people. Most of all, she was going to miss Evan.

# Chapter Twenty-Four

ARY STOOD ON THE SIDEWALK in front of the
Whistle Stop Café, watching the parade go by.
Snow clouds hovered overhead, but the weather was clear
as the parade marshals rolled past on a big fire truck driven
by Marshall's friend Donny. The town council members
smiled and waved at the crowd, and all of them wore
boutonnieres. The mayor did too, and she was ahead of
them waving from the passenger seat of the ambulance.
The ambulance driver let out a short screech from his
siren and people cheered. These first responder vehicles
were at the front of the parade on purpose. In the event
they were needed for an emergency, they couldn't afford
to be hemmed in.

People swamped the sidewalks on both sides of the
street. Mary occasionally spotted Dennis and Itzel stroll-
ing along, while encouraging parade patrons to stay
back from the road. Parents held their children on their
shoulders, and lots of kids waved Mary's Clark Creek
flags. Mary saw Gerald and Geraldine across the way
in front of the Taverna Italiana, and they fluttered their
programs in hello. Marshall appeared behind them,
sending her a thumbs up.

Her walkie-talkie crackled in her pocket and she took it out. It was Evan's voice, asking "How's it going out there?"

"Really great," Mary answered. "The marching band just went by, along with your mom, and then the parade marshals."

"Itzel?" Evan asked.

"Here, boss," she said, her connection crackling. "Looking good over in parking."

Dennis chimed in on the channel. "Gazebo looks clear. Most folks have bought their tickets and gone on to Main Street. Oh, sorry," he added with a chortle. "*Christmas Avenue.*"

"How's it going with you, Santa?" Mary asked Evan.

"Just about to board my sleigh."

Mary made her way through the crowd to peek at Santa's workshop and the animal adoption tent, which was waiting and ready for the animal carriers to be unloaded from the trucks. She turned around and saw the portable library truck approaching. It towed along huge candy cane and book balloons and had a big banner on either side of it saying: *Home for the Holidays and Reading.*

The flatbed truck from the Feed & Seed had large snowflake balloons anchored to its sides and carried bales of hay surrounding a painted nativity scene, complete with a life-size rendering of a donkey and sheep. Mary carefully crossed Three-Notched Pass, then strode by the fairgrounds so she could cross over to the other corner on Main Street and go back the other way.

She heard bells ringing and peered above some taller heads to see the church bus coming with its bell ringers. All around her, people looked happy, and Mary was happy too. Her heart felt full to the brim with the joy she saw on people's faces. There was nothing like the wonder of a Christmas parade.

Her walkie-talkie crackled again. This time, it was Helen. "We have an update on ticket sales. Two thousand so far."

Evan whooped on his end and Mary's heart gave a hopeful leap.

"How are the souvenirs holding up?"

"All out of flags," Helen reported. "Mostly out of magnets. Still a bunch of coasters."

"T-shirts?" Evan asked, and Mary almost wished he hadn't. At the same time, she wanted to know."

"We've moved a few." Helen exchanged words with someone beside her in the gazebo. "Ten."

Mary's stomach clenched.

"Dennis and Itzel?" Evan asked. "Things still good?"

"Yes, sir!" Dennis said.

"That's a roger," Itzel quipped, like she'd been practicing.

Mary got out her phone and removed her right glove, entering the new data from Helen. Two thousand times five dollars was ten thousand dollars. Good. The pertinent souvenirs only cost two thousand, so that was a nice profit on ticket sales so far. Part of those net profits would go to the town and the other portion to parade entries. But only ten T-shirts? She'd forgotten to ask if any of those were budget sales, so she picked up her walkie-talkie.

"Helen," she said, above the parade noise. "It's Mary. What were the proceeds from those T-shirts? Were any of them discounted?"

"Let's see." Helen asked someone else the question, then got back to Mary. "One hundred thirty dollars. That's the total. Eight sold as the sales package, two individuals."

"Okay, thanks!" Mary said, knowing Evan had heard this. She frantically scanned the crowd, mentally willing more people to appear.

Then suddenly, something weird occurred. A big line of trucks and cars moved down Three-Notched Pass from the highway at a slow pace. Mary didn't know why this was happening, but she'd take it. If these were more folks coming to the parade, she'd welcome them with open arms.

The first vehicle turned on its blinker and veered into the parking lot. Then, the next one did too. The traffic was heavy, so moving slowly. A guy rolled down the window of his SUV and shouted to her. "Mary!"

She turned around, recognizing him as Sam Singleton. His lively wife, Angie, sat beside him in the passenger seat. A cute dark-haired boy with big dark eyes sat in back. Beside him was a baby seat, holding a toddler girl with curly dark hair. Next to her, a much older woman with reddish-brown hair wore a stunning printed scarf and colorful parrot earrings. She grinned, her dark eyes sparkling. "*Feliz Navidad*," she said in a light Spanish accent. "Merry Christmas!"

"Merry Christmas." Mary returned the greeting before shouting happily. "Sam! Angie! Hey." She smiled at the older woman. "You must be Angie's grandmother."

"Yes. Nice to meet you."

"I'm Pepe!" the little boy said. He patted the baby on her head. "This is Magdalena!"

Sam leaned out his SUV window. "Sorry we're running late. There was a big backup on our end. Heavy snow on the mountain. People had to wait until the streets were cleared. I hope we haven't missed it?"

"No, not at all. Things are just getting started."

She glanced behind his SUV and saw more people coming, and more after them. The sedan right behind Sam's SUV carried two older couples, who smiled and waved. She guessed they were Angie's mom and her new husband, and Sam's dad with his girlfriend.

She smiled at Sam and Angie. "I'm so glad you and your family made it safely."

Pepe had a question. "Has Santa come yet?"

"Not yet," Mary answered, grinning again. She couldn't believe this good fortune. It was just like Itzel had said. Nothing was over until it was over. Look at all these people coming to her parade!

"Woo!" The child turned to his great-grandmother. "Lita! We haven't missed him."

The older woman smiled sweetly at the boy. "Yes. I heard."

Mary couldn't wait to get on her walkie-talkie to share the news.

"Hey, Helen," she said happily. "Prepare yourself for more ticket sales."

"Yay!" Itzel chimed in. "We seem to be getting a second wave. We're moving into overflow parking now on Nash's farm."

"Yup," Dennis said from his vantage point. "Starting to see them. Lots more folks headed for the gazebo ticket line."

Mary squeezed through parade onlookers, hearing excited yapping sounds coming from the trucks carrying the precious-looking rescue animals. The mascot dogs majestically rode shotgun in the passenger seats of the first two trucks. A big tabby cat pressed his paws up to the passenger window of the third truck, pawing at the glass. And a fourth truck followed.

"Look, Daddy!" a child said. "That kitty's waving!"

Mary glanced up at Chloe's sweet face, seeing she sat on Nash's shoulders. She'd nearly bumped into them when passing by. "Great parade," Nash said.

"Thank you! Hi Nash, Chloe. So fun to see you here."

Chloe waved a tiny mitten. "Hi, Miss Mary."

Nash nodded toward the trucks from the animal rescue. "Bet that adoption tent will get a lot of business today."

Mary held up her gloved fingers and crossed them. "Here's hoping!"

She inched toward Maple Street, spying the stream of newcomers across the street squeezing their way toward the town square by inserting themselves behind the last row of parade watchers and the festively adorned storefronts. Though Main Street businesses had already decorated for Christmas when Mary got here, they'd gone the extra mile in dolling themselves up with more decorations ahead of the parade.

The bake shop float went by, covered with all sorts of yummy-looking Christmas cookies, including gingerbread boys and girls, all of gigantic proportions. Mary worked her way toward the town square, arriving just as Santa's "sleigh" turned onto Main Street. The sleigh was actually Jesse's tractor, but he'd done a really good job decorating it to look like the real thing before he'd gotten ill. Evan smiled and waved at the crowd.

Mary looked up to see a camera crew positioned across the road, taping the whole parade. It seemed to be made up of teenage kids, but then she saw a truck on the far side of the town square near the library, which appeared to be from the local TV station. *Excellent.*

She peered up and down Main Street, spotting an official-looking guy with a shoulder-mounted camera trailing after a female reporter wearing boots and a sleek winter coat, and talking into a microphone. *Wheee! We're making the news!*

"Ho-ho-ho!" Evan shouted in a deeply jolly way. "Merry Christmas!"

Mary's heart warmed. Evan was trying so hard, and he really did make a great Santa, after all. He dug into his Santa bag and tossed a rolled-up T-shirt into the crowd. Then another. "Ho-ho-ho! Merry Christmas, everybody! Merry Christmas!"

When people realized what he was doing with the T-shirts, they gave Evan their full attention, leaping to catch the T-shirt missiles he lobbed through the air. One landed near Mary, and a young boy almost trampled her foot trying to grab it. "Oh sorry, Miss Mary!"

She saw it was Joe. He unrolled his T-shirt and showed it off to his brother.

"Cool," Spencer said. "I want one."

"I saw them for sale on a table by the tickets." Joe nudged Spencer. "Come on, let's go ask Mom and Dad!"

Mary stared in amazement at Evan, who watched the crowd and the group of children playing recorders angled out the windows of the school bus in front of him.

*Better not pout, I'm telling you why…Santa Claus is coming to town!*

Mary could almost hear the lyrics in her head as the kids played their tune, some of them more accurately than others. After a couple of high-pitched screeches, she noted a few grown-ups trying not to wince. They were goodhearted about it, though, and pasted on appreciative grins.

She was grinning too—to beat the band.

And then it started snowing.

Small white flakes twirled down from the sky and Evan *ho-ho-ho*ed even louder. He scanned the sidewalks, looking to the left and then the right. Mary waved and his smile sparkled beneath his fake white beard when he saw her.

He reached into his Santa bag and tossed out more

T-shirts, and people started hollering.

"Choose me, Santa!"

"Over here!"

"I've been a good girl," a woman said in way too flirty tones. Mary scowled in her direction, noting she was about her own age and very pretty. Fortunately, "Santa" didn't hear her, or if he did, he pretended not to.

Instead, Evan caught Mary's gaze and held it. When he was sure that she saw him, he winked and she went all tingly inside. Evan Clark was one amazing man, and totally full of surprises.

People whistled and cheered.

"Pick me, Santa! Pick me!"

Someone else said, "This is the *best* parade. Let's come next year!"

"Look!" another voice shouted. "We're on Christmas Avenue."

"Yeah," his companion chuckled. "Just now noticed that."

Mary experienced a hopeful lift in her heart and she tightly shut her eyes.

*Please, please, please. Pretty please.*

Her walkie-talkie crackled. It was Helen.

"Mary?" she said. "Thought you'd want to know. We're selling a boatload of T-shirts over here."

Mary fist pumped with both hands and did a crazy twirl-around dance on the sidewalk.

*Yes, yes, yes! Yippee! Woo-hoo!*

Then she tucked a lock of her hair behind her ear and answered. "Thanks, Helen."

She put away her walkie-talkie and looked up to see Evan watching her. She gave him a big thumbs up, and he smiled.

"Merry Christmas, everybody!" he boomed. "Merry Christmas!"

Mary caught up with Evan behind Santa's Workshop after the parade. He'd just left his tractor at the fairgrounds and was about to take up his post. A line of kids waiting to see him had already formed, and there was another line for the reindeer rides. Leroy and Austin made very good elves. Hordes of people milled about, happily chatting, yet none were rushing to get in their vehicles and leave. That was great. Mary wanted all of them to stay and have lunch. Then go shopping.

Evan dipped his chin when Mary approached him in the parking area. "Looks like the parade was a success."

She scanned the crowd, her blood pumping harder. Her pulse had been beating wildly ever since she first believed she was going to really pull this parade off. "Yes!"

"What's the word on T-shirt sales?"

"Your marketing idea worked." She checked the app on her phone. "Fifteen hundred sales, so far," she squealed excitedly, "and people are buying more."

"Nice. What's the dollar tally?"

Mary checked her phone again. "Eighteen thousand for first and single sales. Eight thousand at cost."

"Twenty-six thousand all together?" He grinned. "Mary, that's awesome."

"I know. I know. Crossing all my fingers and toes, but—Evan." A family with kids walked by so she quickly amended, "*Santa*. I think we could do it."

"You have done it, Mary. Congratulations!"

Her phone rang. It was Judy.

"Fantastic numbers," she said. "Just saw the update."

"Which update is that?"

"Donation forms! They've been coming in all morning, thanks to that handy 'Support the Parade on Christmas Avenue' link you posted on Clark Creek's town website right under the details about the parade."

She'd been so tuned in to souvenirs and T-shirts, Mary hadn't looked at that section of the revenue spreadsheet. She checked it while talking with Judy…and she nearly fainted.

Several people had given ten dollars. Others twenty. Many one hundred. And—*oh, wow*— at least a dozen donors had given over a thousand dollars each, qualifying them for the Santa's Circle level.

Evan searched her eyes.

"It's, uh." Mary licked her lips. "Judy. She says more donations came in."

"Are *still* coming in," Judy said, "and who are you talking to?"

"Evan."

"Well, tell him 'Great job' too, and Merry Christmas from all of us here at Davenport Development Associates."

Mary nodded numbly.

"Smart thinking to add that comment box," Judy continued, "because people are loving this parade. They want to see another one like it next year."

Mary's throat felt raw. She was so happy she wanted to cry. "That's wonderful."

"A real Christmas miracle, yeah. Congrats on pulling it off! We'll talk later after the final numbers are in. But Mary," she said. "They're only going to get better at this point. Not worse."

"You, Mary Ward, are a world-class Christmas Consultant," Evan said when she ended her call. He gazed at her admiringly. "You've single-handedly saved this town."

"Not single-handedly." She glanced around at the crowd. "I had lots of help. From you, especially, Evan." She gazed up him. "Thank you."

Evan's walkie-talkie sounded and he pulled it out from underneath his tunic.

"Is there a Santa Claus around here?" It was Itzel, but she sounded awfully close, like she wasn't just on the walkie-talkie. She was somewhere nearby. Evan and Mary looked around and found her standing next to Santa's Workshop trying to placate restless kids and their parents.

"Duty calls." Evan shifted on his feet. "I guess I'd better go," he said, like he didn't want to. "Maybe we can talk later?"

"Later? Sure."

He wagged his finger in her direction. "Don't leave town. Not yet."

"I won't." Her cell buzzed in her hand. It was Judy sending a text.

*Just heard from headquarters.*
*You're going to Seattle!*

# Chapter Twenty-Five

*E*VAN FINISHED HIS SANTA DUTIES at the workshop and Itzel left to help manage traffic in the parking area, since some visitors were leaving. Others spilled onto Main Street, filling sidewalks with their happy chatter and lining up at restaurants and cafés. Mary had been right. This parade was very good for business, and it had been great for Clark Creek. Evan was astounded by how much money it had made, and apparently more was pouring in.

He took out his walkie-talkie to check in with the others. Helen had finished her cash box counting and turned everything in to Mary at the courthouse. She and Bernie were about to head home. Mary was in the conference room tying things up, and Dennis was patrolling Main Street. Evan spotted him on his way to the town square.

"Fine parade," Dennis said.

"Saw Linda," Evan said, mentioning Dennis's wife, "with your boys."

"Yeah, they had a great time. Linda bought me a T-shirt."

Evan chuckled. "Nice."

Dennis's cell phone rang, and he answered. "I'm sorry, Evan. That's her."

"No problem. Catch ya later."

Evan nodded and started to walk away. Then Dennis exclaimed, "What? When? Now?" He caught up with Evan. "Linda's in labor."

Evan grinned and slapped Dennis's shoulder. "Well then, go!"

"I'm working the crowd until five."

"I'll take over for you," Evan said.

Dennis's eyebrows rose. "Are you sure?"

"Of course I'm sure. Now go on, get out of here. You don't want Linda having that baby without you."

Dennis gave him a big grin. "No, I don't."

Evan planned to ditch the Santa suit and return to Main Street in his uniform. He'd left it in his office, so that would be a simple task. But first, he had to catch up with Mary. He had so much to tell her, and he didn't want her leaving Clark Creek before he had a chance to say it face to face.

By the time he reached the town square, the gazebo had been cleared. The maintenance crew was breaking down the folding tables and preparing to bring them inside. The ice-skating rink was busy, and a portion of paradegoers lingered in the area, browsing the nearby shops.

Snow drove down harder, pelting Evan with heavy white flakes as he climbed the courthouse steps. His mom scurried up the steps to join him—he hadn't noticed her before. The red carnation on her coat was speckled with snow.

"Evan. How did things go at the workshop?"

He took off his fake beard and tucked it in his pocket. "Great. Everyone wants electronics for Christmas."

His mom shrugged. "That's progress, I guess."

He held open the courthouse door. "Except for Buttercup. She wants a baby sister."

His mom's eyebrows shot up. "Did Nash hear that?"

"Oh yeah, but he pretended like he didn't."

"Poor Nash." She frowned. "I wish he would find someone."

"I don't think he's ready, Mom."

She gave him a thoughtful look. "What about you?"

Evan cleared his throat. "I don't know what you're talking about."

"I've seen how you are with Mary, son," she said as she walked to the elevator. "Happier."

"So?"

His mom turned. "So don't let her get away."

He wasn't planning to, not if he could help it, but he wasn't sharing this with his mom. Not letting Mary get away was all he'd been thinking about all morning. She'd affected him deeply, and he was hoping—oh, how he was hoping—he'd deeply affected her. Evan believed they could build something good together, maybe even a future.

He climbed the stairs to the second floor, removing his Santa hat. He hoped that Mary would be alone, because what he had to say was personal, between the two of them, and didn't deserve an audience.

His phone dinged. It was an incoming text from his mom.

*Think about inviting her to Christmas dinner.*

Mary couldn't believe this day. What a wonderful surprise all those people coming from Hopedale had been. The extra donations at the town website had stunned and thrilled her, too. And Evan's support had been amazing. For a guy who'd put up so much initial resistance to her parade, he'd sure stepped up to play a role in making it such a success. Several roles.

Mary chuckled to herself, envisioning him in that fake beard and big round belly. Even dressed like that, he'd still been handsome, with his twinkling blue eyes and his rugged smile. She packed up the extra coasters, because Connie had said that the town council would find some use for them. There were very few magnets left, and no flags.

Putting these items away reminded Mary she needed to pack her bag at the inn. She'd definitely spread out all over her room, and she wanted to tidy it up as she prepared for her return to Richmond. A melancholy shroud draped over her spirit. Spending Christmas in Richmond alone held zero appeal. But she wasn't going to crash Judy's family party, no matter how kind or well-intentioned the invite had been.

She looked up as Evan entered the room, still dressed as Santa, minus the hat and the beard. "Nice going today," he said, walking over to examine the stacks of T-shirts she'd folded and set on the table. "These all we've got left?"

"Believe it or not, yes." She smiled at him, but her smile was shaky, because she felt all torn up inside. Going back to Richmond didn't just mean leaving Clark Creek. It also meant leaving Evan. Once she was in Seattle, she'd be even farther away. "Thanks for all your support with the parade."

"I'm sorry I wasn't more supportive from the beginning."

"It's how everything turns out in the end that matters."

"Yeah." He gave her a thoughtful look. "What time

are you planning on leaving?"

She checked her watch. "In a couple of hours. Why?"

"Because I was wondering," he said, "if you have time for a walk?"

She scanned the conference room. "I still have a few more things to take care of."

"I've got to change out of my Santa suit. I'm covering for Dennis this afternoon." His blue eyes sparkled. "Linda's having their baby."

Mary grinned at the happy news. "A Christmas baby," she exclaimed. "How exciting."

"Yeah." Evan studied her in a longing way, and Mary's face heated. "So, I was thinking we could take a walk down Christmas Avenue? Might be a little crowded, and it's snowing really hard. But if you're game for one last peek at the town—"

"All right," she said, savoring the idea of spending more time with him. Secretly though, she'd been disappointed by the way he'd put that. Like he was resigned to her saying goodbye.

Well, what did she expect? For him to beg for her to stay? No one had ever asked Mary not to move on before. It was like the whole world accepted her status as a wanderer. She'd accepted that fate for herself a long time ago.

Mary's throat burned hot and her heart thumped painfully. Then she told herself to buck up. This is how it always went for her. How it had always gone. Which was why forming attachments was bad for her in the first place. What was the point in coming to care for someone, when all you were going to do was leave them behind?

"Can you take a break in ten minutes?" he asked her.

"Sure." She was almost wrapped up here, and she could finish any incidentals after returning from their walk.

Evan exited the conference room and Mary's cell rang. She scanned the incoming caller ID, surprised to see it was her mom. "Hello?"

"Mary, hi!" Lila said. "Merry almost Christmas."

"Merry almost Christmas to you. How are things in Portland?"

"Crazy busy. The hotel's doing this huge soirée tomorrow and calling it a Christmas Ball. Lots of important people will be there, big names from the community and such."

"That sounds like fun."

"For them, maybe. For my part?" She laughed. "I'm a stress-mess." Lila was always tense before large events, yet for as long as Mary remembered, she'd done well with them.

While Mary didn't have the closest relationship with Lila, her time here had made her want to do better. Clark Creek's warm and friendly people had made such a lasting impression on her, and Evan's family served as a shining example of a loving, tight-knit family. In the back of her mind, Mary had been thinking that maybe by being geographically nearer her mom, she could bridge the emotional distance between them.

"I know you'll do great with the party," Mary said. "You always do."

"Thanks! How are things in Richmond?"

"Actually, I'm not in Richmond. I'm in Clark Creek."

"Clark where?"

"It's a small town near the mountains." Mary's enthusiasm surged when she recalled the glowing faces of so many adults and kids enjoying the festivities. "I'm here for a work project. Not just any ol' project, a parade!"

"As a fundraiser?" She could hear the doubt creeping into her mom's voice. "Have you ever done one before?"

"No, but—"

"I don't know, Mary. Maybe you should rethink that. Parades are very hard to organize and they're not exactly moneymakers."

"Wait. That's what I'm telling you, I already *have* organized one. And…" She drew in a breath. "It was amazing!"

"So it's over?"

"Yeah, we held it this morning. It was a Christmas parade, and really super." Mary didn't know why she was trying so hard to convince Lila of that, but she felt moved to defend her idea. Just like she'd had to do as a kid. Whenever she'd floated creative concepts by her mom, Lila had relentlessly deflated her balloon, warning her to be realistic about outcomes.

Over the years, Mary had taken that realism and spun it into optimism, which suited her personality so much better. It paid to put a positive spin on things. Hadn't Evan demonstrated that with his stellar T-shirt-typo-fiasco fix?

"We raised lots of money for the town and its businesses," Mary said. "Charities like the animal shelter, too. There were pet adoptions and reindeer rides. Santa's workshop—"

"I don't need *all* the details." Lila was a get-to-the-point sort of person.

"Ah, yeah. So anyway." Mary swallowed her hurt. "I wanted to tell you my news. This assignment went so well that I'm getting promoted to program manager in Seattle!"

"Seattle?" her mom asked. "West Coast?"

"Yeah," Mary said. "I'll be much closer, so maybe we—"

"Not for long." Her mom tsked. "I'm moving to Orlando in January."

"Orlando? What?"

"It's a prime assignment," her mom said, growing elated. "I'll be working at Disney!"

"Oh. Well, I…I'm very happy for you."

"Portland was growing kind of stale, anyway. You know what I mean?"

"Yeah, I think I do."

Her mom was the kind to move on before forming too many attachments, too. She'd been raised by her single aunt after her folks died, and the aunt sadly hadn't been up to the job, showing Lila very little affection. To this day, Lila had difficulty expressing emotions herself.

"Anyway," her mom said. "Since tomorrow will be busy, I thought I'd share my Christmas cheer with you now. You'll have a nice gift basket waiting on your doorstep when you get back to Richmond."

"Thanks, Mom. I sent you something, too." Mary had ordered a fully decorated miniature Christmas tree to be delivered by a florist later today.

"That was nice of you, Mary. Thanks."

Mary sighed, wondering if it her mom would actually appreciate it. Ever since she'd been a little girl, Mary had been swept away by the magic and wonder of Christmas. The grand holiday displays in the hotels where she'd lived had further sparked her imagination. Sadly, Lila viewed all the decorations as window dressing. Mary didn't. She saw them as a sign that there was something in this world larger than themselves. Benevolence. Beauty. Love. And ultimately, renewal. Just like the gorgeous evergreen trees dotting Clark Creek's gazebo and the tall one in the town square.

"Congrats on your new job in Orlando," Mary said.

"Equal congrats to you."

"And Mom?"

"Hmm?"

Mary decided to say it because she hadn't in a while, and it seemed like the moment was right. It was almost Christmas. "I love you."

Lila wasn't a touchy-feely person, and she rarely said it back. Mary's soul ached in anticipation, hoping that this time she would. The notion of leaving Clark Creek was getting her down. The holidays were so much about family, and Mary still wanted to believe she had one, no matter how small.

Her mom was silent a moment before answering. Then, she spoke in a thin, quiet voice. "I love you, too, Mary. I hope you have a merry Christmas. Will you stay in Clark Creek?"

Mary's heart sank when she answered. "I hadn't planned on it."

# Chapter Twenty-Six

*E*VAN CHANGED OUT OF HIS Santa suit and into his uniform, folding the costume and placing it back in the box on his desk. He'd return it to his dad tomorrow at Christmas dinner. Since he had a few minutes before meeting Mary, he decided to give his dad a quick call to check on him.

"Evan!" his dad said when he answered. "I heard you were a big hit in the parade. Might even give me a run for my money next year on Advent Sunday. I hope you don't steal my job."

Evan chuckled. "Not on your life, but I was glad to fill in this time—for a worthy cause."

"Very worthy. Your mom texted me the numbers. Outstanding. You can tell Mary she's really outdone herself as a Christmas Consultant."

"How are you feeling?"

"Much better. I do think it was those jalapeños, after all."

Evan shook his head. "Next time, just use the sour cream."

"Or the tiniest hint of Tabasco."

"Dad."

His dad chortled. "Just joking."

Evan decided to let his dad in on the good news. "Linda's gone into labor. Dennis is on his way to take her to the hospital."

"Fantastic. What a memorable Christmas this will be for his family."

It was turning out to be a very memorable Christmas for Evan, too.

Everything had changed for him since Mary had come to Clark Creek.

When he reached the conference room, she was already wearing her coat.

"Good timing," she said, slipping on her gloves. "I've just finished up—I'm all done here. So I'll be going back to the inn after our walk."

"That's great. So. Maybe I can walk you there?"

"Sure." She shrugged like she was fine with that, and picked up her satchel, slinging its strap over her shoulder.

"Is there anything you need me to carry?" he asked her.

"Nope. All of the parade stuff stays here."

He thought of the decorations she'd delivered to the courthouse on her first day. "And your lan-yap?"

"All of that *definitely* stays." She smiled, and his heart was warmed by it. Evan hoped Mary found his presence heartwarming too, because he didn't want this to be the last he saw of her. After today, he was hoping their relationship could continue.

"Don't forget your umbrella," he said. "It's snowing heavily out there."

She picked up her bright red umbrella and he thought of the way she'd looked when he'd seen her walk out of the Whistle Stop Café after the first time they'd met there for coffee. Evan admitted to himself now that, though he'd been initially opposed to her parade, he'd been intrigued by her determination and positivity from the start.

During their very first meeting in his office, she'd challenged him to use his imagination a little more, and he eventually had. Before meeting Mary, he never could have imagined himself playing Santa Claus in a Christmas parade, that was for sure. Just like he never could have imagined himself enjoying Christmas again, or falling head over heels for someone so amazing.

He opened the door for her and they stepped outside, where activity swirled around the gazebo and town square. The ice skating rink was busier than he'd ever seen it, and there was even a line of people waiting.

"That was a good time we had," he said, his gaze on the outdoor rink.

She glanced in that direction and smiled. "Yeah, really fun. Thank you for that, and…" Her eyes misted. "…everything."

He didn't know what was wrong, but he guessed that she was sad about leaving. He was definitely sorry she had to go. He just wanted to make sure she was coming back. He was also cool with driving to Richmond. Whatever it took.

They reached the sidewalk and she popped open her umbrella. "It's really special what you've done," Evan said, and tilted his sheriff's hat against the snow. "Restored hope for so many people." He counted himself among them.

"With luck, that hope will last."

Evan searched her eyes, thinking about how warm they were and how a man could get lost in them. About how he had become lost in them dozens of times. "My parents were hoping you'd come to Christmas dinner. Actually, so was I." He shot her a cockeyed grin, and she blushed.

She took a moment to process this. "That's very sweet, but I'd planned to leave today."

"I know, but tomorrow's Christmas."

"Yeah."

She turned and started walking toward Main Street and he accompanied her, stride for stride. "What else have you got going on?"

"Judy's invited me to her folks' place in Richmond."

"Judy? Your friend slash boss? That was nice."

"Yeah, but I don't want to butt in." She shared an impish grin. "Judy's got a new boyfriend."

"Ah. Gotcha." Evan smiled to himself, thinking that he wouldn't mind having a new girlfriend, but only if her name was Mary Ward.

"So, I'll probably just have a quiet day at my apartment. Play some Christmas music. Maybe drink some eggnog."

"I'll bet your place is really decked out," he said, trying to imagine how many Christmas decorations she could cram into one space. Probably even more than his mom.

"It is! Except for a tree. I didn't have time to get one this year, but that's maybe for the best with my—" She frowned in concentration. "Post-holiday plans."

Evan wasn't sure what those were, but they sounded kind of ominous.

"Post-holiday plans?"

"It's job-related. I'm going to be really busy."

Evan swallowed hard, wondering if this was the start of a kiss-off. "I see."

"I heard from my mom," she volunteered, and he turned to her.

"Yeah? How's she doing?"

"Okay. She's moving again. To Orlando."

"It's kind of a lifestyle, huh?"

"It is, and Evan—"

"Mary—" he said at the same time. They had reached Main Street. The crowds had thinned and lunch lines no longer formed on the sidewalks, but you could see through their windows that the eateries were packed inside. The various gift and knickknack shops, too.

"I'm sorry," she said. "What is it?"

Evan nodded hello to a few familiar faces, then continued their conversation. "I was going to say that, when things slow down. I mean, after your busy post-holiday—"

"Evan," she said suddenly. "I'm moving to Seattle."

He felt like someone had socked him in the gut.

"Seattle? What?"

"It's a promotion," she told him, as they approached the corner with Maple Street and turned right. "Because of the job I did here."

Evan's head spun. "When did you find out about this?"

"Only this morning," she said. "After the parade and when the numbers were in. I mean, there was a possibility I might get promoted all along if the parade went well, but never a total guarantee. After my run of bad luck with the T-shirts, I thought I'd blown it big-time. I actually feared—" She grimaced, and he could tell she meant this sincerely. "That, instead of being promoted, I was going to get fired."

He put things together, recalling her anxiety yesterday afternoon before he took her to Nash's farm. "That's why you were so stressed."

"Yeah, but you helped me feel better. Trixie did too." She wryly twisted her lips. "Not so sure about Jumper."

Evan repressed a grin. "I'm sure Jumper didn't mean to upset you."

"No, I'm sure you're right."

They reached the front of the Clark Creek B&B, and Evan noted that the newcomer across the street had installed a sign front of her house that read *The Sweetheart Inn*. His brother Marshall was going to have some competition in the lodging department, and very soon.

"Well, here we are!" Mary said. "Thanks for walking me back."

"Mary. Wait." He lightly touched her arm. "About tomorrow, and Christmas dinner. My folks will be so disappointed if you don't come. Nash and Chloe too. Not to mention Marshall."

She tilted her head.

"And…" Evan swallowed hard. "So…so will I."

She hesitated, but he could tell she was wavering.

"My mom and dad want to thank you. It would be nice for them, and all of us, if we could spend Christmas Day together."

"I'd like that, but—"

"Then please say yes." He waited then added, "It's what I want for Christmas."

Her cheeks bloomed red. "Honestly? That's what I want for Christmas too. To spend it with your awesome family. But Evan, I need for you to understand that afterwards…"

"We can make this work," he said. "Find a way to build a relationship. Seattle, okay." He exhaled sharply. This was way more of a hurdle than he'd anticipated, but it wasn't insurmountable. "That's a long way. But airplanes travel between here and there. I'm not opposed to long drives, either. Plus, we've got telecommunications."

She hung her head, thinking. When she finally looked up, she said, "I love that you want to do this, because the truth is, I'd love to do it too. Being with you has been so wonderful and amazing. But, it's just like you said when we went ice skating: I'm a wanderer who needs to keep moving."

"You don't have to move on from me." He hated that his voice cracked.

Regret was written in her eyes. "Long-distance is hard. It's not fair to you."

"Don't I get to decide that?"

"Yes. Yes, you do. By the same token, I get to decide what's best for me."

"And that's Seattle, I get that. It's a promotion. You've worked hard. But that doesn't have to prevent us from trying."

"I'm sorry." Her cheeks sagged. "I just can't see this happening. Me there. You here. I need to feel grounded, Evan. I do that best when I'm on my own."

"Do you?"

Her lower lip trembled. "Yes."

"All right, then," he said stepping back. "If that's what you want." He'd hoped to be taking her in his arms about now and giving her that kiss he'd dreamt of at Nash's farm. He'd also hoped she'd be glad to maintain a relationship with him. On both counts, he'd been wrong. "I'm sorry if I pressured you or made you feel crowded."

She reached out and touched his arm, and Evan had to fight every instinct he had to hold her. "I'm sorry, Evan. If things were different. If *I* was different, but I'm not. I'm no good at relationships. When they're long-distance, it's even worse. I'd only let you down."

Evan's gut clenched when he realized he was losing her, and not just to Richmond or to Seattle, but forever. "If you still want to come to dinner—"

"Won't that be awkward? After this conversation we've had?"

He guessed he'd be a little uncomfortable, but he could tough it out for the sake of his family. They wanted to see Mary, and she'd probably enjoy having a nice Christmas dinner. Nobody would know that he and Mary had talked about this, anyway.

"Not for me," he lied. "If it isn't for you."

"I *would* like to see your parents and tell them goodbye. Nash and Chloe, too." She glanced over her shoulder. "I guess I'll be seeing Marshall."

Evan gave a sad chuckle. "Yeah."

Her eyebrows rose. "What time is the dinner?" Then something in her eyes gave him an unexpected ray of hope, like she was pondering their discussion and wondering if there was a way for them to move forward. He couldn't help himself from wondering too. And hoping. Evan viewed the festive holiday wreath on Marshall's front door, and all the other wreaths hanging in the B&B's front windows, and something in his heart told him not to give up. To have faith.

He so badly wanted her to have faith, too. Faith in the two of them. "Four o'clock."

"Okay then." She blew out a small breath. "Please tell your parents I'd love to."

Evan tried not to let his racing heart get ahead of him, but it beat wildly, anyway.

"Want me to pick you up?" he asked. He knew she could ride with Marshall, but he'd take any opportunity to spend more time with her.

"I'll drive," she said, asserting her independence, and Evan didn't mind. As long as she was coming for Christmas dinner, he was happy. "Can you text me the directions?"

Mary walked into the Clark Creek B&B with a heavy heart.

"Way to go, Mary!" Marshall said in greeting. He sat

behind the reception desk working on his computer. "What a day on Christmas Avenue."

"Yeah." She smiled sadly. "Thanks."

"Are you checking out?"

"No, I've decided to stay on a few more days, if that's all right. Your folks asked me over for Christmas dinner."

"That's excellent. I'm glad that you'll be there, and of course you can stay. The room is yours for as long as you want it." He thumbed through some papers on his desk. "If you don't have plans for tonight, the Community Church has a Christmas pageant at five. The Thompsons are going, and some of my other guests. I'm sure they'd be happy to have you tag along."

"Thanks," she said. "But I think I'll have some down-time in my room, then go out somewhere and grab a quiet supper."

Marshall nodded. "After the busy day you've had, completely understood."

As Mary reached her room, her soul flooded with hurt and confusion. She felt like the most callous person on earth. Evan had been so honest and brave in opening up his heart, probably for the first time in a long while. And she'd completely shut the conversation down.

The Seattle promotion had seemed like such a dream job at the outset. Now, it only felt like something that was ripping her away from the sort of life she'd always yearned for. The type of life people had in Clark Creek. When she'd looked in Evan's eyes and he'd told her they could make Seattle work, she'd so much wanted to believe him. But then, she'd had to take a cold hard look at herself. She'd be leading Evan on to say she agreed. Breaking things off later would be far worse than breaking them off now.

Mary sank down on the bed, her heart aching. She'd

never met a man like Evan, someone so honorable and caring. The kind of guy she could imagine spending forever with. It was precisely because he was so wonderful that she didn't want to hurt him by giving him false hope. But was that hope false if she believed they had a future too?

Mary swept back her hair with her hands, thinking about all the places she'd lived, including probably too many hotels. She'd been uprooted time and time again. Putting down roots anywhere was a scary proposition. Putting down roots with a *person*, in a relationship, was equally terrifying. She just didn't think she could do it.

Mary fell back on her bed and pulled a pillow over her face. Poor Evan. What a horrible mess she'd made of everything. Without meaning to, she must have already led him on, or else he wouldn't have suggested a long-distance relationship.

Mary hated long-distance. She didn't *do* long-distance. Above everything else, she didn't want to do long-distance with Evan. It would break her heart.

Mary pulled back the pillow and gasped as an epiphany hit her. She didn't want long-distance with Evan, because she ached for something more intense and personal. A relationship where he could stand by her and hold her, day in and day out, not over the internet, or by text, email, or phone.

She had to tell him that. It was unfair of her to make him believe he was the only one who'd felt their connection. Because she'd felt it, too. Not only that, she'd fallen for him. Super hard.

Even if they couldn't surmount Seattle, Mary needed Evan to know why she'd said no to his proposal about their seriously dating. It wasn't that she didn't want to be with him. It was more like her heart couldn't bear to be with him in that way. Separated by the width of the country. Evan Clark wasn't a long-distance kind of guy. He was the sort of man you wanted to be with all the time, and the more she was around him, the more she would feel that. Until their circumstances of living at opposite ends of the country tore them apart. That was her fear, and she was just now seeing it.

Evan had been upfront with her, so she was going to be honest with him.

Mary picked up her phone and called him.

When he answered, she could hear the hubbub of others around him and she guessed where he was. "Mary?" he said. "This is a surprise. Did you forget something?"

There was more background noise, so she asked him, "Are you on Main Street?"

"No," he said warmly. "I'm on Christmas Avenue." Mary was glad he could still joke and after what she'd recently said to him. This further convinced her of his good heart.

"I did forget something," she said. "There's something important I've got to say. Something I probably should have said earlier. Only, I hadn't totally processed it through."

"O-kay." He sounded confused, and also a bit wary. "When did you want to talk?"

"I was thinking tonight."

When he didn't respond, she added. "It will just take a minute. Maybe we can meet up?"

"At the gazebo, or do you want me to stop by over there?"

"The gazebo's perfect. Thanks. What time will you be free?"

Mary reached the town square right after nightfall. Evan got to the gazebo at the same time, walking towards it from the courthouse.

"Mary." He tipped his hat. "You all right?"

She'd worked up her nerve to say this and wasn't backing down. "Do you mind if we sit?"

He joined her on a bench in between two prettily decorated Christmas trees. A circle of lights shone dimly above them, and snow coated the darkened stretch of ground extending toward the ice rink. Children laughed and chattered, skating along with each other. Some with adults that Mary guessed were their parents. She questioned if she'd ever become a parent one day. She'd like to, if she married somebody as wonderful as Evan.

"I was worried when you called," he said. "I thought you might be backing out of Christmas dinner."

"Oh no, it's not that." She inhaled deeply. "I just have something to tell you."

His brow creased, and Mary pressed ahead. "It's about…what we talked about earlier."

He looked hopeful for a moment, and she felt like a jerk for making him believe this was something it wasn't.

"What I mean is, Evan." She set her hands on her knees and glanced down at the gazebo floor. "I'm sorry." She met his eyes. "Sorry that I reacted the way I did when you were talking about a relationship. It's not that I don't want one."

"Do you?"

"I would if I could."

His shoulders sagged. "I'm afraid we're back where

we started."

"No. I wanted to tell you. Admit how I feel."

He took her hand and held it. "You can always share your feelings with me. Even if they're not what I hoped. I've come to care for you deeply. I also know from experience that emotions can't be forced. If you don't feel the way about me that I do about—"

"But I do." She squeezed his hand and he held on tight.

"Do you?"

Mary's heart pounded and her lips felt dry. "Yes, Evan. I do. So, so much. Only…" She licked her lips. "I don't think I can do long-distance with you."

"Why not?"

"It's complicated."

"Then explain it."

"All right. It's hard because of who I am."

"I get that." He leaned nearer and her face warmed. "You're afraid of commitment."

Mary knew she'd commit to him in a heartbeat if she could honestly believe he'd be different. That things could be different, and promises could last a lifetime. But they didn't. Her mom and dad were evidence of that. So were all her previous broken relationships. "That's not it," she said. "I'm afraid of not being committed to."

Evan studied her a long while. "Life's been pretty hard on you, hasn't it?"

"I've had a good life. Lots of advantages."

"Yeah, but. Maybe not the sorts of advantages you wanted."

He was so intuitive, and really *saw* her on a much deeper level than any other man had. Maybe he was right about that. Despite the good things she'd been provided, maybe she'd been lacking in other areas: compassion, stability, emotional warmth, and enduring romantic love.

"Anyway." She hung her head. "I just wanted to tell you. It wasn't about not wanting to be with you. It's the opposite. Because I've come to care for you too. Deeply. I have. I just can't be with you like that. Not with us living in different places. I hope you understand."

He sat there a moment beside her, staring out at the skating rink. Then, he turned and met her eyes. "Believe it or not, I do."

Somehow, she felt better, though still awfully sad about going to Seattle. She'd probably feel differently once she got there, and the excitement of being in a new place took over.

"So," he said after a beat. "Are we still on for Christmas dinner?"

"Boy, are we ever!" She grinned at him, her heart feeling lighter. Evan always improved her mood. It was one of his gifts. "Does your mom make a great stuffing?"

"My dad makes the stuffing, and it's delicious."

Mary laughed. "I can't wait to taste it. I wish there was something I could bring. Maybe some wine?"

He shook his head. "Just bring yourself."

They both got to their feet, and Mary felt like something had been settled between them. Things didn't feel awkward anymore. They'd arrived at an understanding, as imperfect as it was. She was still going away, but she'd been honest with Evan about her feelings like he'd been honest with her, and communicating openly had felt so good. Relationships weren't just about finding the right one. Often, they were about timing, too. And the timing for her and Evan just didn't seem to be right.

She thought they were about to say goodnight, then Evan surprised her with a request. "Since you're leaving here anyway, do you think you could do me one last favor?"

Her eyebrows rose.

"Dance with me."

Mary's pulse raced and her cheeks burned hot. "What? Here?"

"I would like that very much."

"But there's no music."

"No?" He cocked his chin. "Listen."

She did, but all she heard were the happy sounds from the skating rink.

"Harder," he urged.

She homed in on her surroundings and then—she heard it. The very faint tune of Christmas music spilling onto the ice…and the sound of heavy wet snow hitting the trees in the town square…the cool wintry breeze sifting through the gazebo and riffling her hair…

And the symphony of emotions written in Evan's eyes.

"What do you hear?" he asked, his voice husky.

Her smile trembled. "Christmas."

"That's what I hear, too." He shot her a lopsided grin and her heart thundered. "Thanks to you." He stepped toward her and held out his hands. Mary walked into his embrace, longing to be near him. Aching to feel his arms around her, even if this was the last time.

They surrounded her with their sturdy warmth, and she slid her arms around his neck. He gently tugged her up against him and held her tighter, as they swayed together—heart to beating heart—beneath the colorful glow of Christmas lights in the gazebo.

Evan was right. They didn't need any music. It was here all around them, and also inside them, although nobody else could hear it. She giggled, loving this moment, but also realizing how they must look to passersby. "People are going to think we're nuts."

He whispered in her ear and tingles tore down her

spine. "Let them."

Mary sighed in his embrace, not wanting to think about Seattle or moving so far away. All she wanted to do was dwell on the present, so she could remember this night forever.

"This is so special." She gazed up at him. "You're so special."

His eyes danced. "So are you."

Her heart felt full to bursting and Mary knew there was no stopping the swell of emotions rising up inside of her. They had been building and building until she couldn't hold them back anymore. "Evan," she said. "I love you."

"I'm so glad." A grin warmed his handsome face. "Because I love you too."

And then, while the music of Christmas rang out around them and sang in their hearts, he kissed her, making Mary believe in miracles of every kind.

# Chapter Twenty-Seven

*E*VAN WOKE UP EARLY ON Christmas morning, because he had so much to do. His first order of business was calling a certain jewelry store in Hopedale. Unfortunately, he received the answer he expected when he phoned: a prerecorded message saying the shop was closed for the holiday and would reopen on December twenty-eighth.

He tried his mom next.

"Evan," she said brightly when she picked up the phone. "Merry Christmas! Your dad and I look forward to seeing you and Mary today. We were happy to get your text that she's coming."

"Yeah, me too. Hey, Mom?"

"Hmm?"

While Evan didn't want to get his mom in on his business, sometimes necessary sacrifices had to be made. "I was wondering if you had a list of those sponsors from the Christmas parade."

"Sponsors?" she sounded perplexed. "Sure, but why would you ask about the list?"

"Because, um…I was hoping to get in touch with somebody."

"Today? Son, it's Christmas."

"Yeah, yeah. I do know that, and that's also part of the rush."

"What rush?"

"Can you please work with me and not ask so many questions?"

She thought on this. "All right."

"I was wondering if you might have contact information for Sam Singleton? Personal contact information, like his cell phone or something."

"Ooh, is this about Mary?"

"Mom." Evan dragged a hand down his face. "You promised."

"I sure did," she said in happy tones. Then Evan heard her whisper to his dad. "Evan's calling Sam Singleton—of Singleton's Jewelers!"

"Not calling yet." Evan sighed. "You haven't given me his number."

"Let me go grab my laptop. Hang on!" A few minutes later she returned. "I'm not sure if he'll answer," she said. "He's probably spending the holiday with his family."

Evan conceded it was an imposition, but in light of the surprise he had planned, he'd decided he needed to try. "Yeah, thanks."

"Good luck, son!" he heard his dad say before his mom ended the call. "We're rooting for you."

But nobody could be rooting harder for a happy outcome than Evan himself.

He dialed the number his mom had given him, and a man answered on the third ring.

"Sam here."

"Sam, hey. It's Evan Clark over in Clark Creek."

"The sheriff, right?" Sam paused. "I hope there's no trouble?"

"No. None at all. I apologize for bothering you on

Christmas. I know it's a family time. I wouldn't be calling unless it was important."

Sam's voice took on a cagey edge. "Is this about a woman?"

"Not just any woman. *The* woman."

"I see."

"I hate to ask you this because I know your store is closed, but I've got a very important question to ask today and I don't want to show up empty-handed."

Sam chuckled. "I can probably sneak away for an hour later this morning."

Sam Singleton had made a friend for life. "I owe you."

"Who is she?" he asked. "Do I know her?"

"Mary Ward."

"Your Christmas Consultant?" Sam sounded very pleased. "Then, by all means, come on over. I can meet you at the shop at eleven o'clock."

Mary followed Evan's directions to his parents' farm, arriving a few minutes early. Even though Evan had said it wasn't necessary, she'd stopped and purchased a bottle of wine on her way back to the B&B last night. She was still floating on air from the romantic time she'd had with Evan. When he'd kissed her, her heart had sprouted wings and flown her to the moon. She looked forward to having Christmas dinner with him and his family. It let her pretend she was a part of them, if only for a little while.

Connie answered the door and gave her a hug. "Mary, I'm so happy you came." Chloe scampered into the foyer behind her. "Hi, Miss Mary. Merry Christmas."

"Merry Christmas to you." She grinned at the child. "Did Santa bring you something special?"

"A new horse!" Chloe said proudly.

"Wow."

"Let me go and get her," the kid said, darting into the living room. Mary watched her lift a toy stuffed animal off the sofa and carry it lovingly in her arms. "This is Annabelle."

"She's beautiful," Mary said.

Nash strode into the room from the kitchen and nodded at Mary. "Hi there, great to see you. Awesome job with that parade."

"It was awesome, wasn't it?" Connie exclaimed, her eyes shining.

"Uh-huh," Chloe agreed, hugging her horse. "The best!"

"Marshall said to tell you he'll be a minute," Mary informed the others. "He's helping some new guests get settled in."

"Arriving on Christmas?" Jesse asked.

"They tried to book earlier," Mary answered, "but he was full up because of the parade. The Airbnbs were taken too."

"It's a good thing we're getting another inn in town," Connie commented.

Nash winked at Mary. "We'll see how my baby brother handles that."

The doorbell rang and Mary peered through the glass insert in the front door. It was Evan. She was so happy to see him.

"Merry Christmas, everyone!" he said, stepping indoors. He handed his mom a poinsettia.

"Evan," she said, pleased. "How festive."

"I would have baked some cookies," he said, "but I

would have burned them."

Everybody laughed.

"I have some news," Evan said, "about Linda and the baby."

"And?" Mary asked with a big grin.

"A little girl, Eliza Jane. Eight pounds nine ounces."

Mary sighed. "They had two boys before, right?"

Evan nodded. "They're all so excited."

"Mary," Connie said, "let me take your coat, then we'll fix you something to drink. Would you like wine or eggnog?" Both sounded so tempting it was hard to choose.

"Why don't you start with one and end with the other?" Evan suggested lightly. He met Mary's gaze and his warmth shone in his eyes, reminding her of the way they'd looked last night in the gazebo. She blushed under his spell and turned away.

"That sounds like a plan!" she told the others. "Evan, what are you having?"

"I think a glass of Christmas wine is in order, don't you?"

"Christmas wine it is." She grinned at him, then at Connie, remembering the gift bag she held in her hand. "This is for you and Jesse."

"Why, thank you, Mary. That's very sweet."

The Clarks had a lovely log home with rough-hewn walls, exposed-beam ceilings, and an enormous hearth. Connie took Mary's coat and Mary peeked into the kitchen, spying a large holiday meal in progress. "Can I do something to help?"

"You and Evan could set the table." Connie gave them both a cheery look, like she knew something, and Mary wondered if she'd guessed they'd fallen in love.

Nash shoved his hands in his jeans pockets and nodded at Chloe. "Come on, Nugget. Let's go and see if your

Paw-Paw needs some help with those biscuits." He shot Mary a knowing look as they left, and she wondered if her feelings for Evan were written all over her face.

Mary stared sheepishly at Evan, wondering if he felt like a fish in a fishbowl too. "Should we—"

"First, your wine," Jesse said, appearing from out of nowhere and handing her a glass. "Is red okay?"

"Red is great."

"It's the right color for Christmas," Evan joked, accepting the other wineglass from his dad.

Evan toasted Mary with his glass. "Here's to a memorable Christmas."

She clinked her glass to his. "It's already been memorable so far."

"It will probably only get better!" Connie chimed in from the kitchen.

Mary sent Evan a puzzled look. "Is there…something going on?"

Evan raked a hand through his hair. "Everyone's just in the holiday spirit."

Mary admired the good-sized Christmas tree loaded with decorations and with stacks of presents beneath it, and the fast-falling snow outside the windows. A cozy fire blazed in the hearth, and the dining area sat at the other end of this vaulted-ceiling room, so you could see the fireplace from there.

"You have an amazing house," she said to Connie and Jesse, when she followed Evan into the kitchen.

"We hope you'll come back often," Jesse said, with a telling edge.

Mary raised her eyebrows and took a sip of wine. Nash stood at the counter helping Chloe roll out biscuit dough with a rolling pin, while Jesse instructed his grandchild on how to use the biscuit cutter. Connie pulled a large turkey from the oven to baste it, and it was already golden brown and smelling delicious. More pots sat on the stove and covered casseroles steamed on the counters.

"This is a feast!" Mary said. "Thanks for including me."

The doorbell rang. "That would be Marshall," Evan said. "I'll get it."

Mary scanned the room, wanting to make herself useful. She addressed Connie, who was still working on the turkey. "Where do you keep your silverware?"

A few minutes later, Marshall passed Mary laying a place setting. "You're very good at that. Do you want a job at the inn?"

"She already has a job." Evan playfully shoved Marshall. "A very good one."

"She could have a good one in Clark Creek!" Connie called from the stove. "Just think about it, Mary. If you put your mind to running other events at different times of the year, you could make a real vacation destination out of our little town."

Mary smiled at her suggestion. "I do love the thought, but I'm afraid I've taken another job. In Seattle."

The room grew so still, Mary could hear the flames flickering in the fireplace.

"Why is everyone so quiet, Paw-Paw?" Chloe asked in the kitchen.

Connie appeared in the doorway, her expression drawn. "Seattle, hon? Is that right?"

"Uh, yeah." Mary bit her bottom lip, feeling like she was disappointing them all. "I'm afraid so."

"Mary's a brilliant Christmas Consultant," Evan said, walking along beside her and laying down the cloth napkins as she placed the silverware. "She's going to be successful wherever she goes."

She smiled at his sweet show of faith. "Thanks, Evan."

"No need to thank me. I meant it."

Mary didn't know when she'd had a more delicious Christmas dinner. Every dish was so tasty, especially Evan's dad's stuffing, and everything was homemade. They had a fun time at the table and Mary loved the banter the adult brothers shared when they teased each other in a warm way. Little Chloe was heart-meltingly adorable, and she could see why Itzel was so drawn to her. She could also understand why the warmhearted brunette was interested in Nash. He was a very eligible bachelor, and so was bookishly romantic Marshall. But in Mary's mind, Evan took the prize.

She loved seeing him with his family, and the way everyone oohed and ahhed over their presents, pretending each item was the very best thing they'd ever received. Even Chloe got into the act, probably because she'd had such good modeling from the adults. It was her turn to open the last present. It was a new scarf, hat and glove set from her grandparents. Though it was a simple and functional gift, the child acted like they'd given her the crown jewels.

"Oh, thank you, Me-Maw and Paw-Paw! They're just what I wanted."

"You're welcome, Chloe," Jesse said.

Connie beamed at her granddaughter. "They'll look fine on you when you're ice skating."

Evan slapped his forehead and stared at Mary. "Oh wow."

She leaned toward him where they sat on the sofa. "Evan? What is it?"

"I had one more thing." He grimaced then whispered confidentially. "That I meant to bring here."

Mary figured it was for his niece or parents. "Oh no. Where is it?"

"I left it at my office. Things were so busy yesterday that I kind of lost track of—"

"It's not too late." Mary touched his arm. "We can go and get it."

Evan glanced around the room. "I'd hate to bust up the party."

"It won't be busted up," Connie said.

"Right," Nash agreed. "We'll be nursing our eggnogs right here."

Evan stood and cleared his throat. "Well, if you really don't mind."

Marshall sat back in the recliner by the fire. "We'll wait."

"Can we play a game until they get back?" Chloe asked. "Or watch a movie?"

Jesse angled forward in his armchair and set his elbows on his knees. "How about we break open that new puzzle your Uncle Evan gave you? The one of Santa Claus with his elves?"

Chloe's toothy grin lit up her face. "Yay!"

# Chapter Twenty-Eight

$\mathcal{M}$ ARY RODE WITH EVAN in his truck to the courthouse. The entire downtown area was quiet after the noise and excitement of yesterday. Storefronts were darkened, and fluttering decorations hung serenely from lampposts. Light snow drifted, turning in lazy spirals toward the ground. No one was out on the sidewalks because everyone was at home with their families. Mary was happy to be included at the Clarks'. They made her feel like she was one of their own.

She noted that *Christmas Avenue* had been returned to Main Street. "I see the signs have come down."

"For the time being, yeah." He paused at the street corner and grinned. "You never know about next year."

"Will Clark Creek have another parade?"

"Hope so."

Mary stared at the closed Whistle Stop Café, thinking of meeting Evan there, and then of the snowball fight they'd had outside it. "Yeah, I hope so too."

"Ya going to write to me from Seattle?" he asked, sounding flirty.

"Ev-an."

"You know you kind of want to."

She giggled. "You're right. I do."

"So, we're rethinking this long-distance thing?"

Mary sighed. She didn't want long-distance with Evan. But after their talk last night and the kiss they'd shared, she didn't want to be completely without him, either. "I might write," she teased. "If you write back."

Evan thumped his steering wheel with his gloves. "I'll think about it."

She shoved his arm. "You'd better think hard, then."

He laughed. "I will."

They drove past the town square, which was just as deserted as the rest of downtown. The ice skating rink was closed and the gazebo stood empty. Mary thought of their romantic dance there, believing she could get used to being in Evan's arms. She hoped he'd come out to Seattle to visit—a lot.

Evan normally parked around back, but this time, he pulled into an empty parallel parking spot close to the courthouse. Most of its office windows were dark, except one. Mary gaped up at a second-floor window, the one that belonged to Evan. It was glowing with Christmas lights. Tons of them, like the entire room was lit up inside.

"What's all that?"

He shrugged, looking nonplussed. "Let's go in and see."

She was really curious now. While she'd been fooled back at his parents' house, Mary questioned if this was really about some forgotten Christmas gift.

"Evan," she asked slowly, as they climbed the courthouse steps. "What's going on?"

He took her hand and whispered. "Maybe my office was invaded by a Christmas elf?"

"Invaded? What?"

He chuckled at her surprised look and tugged her along, hurrying up the steps, while taking care with his footing. "Watch your step."

She glanced down at her high-heeled boots. She'd worn the dressy ones because she'd wanted to look nice for the holiday meal at his folks' house. She hadn't expected this after-dark trip into town. Mary followed him carefully, at one point losing her balance when her heel hit black ice. "Yikes!"

"Whoa there!" He caught her. "Are you all right?"

Her pulse pounded. "Yeah, I'm fine."

Evan took out his pass card and let them into the building. The motion-sensor hall lights automatically turned on.

"It's different in here when it's empty." Mary surveyed the darkened halls. "A little spooky."

He laughed. "Is *not*."

"Okay then." She grinned. "Christmas spooky."

He laughed even harder, and the sound echoed up the stairwell.

"Whoa," she said, gawking up at the ceiling. "Did you hear that?"

"Yep." He smiled. "There's an echo."

She got a silly idea and called up the stairway. "Merry Christmas!"

*Merry Christmas! Merry Christmas! Merry Christmas!*

Her voice tumbled back down the stairs and her eyes widened. "That was pretty cool."

"You're pretty cool." His eyes sparkled. "A bona fide Christmas Consultant."

Evan pressed the button for the elevator, and they went to the second floor. Mary felt like a kid doing something naughty. Like sneaking downstairs early to peek at the gifts under the tree on Christmas morning. She'd never had a family tree, so hadn't sneaked downstairs, but she used to dream about doing that when she was small. She'd also dreamed she'd heard Santa's sleigh once or twice, but Lila told her that had probably been the hotel elevator dinging, not sleigh bells ringing.

"You know," Evan said. "You've changed my mind about Christmas."

"Have I?"

He nodded. "I'm kind of into it now."

They reached his office and he threw open his door.

Mary's jaw dropped. The entire place was decked out—from ceiling to floor! Colorful Christmas lights circled the room while icicle lights dripped from the walls, and a bright strand of tiny white bulbs wrapped around his coat rack in front of the window. The stand of reindeer that she'd given him sat on his desk, and there was a gigantic blow-up snowman beside it. It sort of looked like the one that had been on the Blue Heron Bookshop float.

And—wait! Those huge candy cane balloons resembled the ones that had been attached to the mobile library entry. There was even a life-size painted donkey that reminded her of the one she'd seen in the Feed & Seed's flatbed truck nativity display.

"Hang on." She laughed in amazement and joy at the fanciful site. "Did all these things come from the parade?"

"Not all of them. A few were gifts from somebody special."

"But, how—?"

"I called around this morning to see if anyone could let me borrow a little bit of Christmas cheer."

Mary clapped her hands together and grinned. "Oh Evan, this is fun."

"I had to ask Itzel about borrowing the reindeer." He dropped his gaze and winced. "Please don't be mad, but I...I sort of gave them to her."

"Did you?" Mary laughed, not angry at all. "When?"

"That first day, after you put them on my desk and they tore my ledger."

She giggled, remembering the stony look on his face. "Oh yeah, then."

Mary scanned the room again, taking in the garlands and greenery, including the two Christmas trees she thought had come from Connie's office. She pointed to them. "Your mom's?"

He shrugged. "I'm going to have to give them back after the holidays."

Mary laughed out loud, her heart so light. She did feel like a kid on Christmas morning. This was such a cool surprise.

"There is no missing gift, is there?" she asked him. "You wanted me to see this."

"That's true."

"Well, thank you." Mary folded her arms in front of her, beholding the room again. "I love it."

She could tell he was pleased by her reaction. "The thing is," he said, stepping closer. "I didn't care much about Christmas until I met you. I mean, I cared in a general way, but I guess you could say I'd lost touch with a lot of things." He gave her a soulful look. "Including myself."

He took both her hands in his and her heart melted. "Mary," he said. "You're the best thing that's ever happened to me at Christmas, or at any time of year at all. When I met you, I sensed you were different, impressive. I just didn't know how much, or how desperately I'd come to care for you. How I'd fall for you—so hard."

She tightened her grip on his hands. "I feel the same way, Evan. You've changed me for the better. I feel stronger now, more confident that I don't have to be afraid of loving someone. Not when that person is you."

"I'm so glad you said that." He grinned and released her hands. "Don't go away."

She watched him, mesmerized, as he strode to his desk and slid open the top drawer. "I actually did leave a gift here." Mary gasped when she saw it was a ring box. He carried it over to her and stared at her lovingly. "You're the woman I've been waiting for, and I don't want to live without you. I know Seattle is on your mind, and if that's what you want, I'll go there too."

"What?" she asked in shock. "You'd leave Clark Creek? Your job? Your family?"

His blue eyes sparkled. "I get what you told me, and I feel it too. Us and long-distance? That's no good. I want us to be together. Twenty-four seven."

She couldn't let him do this, make that kind of sacrifice, as much as she wanted this to work. His life was here. His family needed him. Clark Creek needed him. "Evan, no."

"I'm willing to try it for a while," he said convincingly. "Take a leave of absence and see how we like it. Besides which, you told me yourself you never stay in any one place too long."

"But Evan," she said, the full truth hitting her. "I want to stay here."

The realization zapped her like a lightning bolt striking suddenly from above. Of course, that's what she wanted. She knew it now with her whole heart. She didn't want another big-city adventure. She'd found her adventure right here in Clark Creek with the man she loved.

He appeared stunned, but also pleased. "What?"

"I'm saying I don't want Seattle. I want to stay here in Clark Creek with you and your wonderful family, in this amazing small town."

"But, you've worked so hard."

"I'll work harder here," she assured him. Her mind latched onto the idea that Connie had suggested. "I can be good for Clark Creek, like you are. I can help here, serve a purpose. Can't you see?" She sent him an earnest look. "This is where I'm meant to be. In a community that I can contribute to—and be a part of. Not just for the short term, but for a lifetime."

He took her in his arms. "Mary, are you sure?"

"All my life, I've waited for this moment to come along. To feel like I don't have to keep moving because I've found my place. The place where I belong and can put down roots."

He pulled her closer. "And have you?" he asked warmly. "Found your place?"

She nodded. "My place is with you."

"I feel exactly the same."

He popped open the ring box, exposing the most beautiful ring Mary had ever seen. It was a stunning solitaire diamond offset by two sapphires shaped like hearts.

She gasped. "It's gorgeous." Then she noticed the gold emblem on the inside of the lid of the velvet box. *A Singleton's Signature Diamond.* "Is this from Sam's shop?"

"It is."

When had he done this? It had to have been this morning. "But how—?"

"You're not the only one who can work a little Christmas magic."

Mary laughed and he slid the ring on her finger. "It's beautiful."

"Mary Ward," he said. "Will you make me the happiest man alive and be my bride?"

"Only if you'll be my groom."

"If one of my brothers tries to get in the way, he'll

have to fight me."

Mary laughed, her heart overflowing. "Oh, Evan. I love you."

"I love you too."

He kissed her sweetly while snow fell outside the window.

"I can't wait to tell your family," she said as they embraced. "My mom and Judy, too."

"Hmm, yeah," he said. "They'll all be so surprised."

She thought back to how mysterious his family had been acting. "No, wait." She pulled back, laughing. "Did your mom and the others know?"

"It's very hard keeping secrets in Clark Creek."

"Yeah? Well, I don't mind it."

"You know what?" he said. "I don't either." He gazed into her eyes, and she heard that Christmas music playing all around them and in her soul. She smiled up at him, really glad to have stopped her wandering, and he looked extra happy about that too.

Then their lips met again, and she was home.

*The End*

# Homemade Turkey Stuffing

In *On Christmas Avenue*, Evan invites Mary to his family's Christmas dinner, featuring his dad's delicious stuffing. Mary's never been one to put down roots, but as she celebrates with Evan, she imagines what it might be like to settle down. Here's that traditional stuffing recipe for your own table…and you don't have to wait for the holidays to make it. After all, life is a special occasion!

- **Prep Time:** 15 minutes
- **Cook Time:** 45 minutes
- **Serves:** 12

## Ingredients

- 4 cups corn bread, diced
- 8 cups rustic bread with crust, diced or torn
- 1/2-pound (2 sticks) butter, unsalted
- 2 1/2 cups (2 - 3 onions) yellow onion, chopped
- 1 1/2 cups (2 – 3 stalks) celery, chopped
- 2 tablespoons + 1 1/2 teaspoons fresh sage, chopped
- 2 tablespoons fresh thyme, chopped
- 1 1/2 teaspoons kosher salt
- 1 teaspoon black pepper, freshly ground
- 2 to 3 cups chicken or turkey stock

## Preparation

1. Preheat oven to 350°F.
2. Toast bread cubes on baking sheets until slightly crusty, approximately 10 to 12 minutes. Cool and transfer to a large mixing bowl.
3. In a large heavy sauté pan, melt butter and sauté onions and celery on medium heat until vegetables are tender.
4. Add herbs and sauté for an additional minute.
5. Combine vegetable mixture with bread, seasonings and stock.
6. Transfer to a deep buttered baking dish.
7. Bake 45 minutes uncovered until stuffing is hot and crusty on the top.

Thanks so much for reading *On Christmas Avenue*.
We hope you enjoyed it!

You might like these other books from Hallmark
Publishing:

*An Unforgettable Christmas*
*Wrapped Up in Christmas*
*Christmas in Bayberry*
*At the Heart of Christmas*
*The Christmas Company*

For information about our new releases and exclusive offers, sign up for our free newsletter at
hallmarkchannel.com/hallmark-publishing-newsletter

You can also connect with us here:

Facebook.com/HallmarkPublishing

Twitter.com/HallmarkPublish

# About the Author

Whether writing lighthearted romantic comedy or spine-tingling romantic suspense, romance author Ginny Baird delights in delivering heartwarming stories. She is a *New York Times* and *USA Today* bestselling author whose novels include *An Unforgettable Christmas* for Hallmark Publishing. When she's not writing, Ginny enjoys cooking, biking and spending time with her family in Virginia. Ginny loves hearing from her readers! She invites you to visit her website, ginnybairdromance.com, and connect with her on social media.

you might also enjoy

# A Down Home Christmas

## LIZ TALLEY

# *Chapter One*

*I SHOULD'VE COME HOME BEFORE NOW.*

The thought buzzed in Kris Trabeau's head as his car bumped down the winding drive that led to Trabeau Farms. New potholes and overgrown trees greeted him, causing the guilt he continually stowed in the back of his conscience to rocket to the forefront.

At the very least he should have hired someone years ago to help his aunt. The old homeplace was too big for such a slip of a woman to take care of by herself—especially one with a broken leg.

But he knew his Aunt Tansy well. The fiercely independent woman would have sent whomever he hired on their way before the ink was dry on the check. Which was part of the reason he'd driven almost three hundred miles to Charming, Mississippi. It was beyond time to convince his stubborn aunt to give up on living alone and come live with him in Nashville.

Just as Kris crested the hill that would bring the farmhouse into view, a chicken flapped across the drive.

A chicken wearing a sweater.

"What the—" The words died on his lips as a huge beast loped behind in pursuit of the squawking fowl. A leash trailed behind the dog that seemed single-minded in its pursuit of the chicken.

Next came a barefoot brunette, waving her hands and screaming. "Heel, Edison. I said heel!"

Kris slammed on the brakes, the brand-new Mustang fishtailing before jerking to a halt. The woman's gaze flew toward him, her mouth dropping open, before she continued her mad dash to apprehend the dog. Kris unbuckled and climbed out of the car. "Whoa, hey, you need help?"

"I got it," she called back, disappearing down the hill.

Kris lifted his eyebrows and mouthed, *Wow*.

Then his aunt came limping as fast as her crutches would allow. She wore a track suit circa 1995 and a medical boot around her leg. "Think he's gonna get my Loretta, does he? Well, he's got another think coming, is what he's got."

Kris moved then, meeting his aunt who hadn't seemed to notice he stood in her driveway. "Whoa, now, Aunt Tansy. What's going on?"

"Oh, sugar, Edison's after Loretta Lynn again. That dog has taken a fascination with my chickens," his aunt said, her gaze fastened to the spot where the chicken, dog, and pretty brunette had disappeared. Then she jerked stunned eyes to him. "Wait, *Kris*? What are *you* doin' here?"

"Surprise," he said, throwing up his hands. "I thought I would visit for the holidays." *Even though I swore I would never come back.*

Aunt Tansy closed her mouth and wobbled a little. "For the holidays?"

Here in front of him was the very reason he needed to convince her to make a change. Tansy hobbling around chasing a dog was dangerous. She could have tripped again and done even greater damage to her healing leg. Or what if she had a heart attack? Heart disease ran in the family. Or someone broke into the house and Aunt Tansy couldn't get to his great-granddaddy's shotgun in time? So many horrible things could happen to his closest living relative, things he hadn't considered until Thad Cumberland, editor of *The Charming Gazette*, had called his manager and relayed the news that Tansy had fallen, broken her femur, and was in surgery.

The panic at the thought that she could've died alone in that house with things still unsettled between them had sent a load of guilt so massive, Kris had trouble breathing. Guest appearances, tours, and promotional opportunities had occupied too much of his time lately, and he'd put his personal life on the back burner—including his Aunt Tansy. He couldn't put off addressing her situation any longer. Thanks to the new contract, now he could afford to take care of her the way she deserved.

But, of course, he couldn't tell her his plan just yet.

Tansy's dark eyes flashed with something that made the guilt he carried wriggle inside him. Tansy had taken him in at ten years old when his parents had died in a plane crash, sending a terrified Kris from the flat plains of Texas to the gentle Mississippi hills. Living at Trabeau Farms with a maiden aunt he'd barely known hadn't been easy. But Tansy was a determined woman and hadn't given up on him, even when he threw a brick through the front window of Ozzy Vanderhoot's Old-Fashioned General Store or when he drank a six-pack and spray-painted a choice directive on the Charming, Mississippi, water tower.

"Well, boy, I'm glad to see you, but I ain't got time to sit here jawin' when Edison's chasing my Loretta. He may not mean harm, but he might scare her to death.

Wait here. I'll be right back," she said, starting toward the woods to his right.

"Hold up," he said, taking her by the elbow. She felt too thin. Looked too tired and old. How long had it been since he'd seen her? Three years? Maybe four? "You broke your leg. I'm sure you're not supposed to be running after chickens."

"I'm not running after chickens. I'm running after a dog."

"Let me get the dog…and the chicken," he said, carefully leading her to a flat patch where she could balance better. She looked so slight a stiff wind could likely blow her over.

Tansy didn't look satisfied. "You remember how to handle chickens? You're a fancy city boy now and all."

"I'm pretty sure I remember how to pick up a chicken," he said, with a roll of his eyes. Fetching eggs had been one of his jobs growing up. Of course, back then, his aunt hadn't named her egg producers and dang sure hadn't dressed them in sweaters.

"I suppose it's like riding a bicycle," she conceded.

"Probably. I'll be back in a sec," Kris said, before jogging down the slope that led to a wooded copse that held a small creek and good climbing trees. He'd built a fort in those woods when he'd first come to live with Tansy, and the remnants were probably in there somewhere.

He followed the sound of yipping dog and squeaking brunette, pushing through the brush that should have been dead in December but wasn't. Because it was Mississippi and unusually warm for December. Heck, sometimes they even wore shorts at Christmas.

"Ouch, ouch. Please, Edison. Stop. Stop!" the woman yelled somewhere off to his left.

At that moment, the sweater-wearing chicken flew by Kris's head and the dog came bounding after it. Kris ducked as the chicken tumbled by, crashing into the underbrush. He snatched the leash that bumped behind the dog, making the beast's head jerk around when he reached the end of the tether. The huge fluffy dog immediately started yipping at the hapless hen. A few steps behind, the brunette emerged, panting, her curly hair displaying bits of leaf and twigs. With her pointed chin, big gray eyes, and flushed cheeks, she looked a bit like a woodland fairy.

"Oh, thank goodness," she breathed, pressing a hand against her chest.

Edison, who looked like a cross between a Saint Bernard and Chow Chow, whined and strained at the leash. The chicken's sweater had caught on a broken limb and the poor thing flapped and squawked. Kris extended the end of the leash to the woman. She took it and jerked her dog back toward her. "Sit, Edison. And hush! You're scaring Loretta."

The dog sat, tongue lolling out, panting, eyes still fixed on the Rhode Island Red that flopped about pitifully in the brush. Kris went over to the bird and wondered how in the heck he was going to free the terrified Loretta Lynn without getting pecked to death. He started unbuttoning his flannel shirt.

"What are you doing?" the woman asked, sounding slightly alarmed.

"Trying to calm this chicken down."

"By taking your shirt off?" Her eyes grew wide as she looked from him to the chicken.

"I'm going to drape it over her so I don't get pecked. Then I'll try to free her."

"Oh," the woman said, tugging as her beast leapt

against the restraint. "Good idea. Birds have a higher visual stimulus and covering her eyes should calm her down."

*Visual stimulus?*

He shrugged out of his shirt, glad he'd pulled on an undershirt to ward off the early morning chill when he left Nashville that morning. Then he approached the chicken, who grew even more agitated as he moved toward it. Carefully, he drew his shirt over Loretta, then slid his hands around her now-clothed body, pinning her wings to her sides. The hen went still. "There."

"Her sweater's still hung," the woman said unhelpfully.

"I got it," he said, pulling the royal blue yarn free from the branch and looking back at the woman and dog. "Why is this chicken wearing a sweater anyway?"

"That's Loretta Lynn. Miss Tansy's pet. She likes to knit sweaters for her hens. She got the idea off Pinterest."

"Pet? She calls them pets?" Kris arched a brow. "And people make clothes for farm animals now?"

"Haven't you seen the videos of baby goats in pajamas? They're so cute." She paused and then shook her head as if she knew she'd gotten off track. "For some reason, Edison really likes Loretta. I think it's because she's very flappy."

Kris couldn't stop his smile. "Flappy?"

"Miss Tansy sometimes gives Edison dog biscuits, and he remembers. So when he gets loose, he comes here. Unfortunately, the chickens intrigue him. Maybe he prefers Loretta because she makes the most noise."

"That makes sense. He's a dog, after all," he said, turning back to the chicken. He carefully lifted and tucked her beneath his arm. The hen, oddly enough, seemed to sink in relief against his side. Poor Loretta Lynn. "There now."

"I'm so relieved she's not dead. Miss Tansy would have killed me and Edison." The woman let out a sigh.

"And who are you exactly?" he asked.

The woman pushed back the hair curling into her eyes and held out her hand. "I'm Tory Odom. I live next door to Tansy."

"You're one of the Moffetts?"

"No, I live in the cottage on the other side of Tansy," she said as he took her hand. It was small and capable-looking, like she could smooth a child's fevered forehead or hoe a garden equally well.

"Oh, the Howards' old place?" Last time he'd been home, he'd predicted a strong wind could topple what was left of the Howard place.

"I restored the cottage. It's really nice now." Edison took that moment to spring toward the bundle under his arms. She tugged on his leash and pushed him into a sitting position. "And you are?"

"Oh, I'm Kris. Tansy's nephew."

"The country music singer?"

Kris felt pride stir inside. He'd waited a long time to be known as a country music singer. Being named CMA's New Artist of the Year just weeks ago had cemented his position in the country music scene. He'd placed his award in the center of his mantel and made sure the accent light hit it perfectly. The award was the first of many he'd use to decorate the downtown Nashville loft he'd purchased earlier that year with the royalties on his first album. *A Simple Dream* had hit big last spring, but it had taken years of sweat, tears, and sore fingers from playing guitar for his dream to come true. He'd hit number one with two songs on his debut album and was in the process of putting together his second one. Of course, he still had to write some songs for it, but they would come. He prayed they would come. So, heck yeah, he was *the country music star*. "Star is kind of a strong word, but, yeah, I play country music."

"I didn't say star."

She *hadn't* said star. She'd said singer. He glanced away so she wouldn't see that he was embarrassed about the faux pas. He felt really stupid. "Right, right."

"I don't really care for country music. You could be a star and I wouldn't know it," she said, sounding like she offered an apology.

Her admission embarrassed him even more, and he found he hadn't a clue what to say to her. Maybe the sweater-bedecked chicken nestled beneath his arm paired with an ego smackdown had something to do with not being able to find the right words.

Or maybe it was the fact he'd not been able to find the words for the last few months.

And that was what worried him most.

Read the rest!
*A Down Home Christmas* is available now.